MAVIS STEWART

The Frizz In My Hair

First edition

This book was professionally typeset on Reedsy.
Find out more at reedsy.com

To my mother, Sabiba.
for her love, her strength, and her resilience

Contents

Preface

This is a realist narrative that takes place in a remote village in Rhodesia in the 1920s, where much was said about only a few and nothing about so many.

It is about the woman, bent over in the fields with a hoe in her hand, the one balancing a bucket of water on her head with a baby strapped to her back, and maybe even the one sitting outside her hut waiting for the sun to set.

It is about a child dressed in the same ragged clothes as her peers but whose skin is a shade lighter than theirs. It's a study of segregation, a way of life, and the people unseen and unheard, navigating through these waters, in their quest for survival.

I

Part 1 - Esnart and Ahmad

1

Beads in a Mason jar

It was the beads that had attracted Esnart to Ahmad. And there were hundreds of them, creating a kaleidoscope of colour in the Mason jars that lined the counter of his store. There were round ones and square ones and others with funny shapes that made her smile without knowing why. Ahmad had taken his time, choosing only those that he felt she would like, and threaded them into a brightly coloured necklace and slipped it under the yard of fabric she'd come to purchase.

Their fingers had touched a second time during that simple transaction, making Esnart look up at him in surprise. He had looked away quickly then, but not before flashing her a look that told her that the beads were a gift from him and hers to keep if she chose to do so.

Esnart had visited the store on a few occasions, and she'd never thought anything of him, but Ahmad's eyes had been drawn from the very start to this tall, slender woman with the aloof aristocracy of her Mashona ancestry. And now that Esnart knew that he had noticed her, she found herself looking at him with different eyes.

The spell was broken when Ahmad's wife Jasmine, noticing the slight hesitation, came quickly to stand at her husband's side. But before Jamine reached them, Ahmad sprang out of his seat. He brushed past her and went to inspect the merchandise at the far end of the counter.

Ahmad was no longer a young man when they came together, arousing feelings in him that he had long forgotten. And Jasmine knew without him telling her, just as all wives know when things are not quite, the way they used to be.

'I've always been faithful to you,' Ahmad said to his wife soothingly as he reached over to brush away the warm tears wetting the pillow. And he had all those years, resigning himself to the situation he was in and devoting himself to his wife and their store.

The store had a side door that led to a dwelling that adjoined it. It was a spacious building, with many rooms, and too big for just the two of them. It was a house they had built with hope for the future and with enough room to embrace the constant patter of tiny feet and to resonate with the joyful sound of children's laughter.

But the years had gone by, and the little cot, a gift from an adoring parent, received by them with so much joy then, now only served as a reminder of their failure. So, they had packed it up and put it out of sight, but neither of them had the heart to throw it out. Only for that flickering flame of hope that maybe one day, things would change.

A cook with a white apron draped around his waist and with a white hand towel slung over his forearm stood in the doorway attentively. His master gave him the nod and his bare feet padded soundlessly behind the counter. He brought with him a round, white enamel dish in one hand and a tall, white enamel water jug in the other. Ahmad got up from his stool, and Jasmine slipped out through the same door the cook had just come in through.

She ducked under a washing line where several towels, still damp from being dunked for many hours in a bubbling boiler under a wood fire, were now hanging and waiting to be bleached bone-white by the scorching sun above. A dog lying close to the kitchen door rose lethargically to its feet and sniffed at its mistress as she walked past. Then she entered a spacious kitchen furnished with a wood stove and wooden shelves filled with jars of spices.

A table sat in the centre of the room and a tray with a motley of small bowls had been laid out on it. Jasmine flitted between the stove and the table, filling the bowls with portions of coconut rice, split mung dahl, yoghurt curry, rotis, and sprigs of coriander.

The cook's head popped out of the store. He turned to a nearby flower bed and tipped out the soapy water from the dish. Just then, Jasmine's voice rang out, telling him the tray was ready to be carried through to her husband.

Jasmine had lunch on her own in the big house; this was her free time to do as she pleased. And when the cook's wife came to clear the dishes, she told her madam that she had something to say that she might want to hear.

There was talk of a child now, Jasmine heard, and she knew it to be true. As it explained her husband's buoyant mood, his increasingly frequent absences, and that crestfallen look she'd grown to know, between his visits away. But she was still his wife, so she did what she could to try and hold on to what was rightfully hers.

She'd changed out of her everyday clothes and now wore a vivid red saree embroidered with golden thread and studded with shimmery gems. She'd thrown a veil intricately woven with threads of bright red and gold over her head and it fell gracefully to her shoulders. And she looked just as she had on the day of their wedding. The red symbolised good fortune and the gold was for prosperity.

She turned her face, partly obscured by the vibrant colours of the veil, demurely towards her husband, making him hold his breath for a second. He recognised the headpiece against her forehead as the same one she had worn in the photograph that marked that important day of their life. And he knew that this was a reminder from her of the vows they had both taken on that day. His eyes lit up and a smile wavered on his lips to reward her for her efforts, and this in turn gave her a glimmer of hope of winning him back.

'Jasmine means "a flower, a gift from God", and Ahmad means "highly praised"', the priest had stated matter-of-factly.

They were seated under a mandap built for that purpose the day before and surrounded by family and friends. The four pillars that held it up representing their parents, who had given them life.

'Marriage is a holy bond,' the priest told the guests assembled there to celebrate their union. 'It's the binding of two souls into one.'

But it was not always so, and no one knew more than Ahmad that consulting the moon and the stars and having someone beautiful, was not always a guarantee that everything else would by its nature fall into place.

And when the cook brought in his lunch tray, and Jasmine joined him in his meal, Ahmad noticed that the towel he used to dry off his hands was no longer as fluffy or as white as it used to be and the bowls on the tray had lost their shine.

2

A daughter for Ahmad

Ahmad had a name for the child, his mother's name, Khadijah, but he could see that Esnart had something she wanted to tell him, so he waited for her to say what was on her mind.

'See how much she looks like you,' Esnart told him with a shy smile, and gazing down at the baby suckling on her breast.

The child had Ahmad's button nose, and her head was full of her father's hair. But she had her mother's oval face and almond-shaped eyes, complete with her long eyelashes, and cherubic lips. And when Ahmad held his baby against his chest and felt the blood in his veins coursing in unison with that of his child, the love that he felt for both mother and child was like none he'd ever known before.

'My flesh and blood, my beautiful jewel,' he murmured, his warm breath on his daughter's face, and the baby yawned and stretched its tiny limbs before dozing off again.

'A star that shines brighter than all the other stars in the sky,' Esnart murmured contentedly.

Ahmad nuzzled the little chubby face in agreement, and then Esnart said with more confidence, 'I want us to call her Esther,' and he found that he could find nothing to argue with that.

And as time went by, Jasmine found that the fire that she thought was still there, in her husband's breast, was nothing more than a smokescreen. And that the hope that she had harboured of things going back to where they were when they first started, was just a mirage in a desolate desert.

The realisation broke out in a rage that brought down a shelf hanging on the wall of the store. And when Ahmad went to retrieve the goods now strewn haphazardly on the cement floor, she filled his ears with threats to leave him. But he knew that would not happen, not now that he had a daughter, and they both knew who was to blame for their childless marriage.

They reached an agreement, and all of it was executed in silence. This was their home and would remain so, with just the two of them. And the other part, the one with his child and its mother, was his alone.

The cook's wife had been whispering to Jasmine again, telling her things she wouldn't have known otherwise. But this time Jasmine was not prepared for the news that the woman brought.

'There's another child on its way,' she said, 'Ahmad is to be a father again.'

With her heart pounding and her mouth resolute, Jasmine told her husband it was time for them to sell up and leave. They were standing opposite each other with the counter between them and his back towards her. He lined a shelf with the newly arrived tobacco pouches. Then he shifted the tinned groceries and bottles of petroleum jelly around so that they were more visible to his customers. He took a step back to appraise his work before turning around to face her.

'Do our families at home go without?' he wanted to know, with his glance locked on hers. 'I play my part. I do what I can.'

'This is my dowry,' Jasmine retorted, her arm stretched out to encompass the store and everything in it. 'All this came from my family. I have a say in where we live.'

The anger swirled around them as the yards of tired chiffon, with their sweet and spicy aroma, trailed gracefully over the rough floor. They brushed past sacks of grain and baskets of fresh produce, all received in exchange for packets of sugar, candles, and matches. Bartered merchandise now waiting to be sold off to some lone traveller in pursuit of riches or an aloof housewife forced to go where she must for her household needs.

The door to the store was shut earlier than usual that day, and the customers, accustomed to always seeing it open, gaped at it with disbelief. Inside the big house, Ahmad sat alone, waiting. One hour went by, two hours, and still no sign of her. Then he heard the back door open, followed by footsteps, and he remained where he was, seated on the edge of their bed.

Jasmine came rushing down the passage and when she saw him there instead of in the store where he almost always was, she pulled back in the doorway with a cry of surprise.

'I'm sorry,' he said, because he knew where she'd been, and he accepted the blame for forcing her to go out and do the same thing he was doing.

She saw that his mouth was trembling as he struggled to speak, and an icy cold wave of dread washed over her, as she feared the worst.

'I'm sorry,' he repeated, and she realised that she'd made the wrong assumption and that he was not trying to break things off with her. She felt a sudden flash of anger that was for the first time mixed with pride.

She raised her chin and with her blazing eyes on him asked, 'Sorry for what? Sorry that our marriage has come to this? Sorry about your absences and the times that you've left me here on my own. Sorry that I can't give you what is beyond my control?!'

Ahmad sat in the lounge room as Jasmine began to pack, listening as she moved from one room to another. Picking up something here and another thing there, small noises echoing through the silence. And he couldn't help noticing how she avoided the room with the box that held all the bits of wood that made up the little cot they had received all those years ago.

'I'm going,' Jasmine said, lifting her face over a wooden crate that was slowly filling up, 'with or without you.'

She got her way, this time, 'but not right away,' Ahmad begged, torn by the choices that were being forced on him, and trying desperately to hold off the inevitable for as long as he could. 'I have to make arrangements for the sale of the store, and there's still that order that should be arriving any time now.'

3

A new wagon

Ahmad had paid for a new wagon and two horses because that's what his wife wanted in exchange for the time, she had granted him before they departed for good.

'If you can have what you want,' Jasmine said, referring to his other family, 'Then, why can't I?'

The wagon arrived, drawn by two brown horses, which did not appear to be as sprightly as the ones he had paid for.

'I think they may have been switched,' Ahmad said, sharing his suspicions with his wife.

'Mr Potgieter is a reputable man,' Jasmine insisted, vouching for someone she had little knowledge of. 'He'd never do anything like that.' Ahmad gave her a look that said he knew the Boer in question, and he knew otherwise.

A name previously sketched on the side panels of the newly acquired carriage had been poorly painted over. And the leather seat had been refurbished so that it now gleamed enticingly at its new owners.

'Horses are no different from donkeys,' the dusky driver who had come to deliver the purchase told him with a grin, but Ahmad was not so sure and eyed the whole contraption dubiously. 'Jump in,' the driver invited as he held the reigns to keep the horses steady.

Ahmad took a step forward and the horses blew through their nostrils defiantly, but the driver's peal of laughter reassured him. So, he jumped in beside him, conscious of his wife and the cook in his white uniform standing on the porch and watching him.

Up and down the gravel road they went. The spectators outside the doors of the store soon lost interest and turned back indoors. The driver's glance darted towards the horizon, where the sun was heading steadily, but Ahmad gestured to him to go another round. So away they trotted, back and forth, and going a little further out each time. The confidence came at last, pasting a smile on Ahmad's features, but it had been long in coming and the horses were tired and covered in sweat.

'I told you; you could do it,' Jasmine said a few days later when they were returning from a short test ride in the vicinity of their dwelling. 'And now that Cook has found a groom to take care of the horses, you have nothing to worry about.'

Back in the village on one of his many visits, Ahmad stood in the doorway of the round thatched hut, his worried eyes on the mother of his child.

'Are you sure you don't want me to take you to the clinic?' he asked with a crease on his forehead.

'It's nothing,' Esnart replied with a small shake of her head.

Esnart hadn't been herself since her miscarriage and Ahmed scrutinised her face for clues, but he found nothing there that he didn't already know. And Esther, now almost four, skipped about nearby as Ahmad packed his bag reluctantly and got ready to leave.

Ahmad had not been back in his store and his other life for long when Esnart, clutching her stomach, collapsed to the ground. She bit her lip as she crawled painfully back into the hut she shared with Ahmad on his visits to the village. And when darkness fell, Esther crept into the hut and snuggled up to her mother. Outside, the cock crowed as it heralded the new day, and when it grew light, Esther peered into the serene face lying next to hers.

'Mama, Mama,' she called out urgently, shaking her mother gently at first and then more rigorously as she tried to get her mother to open her eyes.

The sound of horror that followed pierced the air, and a neighbour came running to investigate. Ahmad had been sent for and he arrived as soon as he could. And when he called out to his daughter, Esther recognised the voice as her father's but recoiled from the gaunt figure with hollow eyes who came rushing to embrace her.

After the burial, when the neighbours had returned to their homes and only a trusted old woman remained behind, Ahmad took Esther aside so that he could speak to her in private.

'I've made arrangements for you,' he said to the child sitting on his lap, his eyes moist and his voice gruff.

Silence followed as he grappled to stop the emptiness from enveloping him and frightening his daughter with a fresh flood of tears. He put his hand in his pocket and with a forced look of cheer on his face, held out some candy to her.

'Tell me about your hen,' he asked instead. 'Is she still sitting on those eggs of hers?'

Esther's face broke out into a wide grin, and she scrambled off his lap and raced off to the fowl run. He leaned over the wire mesh and they both watched as the new mother proudly strutted around her three yellow chicks.

'I'm taking you to my brother's house,' Ahmad told Esther a few days later. 'He has a farm, and you will stay there with his family. He knows you're coming.'

Esther looked towards the graveyard where her mother was buried and Ahmad said quickly, 'You'll be happy there and I'll still come and visit you, just as I used to.'

'Just one more order, I promise, then we'll go,' Ahmad said to Jasmine, more eager than ever now to buy that precious commodity of time.

It had been almost four years now, and with Esnart gone, Jasmine had nothing to fear, so she smiled and nodded her head to show that she was okay with that.

4

The consignment note

The station master's messenger 'boy' arrived at Ahmad's store with important news.

'The train from Bulawayo has arrived, sir,' he told Ahmad with a smile.

'And my order,' Ahmad returned, with a stern glance at the young man, as a forewarning that there would be consequences if this turned out to be a wasted trip. 'Are you sure it was on the train? You saw it with your own eyes?'

'The boxes are all there, with your name on them,' the 'boy' reassured him with a jovial smile, holding the consignment note out to him.

'Tell the groom to get the carriage ready,' Jasmine called out gaily to the cook when Ahmad passed on his news to her.

Ahmad and Jasmine were returning home from the train station with their wagon piled to the top with goods for the store. The horses came thundering down the narrow road, and the wooden wheels trailing closely behind, crunched the gravel beneath them. A hawk caught napping in a low-hanging bough started up with a loud screech. Its wide wings spread themselves out and then began to flap furiously as it fumbled its way out, into the open sky. The unsuspecting horses pulled back with fright and then turning off the road, charged over loose rocks. Ahmad pulled hard on the reins instinctively, and the beasts, believing themselves under attack, took off wildly up a granite kopje.

Jasmine turned a horrified look at her husband and seeing the terror on his face, clutched the side of the carriage with both hands. Ahmad tugged at the leather straps in his hands as they careened up an escarpment. One of the wagon's wheels mounted a boulder and swerved erratically before the whole contraption toppled over. The wagon slid for a short distance before it brought down the horses.

A crash like thunder burst into a field and a group of farmhands bent over a potato crop straightened up abruptly just as a cloud of dust broke through the air and began to chatter excitedly. A cry rang out and figures with curious faces abandoned their tools and rushed through the bush towards the road. They saw the wagon first, with its three wheels turned up towards the sky, and lying beside it were the two unconscious horses still harnessed to it.

A loud gasp was uttered and all eyes turned to a body draped in chiffon that was matted with blood and dust and lying half-buried in some shrubs. They found the owner of the store, just a short distance from his wife and with his blue tunic soiled in the same way. Not far from him, someone located the fourth wheel of the carriage wedged between the lower branches of a tree.

The labourers turned back to the bodies and finding no sign of life in them, descended on the merchandise. The women gathered cartons of tinned food, bottles of cooking oil, and other types of goods too numerous to mention in their aprons. The men removed their shirts and turning them into grocery bags, stuffed them with goods.

'Leave a few things behind,' the boss boy advised, 'Or the law will catch up with us.'

They rushed to hide their loot in nearby bushes and when the boss boy went in search of the manager, to report the accident to him, there were only a few items left scattered about on the ground.

The manager came rushing over, and bending over a carton of cigarettes, picked it up and stuffed it in the huge side pockets of his jacket. Then he took his rifle to where the two horses were lying and put them out of their misery.

5

A young orphan

Back at Rajesh's farm, Esther lowered the bucket of water from her head and placed it near the vegetable bed she was attending to. Accustomed to being pulled off one task only to be given another, she ignored the child her uncle had sent to call her. She took her time as she rinsed the dirt from her hands and then unrolled the turban she'd used earlier to balance a bucket of water on her head and began to dry her hands with it. And then with no other excuse to detain her further, she turned to the boy waiting for her patiently and followed behind him at a leisurely pace.

She found her uncle sitting in an armchair on the front porch of his house and looking out for her. She curtsied and clapped her hands in greeting, and Rajesh noticed with surprise how tall she had grown. He gave her a brief nod and she took her seat on the top step of the porch with her hands clasped together. Rajesh opened his mouth to speak with his gaze on his niece but on seeing his brother in her features, he paused and swallowed hard.

'I'm afraid that I don't have good news for you,' he said eventually, with his eyes turned to his feet.

Esther's eyes flew open with fear.

'Tell the child!' his wife cut in impatiently from the doorway where she had suddenly appeared before going to take a seat beside her husband.

'A terrible accident. They didn't stand a chance. Bad business,' Rajesh added without looking at Esther.

Esther turned her startled eyes from one to the other, not quite comprehending what her uncle was trying to tell her.

'Your father and his wife are dead,' Amina told her, before turning her glance down and dabbing her eyes with the end of her turban.

Rajesh cleared his throat and shifted uncomfortably in his seat.

Esther gasped as the news smashed into her belly. Then, she was up on her feet, without knowing how, and running with the wind. She flung her hands over her ears to block the awful noise that surrounded her, unaware that the sound that plagued her eardrums was what was spilling out of her.

Her uncle's harsh tones tore through the horror as a brusque order was hurled out at a gardener standing close by. The man turned to the fleeing figure and his footsteps soon caught up with those in front of him, and strong arms bundled Esther up.

Then Rajesh's voice, louder and more chilling than the sound she was enveloped in, made her clamp her mouth shut. A stern voice ordered her to quieten down and to bear her sorrow with dignity. And Esther did what she was told to do, because it was bad luck to announce your heartbreak to the rooftops, no matter how much blood your heart was shedding.

6

A tractor is purchased

Rajesh's old lorry rattled over the uneven ground, slowing down as it reached the main entrance of the showroom, his eye picking out the farming equipment on display in front of the building. Then he drove further down the road and took a rough track that ran alongside the wire enclosure until he came to a small gate behind the business. This was where all the second-hand items were kept. Normally, he would just drive down slowly before turning back around and heading off back the way he'd come, but not this time. The man guarding the back entrance stood up from the empty crate which served as his stool and strolled over to the parked lorry.

'Which one are you interested in today, boss?' the man asked, with a wide grin at his potential customer.

Rajesh swung his car door open and after shaking the man's hand, swaggered towards the diamond mesh fence to look inside the yard.

Pointing at a well-polished tractor that he'd admired from a distance for a few months now, he said, 'That's what I'm after, is it for sale?'

'Everything in here is for sale,' the gatekeeper replied with a chuckle and held the small gate open for Rajesh to enter.

Rajesh strutted up to the tractor and began to inspect it, kicking a tyre here and fingering a panel there. Then he climbed into the cab and while inspecting the interior, he noticed a small cardboard tag taped to the gear of the tractor with the price written on it. He agreed with the price mentally, but a price was only acceptable if it was affordable. And the look on Rajesh's face when he jumped off the tractor told the salesman that the price was out of his reach.

'Can you imagine how jealous all the other farmers will be when they see you ploughing your fields with something like this?' the salesman baited.

Rajesh's pulse quickened with excitement but experienced at bargaining himself, he turned away from the tractor as if he were no longer interested. And the aspiring salesman, now afraid to see his customer walking through the gate empty-handed, trotted hurriedly beside him saying, 'You won't find a tractor in this condition and at this price anywhere, I can assure you.'

'How much?' Rajesh asked, pausing in his stride to turn to the speaker.

The man named the price and when Rajesh purposely dropped his face, the seller was quick to say, 'I can give it to you for a good price! Just let me check with my boss.'

He walked towards a door that led to the showroom before turning around and saying, 'How much do you have?'

Rajesh named a number that was lower than the asking price, and which he knew to still be more than he could afford to pay. The security guard gave Rajesh a hard look before disappearing behind the door and leaving Rajesh to figure out a way to come up with the funds. He had already reached out to family and friends, but the story was the same, things were tight for all of them. And when he approached the banks, they spoke about collateral and unencumbered property, things they knew he didn't have.

A look of bravado erased the worry lines from his face as soon as the door swung open to eject the gatekeeper, accompanied by a tall lanky man with red hair, who Rajesh assumed correctly to be the manager. Some serious bargaining ensued, and after much talk and Rajesh's reassurances, the lanky man said, 'Deal!' before shaking Rajesh's hand. Then, with a look of self-importance, Rajesh swaggered back to his old lorry and drove off.

And when the security guard, now back on his stool, was just a blurry image in his rear-view mirror, the smile Rajesh had kept on for the benefit of the two men faded, and his brow creased up again with worry. He drove home slowly and then, with a sudden but characteristic impulsiveness, he swung the lorry around and headed off towards the town centre. Before reaching it, he turned off the main road and skirted around the town fringe to the rough side of town, with its untidy and dilapidated buildings.

He parked his lorry under some trees and left the engine to run as he surveyed the area. Then, making up his mind, he turned the engine off and with a determined gait, pushed his way past a group of unsavoury men loitering about. He reached the buildings and ducking under a board declaring 'Cash for Stash,' slipped into the store quickly.

'Mr Kumar,' the owner of the store, a large lumbering man with shifty eyes, called out to Rajesh in greeting as he ushered out a furtive customer clutching tightly to a package wrapped in old canvas.

'Mr Riley,' Rajesh replied, pumping the store owner's hand in his.

Rajesh walked around the room and commented on one or two items sitting among an assortment of goods that filled every corner of the store. Then he stopped and facing the shop owner said, 'Remember that business we spoke about?'

Brett Riley gave Rajesh a puzzled look and then shook his head.

'Come now, you know what I mean,' Rajesh insisted.

'Are you talking about your niece?' Brett inquired with a dubious look.

Rajesh nodded his head with a smile.

'You're serious, aren't you?' Brett said, in half disbelief, but with a smile growing on his face. 'What's changed your mind?'

'A tractor!' Rajesh replied with a twinkle in his eye. 'So, do we have a deal?'

Brett stood up straight and with a firm grip, shook Rajesh's hand.

'How will you pay for it?' Amina inquired with a curious look when Rajesh told her about the tractor.

Her husband's eyes turned towards the kitchen where Esther was preparing dinner for the family. Amina's jaw dropped and then with a swift gesture from Rajesh, they retreated to their bedroom in silence.

And when they were back in the lounge room again, Amina asked, 'When?' to which Rajesh replied, 'Tomorrow.'

7

Debt for tractor repaid

The next evening Amina called out and Esther bent over the kitchen floor with a short broom in her hand straightened up and with a low sigh went to find her.

'When you're finished sweeping, you can knock off,' Amina told her.

'What about the dishes?' Esther asked.

'Don't worry about them,' her aunt interjected briskly, 'I'll get someone to wash them. You can knock off now. There's hot water in the kettle, you can take that for your bath.'

And then to Esther's great astonishment Amina, who was not known for kindness especially towards her, handed her a cake of Lifebuoy soap. Esther's face broke into a bright smile. She murmured her thanks and curtsying, held out both her hands to receive the gift.

Moments after, carrying a pail of warm water in one hand and the treasured red soap in the other, she bounced off gaily down the path. Amina waited until the girl had entered the simple reed and straw structure that served as her bathroom, before rushing off to find Rajesh.

Half an hour later and with the sweet scent of Lifebuoy soap still clinging to her, Esther emerged from the small cubicle. Then she headed towards a solitary brick structure that stood behind the main house and hidden from it, by an overgrown bougainvillea bush.

She pushed open the rickety door and dropping to her knees, searched the floor with her fingers. Her hand folded around a small box. She pulled out a match and lit it. Then a candle flickered to life and revealed a reed mat leaning against the mud wall. And beside that was a small wooden suitcase that contained her worldly belongings.

The suitcase belonged to her mother once, and it was the only reminder Esther had of her. She unrolled the mat and lowered her weary limbs on it. And then, pulling a thin blanket over herself, she soon fell fast asleep.

Outside her room, a man climbed a ladder and fiddled with the window latch. Then he pushed his way through the opening before springing towards the figure lying on the mat. Esther started up with fright as two booted feet landed beside her with a loud thud. She opened her mouth to scream but a large hand beat her to it. It fastened itself over her face and stifled the cry behind it, while another tore at the thin calico wrapped around her body.

Esther lashed her arms and legs out at her attacker and the man held one hand out to fend her off. Then with his face tightening, he rolled his hand into a ball. His clenched fist smashed against her cheek, and her head lolled to one side. She groaned as rough hands clawed at her flesh.

The room filled with the sound of heavy grunting, and she shut her eyes tightly as each thrust tore at her young flesh. Then the heavy weight over her shuddered and lay still before finally rolling off her, its owner shoving her off with the contempt that people like him had for people like her.

Esther's face creased with pain and drawing her legs up, lay on her side with her face turned towards the wall. The man stood beside her with his legs apart and with his eyes fixed on her as he strapped his leather belt back around his waist. Then he brushed his hair away from his face with his hand, and chuckling softly to himself, yanked the door open and strode out confidently. Esther flinched as the door swung back and closed with a loud thud.

Her body felt raw and stiff, and even if she had been able to move it, what was the point of running to tell those in whose charge she'd been left what they already knew?

Outside, the sound of voices drifted back to her, and when this was followed by light laughter, her misery was complete.

All too soon, a rooster crowed outside. Then the sun rose, and a truck came down the driveway. The driver who Brett had sent to collect Esther spoke briefly to Rajesh and then sat back in his seat and waited patiently.

'You will pack your bags and go with him!' Rajesh stormed, before smashing his fist against the crooked stick holding up Esther's door, his face flushed with irritation.

His bulky frame filled the doorway, and Amina leaned forward to peep curiously at the inert figure curled up on the mat.

'Did you hear me?' Rajesh demanded before spinning away abruptly and leaving his wife to deal with his niece.

Amina entered the room and put the pail in her hand down before kneeling beside Esther. Then she gently removed the blood-stained fabric still attached to her body to reveal the torn flesh beneath it. She began to dab the bruises tenderly with a towel, erasing the horrors of the night, and exonerating herself from the guilt she shared equally with her husband.

Despite her past insensitivity to her spouse's niece, Amina now felt a stab of anger at the brutality of the man who was responsible for Esther's injuries.

Later that evening, when Rajesh returned from the fields, she confronted him even before he had a chance to reach the front door.

'Did you tell him that the child was untouched?' Amina blurted out, her ice-cold eyes on him.

'He knew,' Rajesh replied almost inaudibly, with a perplexed look on his face.

8

A new occupant for the cottage

The lorry pulled up the driveway to the Riley's homestead and Brett, giddy with excitement, rushed to swing the door open for Esther. When she was back on solid ground, he hovered around her protectively and chuckled with nervous energy.

'Come,' he said feverishly with his hand on her shoulder, 'I'll show you where you'll be staying.'

Esther's frightened glance leapt towards Brett's driver, and then she withdrew with fear when she saw his back already turned towards her.

'Come on! I don't have all day!' Brett snapped, excitement turning to anger.

Esther picked up her suitcase and with her heart beating rapidly, trailed behind as he stepped to the other side of a hedged wall that separated the homestead from the servants' quarters.

'That's Mpofu's cottage, you know, the driver who brought you,' Brett told her with his arm stretched towards a small brick building.

Outside the cottage, a woman hanging out the washing with a toddler clinging to her legs stopped to stare at them before picking the infant up quickly and disappearing behind the building.

Brett pointed to a forested area and said, 'That's where the farmhands live,' as he led the way down a path that took them to another cottage, that stood apart from the other outbuildings. He rushed ahead and when he reached the door, Esther stood still and watched as he fiddled with the lock. He pushed the door open and strolled back to where Esther was standing.

'This is where you will live. Close enough to the main house so that you can assist the madam whenever she needs you, day or night. Do you understand me?' he said with his eyes fixed on her.

Esther turned a sullen face to the ground.

'Always keep the door bolted, no matter what time it is, you hear me? Anything can happen, especially to a young girl on her own,' Mr. Riley said fingering the bunch of keys in his hands.

He removed one of two identical keys from the silver ring and when he looked up to hand it to her, he found her staring at him. And the look on her face said that she wanted to say something but didn't quite know how to say it. Their eyes locked and hers told him that she remembered what he did to her that night. And in the end, it was his gaze that yielded to hers. And when she still did not attempt to enter the cottage, Brett turned away abruptly and disappeared through the secret opening in the hedge, that led him back to his house.

After a short pause, Esther stood in the doorway and surveyed the room. It was empty except for a coir mattress lying on the floor. She entered the room tentatively and wavered beside the windowsill where a half-burnt candle with a thick coat of dried wax spilled over its sides, was perched. She wondered who it belonged to and where its owner was now. Then pushing the window open, she tossed the candle out, and with rushed movements, retrieved the one she brought with her from her suitcase and placed it where the other had sat.

9

The treadle sewing machine

The quiet hum of the workers in the fields drifted back to Esther and reminded her of how much she missed working outdoors. She loathed being cooped up indoors, with the endless chores of dusting and washing and cleaning and the boredom of having just the cook boy for company.

'Esther!' Mrs Riley's voice bellowed out, bringing her back to the present. 'Get in here, right this minute!'

Esther gave a great sigh and then ambled toward the sound of chugging metal.

'Well, don't just stand there!' the madam muttered from behind a treadle sewing machine as she pumped her legs furiously.

Esther twisted her fingers nervously as she edged forward, and stood with her head bowed.

'Here,' the madam said after a short pause, throwing a piece of calico at her. The simple frock bounced off Esther and landed at her feet. 'Try it on!' the madam ordered, her voice raised with resentment.

Esther picked up the frock from the floor and held it up in front of her.

'Not good enough for you, eh?' the madam said, with her lips twisted. 'You're ungrateful!' she added with irritation.

And then with a swift movement, she got up from her chair and Esther tensed as she grabbed the tunic back.

'It just needs a little taking in, no need to waste precious money when this is still good enough for the likes of you,' the madam seethed, as she glared at Esther's slim figure with disapproving eyes.

The madam dropped back in her seat and stretched across the table for a large pair of silver scissors and then they both watched as its blades crunched their way through the faded and shapeless fabric.

The jagged part of a sleeve was nipped off. It slid off the cutting table and landed gently on the cement floor. A few moments later a frayed hem slipped to the ground to keep it company. The room was tense as the bits of fabric on the floor steadily increased.

The madam leaned forward and with her feet paddling the treadle, guided what was left of the tunic through the jaws of the machine.

After several minutes had elapsed the sewing machine shuddered and whined before coming to a gradual standstill. A metallic click rang out, the tunic was unclamped and released from its torture.

'Here!' the madam said with gritted teeth, as she held the frock up in the air. 'Here, take it! Take it!'

Esther clapped her hands and curtsied in the way of her mother's people before accepting the tunic. Because in her custom, a gift was sacred, no matter how one might feel about it.

'You make sure you wear it. I don't want to see you coming into my house dressed like that!' she added, gesturing at Esther's brightly patterned frock.

Esther nodded, with her eyes on the ground.

'And make sure you clean up in here after you've changed. Do I have to teach you everything?' the madam snapped again, expelling all the anger eating her up.

Esther left the main house and when she returned, her newly altered but still faded tunic met with her madam's approval.

10

Mail has arrived

Small things had a way of triggering the madam's anger and today, among the letters Brett had brought back with him from the post office, was a letter from her sister, transporting her back to her younger self, and her dreams.

Hilda had worked as a washerwoman then and was stuck in a dingy boarding house with little hope of leaving either when a friend showed her an advert for a mail bride in the Sunday Mail.

'I have to get away from all this,' Hilda had told her sister with her arms submerged in a tub of soapy water. 'Otherwise, what was the use of all that learning?'

And when Brett had paid for her passage on the ship, Hilda remembered how her father had turned his nose up at her with unjustified snobbery for someone who thought nothing of living off the meagre earnings of his eldest child.

Hilda had happily endured the months of sea sickness and boredom, glad to get away from it all and confident of the better life that awaited her.

Memories of the end of their long journey came flooding back to her, as they often did and brought a smile to her face. She remembered how they'd all stood squashed on the deck and waved back at the jubilant crowd below, carrying welcoming banners.

She had worn a pale yellow silk dress that day, with a matching shawl, and had swept her chestnut shoulder-length hair, up into a bun.

She had spotted Brett immediately, dressed in a khaki bush shirt that was tucked neatly into a pair of khaki trousers and with his eyes busily searching the deck for her.

Then his face had lit up, and in that instant their eyes met, recognising each other anew from the photographs they had exchanged.

Then the sea of silk dresses had surged forward, taking Hilda with it, and coming from the opposite direction was Brett, tall and lean, pushing his way through the crowd to claim her for his own.

They reached Fort Victoria a few days after, and Brett had shown her around his farmhouse with its wood stove and sand floors, and the wood crates he used as chairs.

'Where does the water come from?' Hilda had asked then with a worried look at the barrel of water against the kitchen window, and Brett had pointed to a creek that ran at the edge of the garden and the colour had drained from her face.

'Don't worry,' he had reassured her soothingly, 'The servants will take care of everything, you just have to tell them.'

But even that wasn't as straightforward as she'd expected. She didn't understand their language, nor they hers.

'I love it here,' she'd written back to her sister then, although, in truth, she felt alone, surrounded by people she couldn't communicate with.

Gradually, Brett had taught her Chilapalapa, a bastardised mixture of English and Southern Rhodesian native dialects.

'Don't worry, it will take time, but you'll be fine,' Brett murmured, his arm drawing her close to him, and she'd smiled and nodded, happy that she was there with him.

Then an old pastor who had spent many years in the country told her the true meaning of some of the words of this new language that she was trying so hard to learn and she had shrunk back in horror at how belittling some of the phrases were.

'You can't go soft on them, they're not like us. Always show them who's the boss,' Brett had warned her, with his face set.

In the years that followed, Brett was everything his letters had promised, and then the children came, and gradually things began to change between them.

'It doesn't take long for the blinkers to come off,' Helen had said at one of their regular tea parties, 'And the wife is always the last to know.'

And although Helen was talking about herself then, she could've just as well been saying that of Hilda. But Helen was like that, saying things that were best left unsaid.

Hilda blamed the heat for her rounded figure, and her hair, that she now wore in a short crop, which was a far cry from the slim bride of all those years back.

'Esther!' she yelled from her bedroom, her voice echoing menacingly in the almost deserted house. 'Don't just stand there!' she snapped at the young woman in the doorway, her dark blue eyes flashing. 'Come here!'

The bed had been stripped bare and the used linen lay in a heap on the floor and Esther sensing her madam's mood stiffened and prepared herself for what was to follow.

Hilda walked to her wardrobe and brought out a fresh pair of sheets and Esther stepped forward instinctively her arms reaching out to assist her.

Hilda raised her arm to stop her and Esther stepped back. Her eyes followed her madam's hands as they smoothed out the ripples in the under blanket.

Hilda pulled her mouth tight as she spread one pink sheet and then another over the bed. She snatched a blanket hanging over a chair and placed it carefully over the sheets then walked around the bed, neatly tucking the bits hanging loosely over the bed under the mattress.

'The patterned sheets are for the children's rooms,' Hilda had told Esther when she had first arrived. 'The different shapes and colours stop the dirt from showing too soon.'

She draped a quilted patchwork over the bed as her mind sought an opening to what she'd planned to say to her maid.

'It doesn't matter how many times I teach you anything, you never learn. You are all just the same, empty-headed and ignorant,' Hilda said straightening up.

Esther met the two wells of raging fire directed at her for a brief second before dropping her eyes.

'I wanted to serve apple pie for afternoon tea, but the cook boy told me we'd run out of flour.' Hilda's words trickled out like honey from a jar as she gently slipped a pillow into its cotton case. Then she hunched herself forward and fluffed it out before placing it neatly at the top of the bed.

'How many times have I told you to tell me when we're running out of things? How many times, hmm, hmm? It just so happens that I am expecting visitors today and what do you propose I give them? You tell me.'

Esther had learnt to keep perfectly quiet at times like this. She retreated into her shell and dropped her gaze on the white canvas shoes wrapped around her feet.

'You are all the same, no shame, no loyalty,' Hilda persisted, in a harsh tone.

Esther's eyes flicked up briefly before she bowed her head down again.

'You're not the first, you know, so don't think that you're special, because you're not. It's just an urge he has. He can't help himself. But he despises you more than I do,' Hilda assured Esther in an even tone.

A slight tremor passed through Esther and the madam's quick eye caught it. Satisfied that the arrow had hit its mark, Hilda turned back to the bed and began to smooth out the creases in the quilt, before turning the top bit over to create a neat pleat.

When she was done, both women stared at the frilled pillows and the embossed quilt cover, and the bed looked prim and proper and so out of place in a room like this.

Then, with her mind temporarily purged, Hilda pushed her way past Esther, leaving her maid to bear the weight of her quiet outburst.

11

An act of kindness

Mr Riley sat next to Esther as she bathed the baby in the new plastic bath he had brought with him and he watched as a cotton nappy was wrapped around it before its tiny limbs were eased through a laced cotton tunic. Then he tilted his head down and kissed the newborn before shaking his head as if in disbelief

'We'll call her Clara,' he told Esther with a proud smile picking up the baby and cradling her in his arms.

'She won't stop crying and I don't know why?' Esther complained to the compound midwife when she came to check up on the new mother, her head swimming with lack of sleep.

'It's because of the father's blood that runs through its veins,' the old woman replied. Then she gave Esther a toothless grin to show, that she was not serious.

'It's colic, nothing more than just a little wind,' the midwife murmured after, holding the baby's chest against her own and rubbing its back gently to relieve its distress. The minutes ticked by and the child settled down and went to sleep.

But to Esther's dismay, Clara cried often, and at times even after she had followed the midwife's instructions, Clara still wouldn't stop crying.

'Shut her up, for heaven's sake!' Brett seethed, unable to bear the noise. 'Can't you people do anything right?' he asked, unleashing his temper on Esther. And then on a good day and holding the baby gently in his arms, he said, 'She's a pretty little thing and can easily pass for white.'

But Brett was the only one who had anything nice to say about Clara. Esther's head drooped with shame at the way the other workers looked at Clara and at the way the madam twisted her mouth with distaste at the sight of her.

Esther loved Clara with all her heart, but there were many times when she wished that Clara looked like all the other babies in the compound. 'I look different and look what looking different brought me,' she said to herself.

'I want Clara to go to the same school as my boys,' Mr Riley said in one of his happy moods.

Esther gave him a long look which made him put the baby he was playing with back on the mat gently. And when his hands were free, he brought out a small red book from his back pocket.

'You think I'm not serious, hey,' he said, holding the book out to her. 'Well, look here, see for yourself! I put it in your name, Esther, so you can take care of Clara.'

Esther looked at the book he was holding out to her and saw her name written on it.

Then he said with his eyes on her, 'Both my sons have their own books, and I don't see why my daughter can't have one too, no matter what anyone else says.'

Esther turned her face away from him, and Brett said, 'You think I'm joking, hey?' When she still did not say anything, he said, 'Here, take it, take it. You keep it for her!'

But the good days were few, and after one of those days that were not so good, Esther waited until Mr Riley had driven out in his truck before she packed her suitcase. A scotch cart on its way to the grinding mill stopped to give her a lift. And Rajesh was summoned home from the fields by his wife when Esther arrived back at his farm with a bruised face.

'Have you no shame? What will people say if I allow you to leave your husband and come back here?' he said to Esther with a snarl on his face.

Esther told him that she had nowhere else to go, and when he remained adamant, she summoned up the courage to remind him of his promise to her father that he would take care of her.

'It does not matter what you say he does to you,' Rajesh said after reflecting for a moment, and the sting in his tone was now gone. 'You are his wife, remember that! Your bed is made, and you must lie in it!'

Esther stared in front of her, her eyes gloomy with desperation, and the baby stirred restlessly in her arms, and she knew that she had no choice in the matter. And when the boss came to see her at the time that he usually did, it was as if she'd never even tried to leave.

12

Returning from a hunting trip

Mr Riley was on his way home after a week of successful hunting. The excitement of the hunt had left him, but another feeling, more intoxicating, overcame him as his Land Rover bumped its way homewards. He stopped at the compound gate to drop off the men he had taken hunting with him and then continued down the road to his homestead. Before reaching it, he slipped off the road and took a side track that only he ever used.

After a short drive that circumvented his homestead, he parked his vehicle and retrieved a parcel he'd carefully wrapped up earlier from under his seat. And then, with an animated gait, he continued his journey on foot. The exhilaration in him grew steadily as he pushed his way through the long grass and overhanging branches until at last the little cottage came into view.

He stopped abruptly and peered ahead at the two people standing in the doorway and his face tightened as light laughter danced its way to him. Brett recognised the tall well-built man as Bernard, a contract builder he had hired to extend the rooms to the cottage he was now staring at.

Bernard had arrived on the farm one day after Brett had let word out that he needed a bricklayer. It didn't take Brett long to find out that not only was Bernard a good builder, but that he also had a good understanding of machinery and livestock, and he had kept him on. But, looking at the pair at the cottage now, he wondered if Bernard had reasons of his own for his extended stay.

He waited until the two confidants had parted company and then, with his manner now somehow subdued, crept on ahead. When he reached the threshold, he tested the doorknob, and finding it locked, slipped one of the keys from his bunch and gained entry to the cottage.

'Dada!' Clara, who had heard the jingle of keys outside and who had been watching the door now cried out with glee on seeing him. She threw the doll she'd been playing with aside and went bounding up to her father. Brett dropped the small parcel in his hand on the table Esther was working on and scooped the child up in his arms.

'How's Daddy's girl?' he chuckled, holding her up high. Clara giggled happily as she sailed up and down the room. Then, placing Clara back gently on the floor and going to sit on the couch with her, he turned his attention to Esther and said, 'I brought something for you.'

'Thank you,' Esther replied, smiling shyly at the parcel, before unwrapping the fresh chunk of duiker steak.

The room was silent except for the sound of Esther's knife as it touched the cutting board at times. After a short pause, Brett left the couch and went to stand in the middle of the room.

'Leave that and come here,' he said to Esther in an even tone, his finger pointing to a spot close to him.

Esther looked at him sullenly and remained where she was, which made him raise his voice a little. Esther left the table and did as she was told.

'You've been getting visitors, I see,' Brett announced looking pointedly at a bunch of spinach leaves sitting on the kitchen table.

Esther followed his glance, before fixing her eyes back on him.

'Where's that from then, hey?' he stormed, as he glared at her. And when Esther still did not answer he asked, 'And what do you give that young buck in return for the gifts he brings you? Hmm, hmm, what?'

Esther stared at him hard, refusing to accept the accusation being thrown at her. But she could see that he was slowly slipping into that other side of himself and that whatever she said now wouldn't make a difference to him.

'Do I have stupid written on my forehead?' Brett asked, his blue eyes flashing with anger, and thumbing her chest with his forefinger. Esther shook her head and took a step back to steady herself. 'Answer me!' he yelled as he grabbed her with one big hand.

'No, Brett!' Esther stammered.

'You think I don't know what you get up to when I'm not around!' he said, striking the side of her head with the back of his hand.

Esther crumbled to the ground and Clara, yelling incoherently, tried to throw herself at her mother, but Brett was ready for her. He swung his arm out and she stumbled back in fright.

'Go to the bedroom!' Esther yelled out to her daughter, who scrambled to her feet and standing at a safe distance continued to howl.

Brett now crouched over Esther's body, pummeled every part of the prostrate form under him with his clenched hand.

'No, Daddy, no!' Clara yelled as Esther gasped for air, and when he was still deaf to her cries, she wrenched herself away from the safety of the doorway and threw her tiny body between her parents.

Her cries pierced the veil that separated insanity from sanity and Brett, with his fists covered in blood, staggered up to his feet. He went to stand a short distance away, his chest heaving as the thunderstorm subsided.

Esther's arm came up, and she pushed Clara off her before rising slowly to her feet. She limped into the bathroom and pulled the latch shut. Clara pressed herself against the closed door and waited.

Brett's heavy footsteps strode to the kitchen tub. He picked up a mug and scooped out water from the barrel beside it. Then he picked up a cake of soap and lathering his arms, washed off the blood staining them. Then, wiping his hands against his hunting gear, he went to stand behind Clara. And with his head leaning on the door, he began to pound the door with his fist.

'I want you out of there in five minutes before I kick the door in,' he yelled. 'Hurry up and go and finish your cooking. It's past lunchtime.'

He turned his gaze down to Clara and her little body tensed. Then he held his hand out to her, before leading her back to the couch they had been sitting on earlier.

'Here,' Brett said, holding a fork with a piece of game attached to it out to Esther when they were now seated around the kitchen table. 'I don't think I've ever tasted steak this good before!'

Esther took the piece of meat from his fork with her fingers and slipped it into her mouth. And it was as if everything that had happened earlier hadn't happened at all. Except, of course, for the bump and the bruises on Esther's face and the wet smear left by Esther's mop, where she'd wiped the floor clean.

As the days went by, and things only got worse, Esther said she'd had enough and that she wanted to leave.

'You can leave any time you want,' Brett said, holding the door open for her to go.

Esther turned to where Clara was standing and held her hand out to her. The child rushed towards her mother and buried her face in her mother's skirt to shut out the sobbing and the angry words. Esther stepped towards the opening and Brett moved swiftly, planting himself in the doorway.

'Not with my child. You can go, but just you. Come on, out with you,' he said, grabbing Esther's arm and trying to force her out through the open door.

Clara was crying with her face against her father's leg and Esther wouldn't leave without her child. Brett tried to shove her out and she dug her fingers into the wooden door frame to stop him from achieving his purpose. Clara began to howl at the top of her voice, scratching and clawing her father to stop.

'Okay, okay,' Brett said with a laugh as he stepped back inside.

He shut the door and locked it, before removing the key from its hole. And Esther scrambled away from him, taking the child with her.

'Come, Clara,' Brett said, smiling and crouching to unfasten the child's fingers from her mother's dress. 'Mummy can go if she doesn't want to live here with us anymore. But you are too precious to me, and I will not let her take you away from me.'

He straightened up with the child's hand in his and then turned to peer into Esther's face. 'See, Esther,' he said to her, 'The child is happy here with me.'

He let go of Clara's hand and went to where Esther was, and Clara's eyes followed his movements. He touched Esther's chin gently with one finger and scrutinised her face as if trying to read her thoughts.

'You're a wild one, Esther. I knew that from the beginning. Your uncle took the trouble to warn me. To prepare me. And you know what, I like a good fight, and I was determined, more than ever to take what I wanted. And now I have you where I want you,' he said, nodding towards Clara.

13

A forced relocation

The whispers concerning Mr Riley's other business ventures and the cruelty to his workers were growing louder.

'Is this something I should be worrying about?' Hilda asked her husband when some of the rumours reached her at her tea club.

'It's all gossip,' Brett replied. 'You should be standing by my side, and not listening to idle chatter!'

'It's the pilfering we can't condone,' the directors told Brett when the news finally reached its intended audience.

'Have you heard?' Helen said to the tea club ladies, just before Hilda arrived. 'Brett's been relieved of his duties. Fired!'

'Poor Hilda,' some of the women murmured.

'He's a piece of work, I don't know why she puts up with him,' another added.

The farm truck had been loaded with the Riley's household goods and Hilda and her two sons lingered beside it as they waited for Brett to drive them away.

There was the smell of alcohol on Brett's breath, and he held a whip in one hand.

'You're mine, damn you!' Brett said to Esther in a fit of ungovernable fury. 'Paid for, lock, stock, and barrel. You will come with me, do you understand?'

He stood facing her, angry at her for making him almost beg her to go away with him. She kept her eyes on her tormentor, watching his every move. Then she turned her glance towards a handful of men milling in the background, and Brett turned his head back to follow her gaze.

'The lorry is ready and waiting, sir,' the farm's boss boy said.

Brett looked past him to the men now standing in a group behind the boss boy and smiled at the small show of rebellion. Then he held his whip up defiantly, confident of the power he still wielded over the farm labourers, and then, as if reaching a decision, dropped his hand again.

He pulled himself up to his full height to show that he was still the boss, and then he stormed past the boss boy. The knot of men opened and gave him a free pass to the waiting lorry. A few moments later, an engine started up and the truck rumbled down the driveway, leaving behind it a deathly silence.

14

News travels fast

The scotch cart stopped outside her uncle's gate, and the children were the first to see Esther and Clara alighting from it. Esther smiled at their excited chatter, glad to be finally free. And Clara, unused to company, peeped from behind her mother's skirt at the children, barefoot and dressed in ragged clothes, racing up the driveway to meet them.

'Now, now, have you forgotten Maleek and Anesu already, after all the time you spent playing with them? Stand up straight and don't be shy now,' Esther admonished her daughter.

The children were nearly halfway up the driveway and filling the air with their laughter when a window suddenly rattled open, and a head popped out from behind the curtain.

'Get back here this moment,' a voice lashed out.

The children stopped abruptly with their heads turned fearfully towards it. Amina's voice rang out again, and the children, now quiet and sullen, skulked back down the driveway and then disappeared into the garden where they'd been playing earlier. The window banged shut and the head behind it vanished as the drapes were drawn.

Esther rapped the front door with her knuckles and then stood back. After a short pause, she knocked again, and when there was still no answer, she was quick to conclude that the news of Brett's forced departure had preceded her. She went to the back of the house and continued her knocking on the kitchen door.

After a long pause, the door creaked, and a woman took a long peep at Esther through the narrow gap, before asking, 'Can I help you?'

'You know who I am, Rudo,' Esther retorted irritably. 'I can hear movement inside the house and yet not a single person seems to have heard me. How long do you intend to keep me waiting outside?'

'Tell me what you want,' Rudo repeated but with less conviction than before.

'Why do you stand there pretending not to know me, Rudo? Is my uncle at home?'

'Madam, you know that I only work here.' Rudo relented as she stepped through the doorway, before closing the door behind her. 'I am obliged to do what I am told, otherwise I risk losing my job. The big madam is in the house, but she's been instructed by your uncle not to speak to you.'

'Go back inside and tell her I have nowhere to go. I have a small child. Where does she expect me to take her, at this time of the day?'

'Please wait here, Madam, and I will go in and ask the big madam what to do,' Rudo offered reluctantly.

Esther found a stool under an avocado tree and waited there with Clara flopped at her feet.

'You want to sit on my lap now?' Esther murmured to her daughter, who was drawing shapes in the soft sand with her finger.

Clara shook her head without looking up. The child shifted her body on the ground as the shapes began to take form. A circle with a hat on it, two sticks for the arms, and then a bulky boot on one leg. Esther turned her face away from the drawing abruptly when Clara added another boot to her artwork.

'Is Daddy coming to pick us up in his lorry?' Clara asked, turning to gaze up at her mother earnestly and Esther was saved from answering her when the kitchen door swung open at last.

She looked up expectantly, but the maid's crestfallen face and the reed mat and blankets in her arms made her look down again. They followed Rudo down a winding path and when they entered a brick shed, Rudo found room between stacks of sacks filled with cobs of corn and spread out the mat on the floor. Esther went to stand in the doorway with her back to the room and with her eyes fixed on a solitary structure a short distance away.

'That's where I sleep now, Madam, but if you like, I can take your bedding to your old room, and I can sleep here,' Rudo offered as she went and stood next to Esther.

Esther shuddered at the memory of that room and what happened in there, and she shook her head resolutely, saying, 'No, no. This is fine, thank you.'

'Why are you crying?' Esther asked, wiping the tears streaming down Clara's cheeks with the back of her hand. 'Are you hungry? Do you want something to eat?'

The child shrugged her shoulders, but the tears kept coming.

'Are you cold?' Esther persisted. This time, a shake of the head. Esther lifted the child onto her lap and cuddled her. 'Okay now?' she asked. Clara nodded with her eyes shut, and her head on her mother's chest.

Outside the shed, Esther could hear the faint chatter of the household as they went about their daily business, but no one approached the shed, except for Rudo, to bring them first their breakfast then lunch, and then supper.

'The boss wants to see you before he leaves for the fields, Madam,' Rudo told Esther on her next visit.

Inside the homestead, Esther stood in the doorway with her hands clasped together and her head bowed as she waited for permission to enter.

A figure seated at a small desk at the end of the lounge room tore its eyes away from a blue hardcover ledger lying open in front of it and scowled at the brightly coloured frock sheltering the bony figure inside it. Curious eyes hovered over the hollowed-out cheekbones and the dark rings circling each eye. And then, with his eyes still on his niece, Rajesh howled, 'Amina!'

His wife, who had been forewarned about the meeting, arrived promptly. She brushed past Esther and Clara before dropping herself down on a couch, where she regarded the pair in the doorway with a neutral expression.

The ledger snapped shut decisively and Rajesh returned it to the top drawer of his desk. He left his seat, sauntered across the room, and went to lean on the back of an armchair with his face turned towards his wife.

Amina beckoned towards the door, and Esther entered the room tentatively and sat on the floor in front of the couple. Clara still holding on tightly to her mother's skirt, dropped down with her.

'Why are you not in your husband's house?' Rajesh demanded, going straight to the heart of the matter without beating around the bush.

'Boss Riley is gone away, and there's a new boss at the farm now,' Esther replied in a low tone.

'What about money? Did your husband leave you money?' he interjected. Esther shook her head. 'Nothing?' her uncle stormed. 'You live with a man for all this time, and you come back here with nothing?'

'He gave me nothing,' Esther agreed through quivering lips.

'That's because you're stupid!' her uncle thundered. A tremor passed through Esther, and Clara gave her mother a terrified look. 'You are no different from your mother!' Rajesh declared in a severe tone before going off on a tirade. 'I always knew you would come to this! There is a name for people like you and mark my words, the same thing that's happened to you will happen to that child of yours!'

Rajesh paced the room as he berated his niece for not going with Brett to his new home. Fresh tears rolled down Esther's cheeks and Clara whimpered with her face buried in her mother's bony lap.

'Raj! Raj!' Amina implored at last.

Rajesh emerged from his outburst and after uttering a final curse, went to sit in an armchair opposite his wife.

'Your uncle is concerned about your welfare,' Amina began in a quiet tone, addressing Esther for the first time. 'I want you to think carefully. Did your husband give you anything, something, no matter how small? Did he talk to you about his other business? About things that concern the welfare of the child?'

Esther kept her eyes downcast to avoid the inquiring ones fixed on her and shook her head at the floor.

'Use your brain, woman! Can you think of anything?' Rajesh, unable to contain himself any longer, hissed. Esther cowered under his wrath.

'Speak!' Rajesh thundered, and even though Esther knew that this included the small red book Brett had given her, shook her head even more resolutely than before.

15

A visit to the post office

Esther stood in the tall grass with her hand shielding her eyes from the sun and scanned the buildings spread alongside the dirt road. Her gaze rested on a stout brick building with a large red jerry can mounted on a stand in front of it.

She secured the small bag hanging from her shoulder under her arm and with her daughter's hand firmly in hers, waited at the edge of the road. She turned her head up the road and then down it again. She gave a small cry to Clara before they both bolted across the deserted road.

They walked past a patch of mopane trees where Brett had parked his lorry, that one time he had brought her here. Brett and Clara had walked off hand in hand then and she had remained behind, seated between the crates of produce at the back of the lorry. From there she watched as a man dressed in khaki shorts with a matching shirt and holding a wooden baton in one hand rushed out into the open. He ran ahead of Brett and Clara and with a broad smile playing on his face, swung the door open for them to enter.

He opened the door again a short while later and the pair emerged from the building, Brett with his head bent towards the bundle of letters in his hand and Clara chewing a toffee and cradling a pink plastic doll in her arms. Then they'd both jumped back into the cab of the lorry, without even a backward glance at her.

Esther now watched as the same security guard clicked his heels at an old couple and then performed an elaborate salute for them, his pearly white teeth contrasting deeply with his beaming face.

Then he whizzed ahead of them with his hand stretched out towards the door. The couple entered the building, chuckling happily.

The doorkeeper strolled back to his post smiling when he suddenly tensed at the sight of Esther approaching the main entrance. He moved quickly and intercepted her.

'Where to?' he snarled, resting the end of his baton on Esther's chest and with his bloodshot eyes trained on her.

Esther held the red book up to him and he pushed it aside contemptuously with his baton. 'Please,' Esther pleaded. 'The child's father…'

The man turned the end of his baton aggressively at a long queue that started from a window at the back of the post office building and Esther stared back at him with confusion.

'Are you challenging me?' the man demanded in a threatening manner. 'You want me to drag you away by your hair?'

The security guard suddenly cocked his ears and then, elbowing Esther off the walkway, arranged his features into a beaming smile. He clicked his heels at a middle-aged gentleman wearing a wide-brimmed hat, and dust rose around his feet as they scuttled off towards the entrance. Esther and Clara redirected their footsteps to the back of the post office.

An hour later, Esther held the red book up to a man behind a serving hatch. The bank teller flipped through its pages with little interest, before becoming more alert. He fixed his glance on Esther for an instant before disappearing hastily into the back of the room.

A sudden chill overcame Esther. 'What if Brett had gone back on his word and reported the book stolen?' she thought, clutching her bag nervously. A slight tremble began to build up inside her as a woman with a bright pink face, yellowish hair, and dressed in a red blouse appeared suddenly at the window.

'Esther?' she inquired in a rich Irish brogue, looking at Esther and Clara in turn.

'Yes, Madam,' Esther replied quietly, her voice quivering.

'I want you to go to that door,' the office manager said, leaning out of the hatch and pointing at the heavily guarded door, whose sentry now pretended not to be eavesdropping on the conversation taking place at the window.

Esther and Clara reached the door, and the woman held it open for them to enter. She took them to a small room and gestured at a chair beside her, before sitting down but Esther, unaccustomed to such civility, remained standing with a frightened look on her face. The post office official insisted and Esther slid into the chair awkwardly.

Clara kept her eyes locked on the strange woman's face, and then losing interest, went to play with the small handbag at her mother's feet.

'This is a lot of money,' the office manager told Esther in a friendly tone. 'Too much to take out at one time. What do you need it for?'

'Transport and food, Madam,' Esther murmured.

'I tell you what,' the bank official responded with her pen poised. 'Tell me how much you need for these things you mentioned.'

Esther named a figure, and the woman entered into a conversation with her customer. She made a list on a notepad, and stopping now and then, revised the numbers she had jotted down. Then she retrieved a calculator with a roll of paper attached to it from a shelf and Esther looked on curiously as she tapped on it.

The keys rang out, and Clara sprang up from under the table with rounded eyes. A strip of paper edged out and then lolled like a tongue from the calculator's mouth.

'You see here,' the woman said, tearing off the tongue and squinting at it, before showing it to Esther. 'This is all you need for now. The rest you keep in the book until you need it.'

Esther nodded in agreement and when they were alone, she grinned widely at her daughter.

The woman returned with a small tray a short while later. 'This is what you are taking out,' the manager informed Esther, her pen hovering over an amount reflected in the book. Then she counted out the notes and laid them out on the table, before giving Esther a hard stare for confirmation. Esther nodded her head.

'This is for transport,' the woman said, arranging the notes in a pile. Then she made another pile and said, 'And this is for food.' Gesturing to a third pile, she said, 'And this is for accommodation.'

Both women eyed the small fortune in front of them, then the bank manager leaned back in her chair to show that she'd done her duty. Esther took the first pile of notes and put it in an outside zipper of the small bag she carried. She put the second pile in an inner pocket of the same bag. She unbuttoned her blouse and hid the rest in her underwear, much to the amusement and approval of the woman, who had seen it all before.

Back at Rajesh's farm, they avoided the main house, and with her heart thumping wildly, Esther led Clara to a pile of scraggy stones, where a watermelon stall once stood and beside which was a cage where the watermelons were stored at night. The cage and the steel gauze that was fitted over it were now gone and all that was left was a hole that was now covered with mimosa branches with sharp white thorns clinging onto them.

Esther glanced around cautiously and then quickly dragged the branches aside. Then kneeling beside the hole and leaning down, she retrieved the suitcase that she had secretly deposited there the night before.

She spoke to Clara quietly but urgently, as she brushed the dust off the wooden case with her hand. Then they set off swiftly in the direction they had come.

Back on the main road, they took shelter from prying eyes and the sweltering heat under a wild hedge.

The sun had not risen far when a middle-aged man servicing this part of the road approached, walking behind two donkeys drawing a cart.

II

Part 2 - Bernard and Esther

16

Bernard rescues Esther

The cart driver who had spoken little during their relatively long journey cracked his whip. The donkeys stood still as he helped Esther and Clara out of the cart. Then he turned back to the cart to retrieve his passenger's suitcase.

Esther had thought only of getting as far away from her uncle's farm as she could, but now that the trip had come to an end, the enormity of what she had done hit her. 'What to do now? It's not just my welfare to worry about, but Clara's too,' she told herself with panic.

'There's a mission school not far from here,' the driver offered, seeing the dilemma playing out on her features as he placed the wooden suitcase down beside her. 'They're always looking for workers.'

Esther turned an anxious look at the speaker and the driver's heart lurched with compassion for the young and troubled woman.

'I know that look,' the man thought to himself. 'She's running away from something or someone.' Then he said to himself angrily, 'There's nothing more I can do for her, except keep her secret.'

As he pulled and pushed at the reins to turn his donkeys around, Esther couldn't help noticing the great pains he took to avoid all eye contact with her before he cracked his whip in the air and began walking briskly without a backward glance.

Esther picked up her suitcase and then after a brief hesitation, turned to walk in the direction the man had pointed to.

It was October, and at this time of the year, the heat can be unbearable. And Clara, despite them having taken several short breaks to rest, found herself unable to walk any further. She sat on the hot ground and began to cry. Esther took the cloth wrapped around her waist and used it to strap the child on her back. Then picking up their belongings, walked on, her body growing weaker with each step.

'The mission can't be much further, just a few more steps,' she murmured, reassuring herself more than she did the child clinging onto her.

An hour went by, and then a sudden giddiness came over Esther. Her legs buckled and the ground came up fast to meet her. Clara let out a weak wail before it all went quiet.

Another hour went by.

'Whoa!' a man riding a horse called as he peered ahead curiously. He cantered over to what looked like a heap of rags and then started with surprise when a small head showed itself.

'Clara!' he cried, dismounting his horse and rushing over to the child who sat beside the road crying.

He lifted her up in his arms and wiped the tears trickling down her cheeks. Then something caught his eye and he placed the child back on the ground slowly.

His heart thumped wildly, as he rushed over to a ditch that ran alongside the road. Then crouching beside a still figure that lay there, uttered, 'Esther,' in a voice that was heavy with anguish as he bundled her up in his arms.

'Bernard!' a woman cried out with surprise as she rushed towards the door to let him in. Then, turning her head back, she yelled out,

'Mr Ndlovu! Come quickly, it's Bernard!'

A tall thin man with a clean-shaven face and wearing spectacles came rushing behind her.

'I found them on the side of the road,' Bernard said as he followed Mrs Ndlovu into the house with the semi-conscious woman in his arms and the child clutching the side of his trousers.

Bernard lowered Esther on a mat, and just then her glazed eyes flew open, and she began to fight him off. It took both men to hold her down before her eyes rolled back and she went back into a deep sleep.

'What's wrong with her?' Mr Ndlovu asked when her breathing had become more even.

'She has a fever and it's making her delirious,' Mrs Ndlovu replied.

When both mother and child were now sound asleep on the mat, the three adults retired to the lounge room.

'And the child?' Mrs Ndlovu asked as they sipped their tea.

'What about her?' Bernard replied wearily.

'Is the child hers? We don't want trouble here.'

'The child is hers. I know her. We worked for the same man once.' Bernard replied.

'His child,' Mrs Ndlovu murmured knowingly, and Bernard nodded with his face averted.

'No, no,' Esther moaned in the early hours of the morning. 'I won't let you take my child!'

Bernard slipped out of his chair and went to wrap his arms tightly around her. She mumbled incoherently for a while, then she closed her eyes and went back to sleep.

At another time, Esther opened her eyes and saw a woman with a kind face who reminded her of her mother.

'I can't stop, he'll kill me for sure this time!' she confided to the stranger. And then her voice became more urgent. 'Please don't tell them where I am,' she pleaded. 'They want to send me back to him.'

A week went by, days and nights merging into one, as Esther's life hung in the balance.

'Just one more,' Mrs Ndlovu coaxed, with one hand circling her patient's frail shoulders, and the other holding out a spoonful of watery warm porridge.

'Clara,' Esther murmured faintly, her feverish eyes searching the room, in one of her lucid moments.

'Clara is fine,' Mrs Ndlovu reassured her. 'She's at the school creche where my husband works as the headmaster. Don't worry she'll be back soon.'

Esther sighed with relief and then parted her lips to accept the sweet warm liquid.

'How is she?' Mr Ndlovu asked from the doorway, one day. 'Should we send for Bernard?'

'The worst is over,' his wife replied, rising to her feet. 'Hush now and let her sleep.'

17

A marriage proposal

Bernard leaned forward and pressed his lips gently on one side of Esther's neck and then, turning his head slightly, locked his dark eyes on hers, sending a tremor up her spine. He moved his head ever so slightly and gave the other side of her neck the same treatment as the first. Esther sighed contentedly.

Then he let his glance travel further up, to a scar behind Esther's right ear. He wanted to reach out and soothe the welt with his fingers, but he held back, afraid of what that might do to her.

Esther had told him about it, and he had pictured Mr Riley stumbling into the cottage and dragging her away from the wall where she'd been cowering, to the middle of the room. He saw the man's hand swing out and the ring binding that man to his wife, colliding and melting into the smooth flesh it made contact with and leaving its mark there. He pulled away involuntarily and Esther knew what he was thinking, and she regretted having told him that part of her, because of what it did to him.

'Come,' he said, pulling her up to her feet. 'We've known each other long enough and I want you to meet my mother.'

'No!' Esther shrieked playfully. 'You know your mother doesn't like me!'

'What's there not to like about you?' he asked, holding both her hands in his and appraising her with his eyes.

'You told me yourself; she wants a plump Matabele woman with big hips and big breasts!'

Their eyes met, serious for a second, and then they both broke out in laughter. His face became earnest, and he let his fingers trace her dark eyebrows and the bridge of her perfectly shaped nose, skirting the contours of her oval face and then around her full lips. And then he leaned in closer to breathe in the spicy fragrance of Bantu mixed with Asian, and he knew that there was no one else in the world that he would want to spend his life with.

'Hop on,' Bernard said to Esther, holding his bicycle steady as she slipped onto his back carrier. The bicycle wobbled as he swung onto it, and then he said, 'I want to show you something,' as he began to pedal.

They jostled over the rocky terrain, and the khaki landscape rushed past them and Bernard felt complete with Esther's arms tight around his waist. They left the bicycle hidden in the long grass, and when they were on top of a granite outcrop, Bernard pointed down to a creek in the valley below.

'We used to fish there when I was a young boy,' Bernard told Esther fondly, 'But see that fence there, that says it's private property, and only the owner can fish there now. A whole river, for just one person.'

They walked to the other side of the summit, and he put his finger over his mouth with his eyes on her. A ripple of fractured voices riding on the waves of a light breeze reached them, and they crouched low in the bushes.

Then lying flat on their stomachs, Bernard pointed to a flurry of half-naked men drenched in sweat. Now and then a glint of steel flickered from the various lumber tools in the men's hands. Just then a shout rang out and a tree came crashing down to the ground, its branches reaching out to its neighbours as if crying out for help. Men wielding hand saws converged on it and the air vibrated with the sound of serrated steel blades cutting into wood.

A warning rang out and yet another tree tumbled down, and then another, so that the sun now found itself glaring down in shock at a part of the countryside that had been long hidden from it. Mopane, msasa, and mfuti trees, and many others succumbed to the brutality at hand, amid loud chatter and excited laughter.

Then the ant-like figures darted around, dragging branches across and stacking them up into a pyramid, where another pile of branches now reduced to ash, had previously stood. Dying coals flickered avidly as the weight over them grew. A hungry flame leapt up, hissing angrily as it devoured branches in an orange glow.

The sound of a tractor engine starting up attracted the attention of the observers above. They followed its progress as it rumbled forward, its driver perched high on his seat, and with his body twisted towards a plough wedged between its back wheels. The tractor driver bounced on his seat as the sharp blades of the plough left gaping wounds in the earth behind him.

'Nothing is like it used to be,' Bernard said, shaking his head despondently. 'I used to hunt there with my father. We only took what we needed, which wasn't much. We took care of the forest, and it took care of us.'

'Tell me about your father,' Esther said when they were back on the road to the mission school. 'What happened to him?'

'They took away his chieftainship, his livestock, everything. And then they banished him. We had to leave our homeland, but I vowed I would come back one day, and I did,' Bernard murmured.

'Why?' Esther asked in despair. 'What did he do?'

'Stood up for his people,' Bernard replied with a bitter smile. 'Stood up to authority. They wanted cheap labour, and he wanted fair wages for his people, so they made an example of him, and punished him.'

'What about your mother?' Esther asked, and Bernard laughed and said, 'She has the warrior blood of our ancestors running through her veins. She still hasn't accepted her loss of status, even after all these years. She still believes that one day I will be installed as the rightful heir to the throne and restore her to her former glory.'

'Is that what you want?' Esther asked. 'To be chief like your father?'

'That would've been my right as the eldest son, but I can't be a chief now, because of what they did to him. But he was also a rancher, so why can't I be that, if nothing else? Cattle and plenty of land for them to graze in is what I want,' Bernard told her stubbornly.

He was standing with his chest puffed out against his frayed shirt and Esther saw the man that he was under those rags and her heart wanted to burst with all the love she felt for him. A look came into her eyes, that he knew well, because it was the same look he had, whenever he looked at her.

'You don't need acres and acres of land to feel free, Bernard,' Esther told him.

Back at his homestead, the sound of hammering stopped, and Bernard stepped back to examine his workmanship with a keen eye. Then, resting his arms on the beams of the cattle kraal he was repairing, he waited for his mother to reach him.

'Nkosazane,' Bernard murmured, as the regal woman approached him.

'My son,' his mother responded, with a slight bow of her head. 'I have thought hard about your request, and I am now ready to give you an answer.'

Bernard picked up his toolbox and returned to the homestead with his mother.

'You'll work and raise enough money to pay for lobola, and then you will marry as planned. Your bride-to-be is here with us, one of our own,' Nkosazane told her son when they were seated.

'What about Esther?' Bernard asked. 'Have you forgotten the last conversation I had with you?'

'Will you throw away all we'd hoped for on account of a fling with someone of no consequence?' Nkosazane countered, with suppressed rage. 'Someone with a child of her own?'

'You have two other sons, Mother,' Bernard replied in a quiet tone. 'I won't give Esther up.'

'So be it, but don't come running back to me when things go wrong,' his mother warned with a thunderous face.

18

A goat is rescued

Bernard grabbed some leaves off a tree without breaking his stride and went to crouch beside a brown and white goat lying helpless on its side. The goat, forgetting its distress for a moment, stuck out its tongue and snatching the leaves from his hand began to chew on them greedily, with its head turned to one side.

'What have you got yourself into this time, Betty?' Bernard whispered as he slid down on his knees to examine her.

Betty made a feeble attempt to scramble up and Thoko held her down and then began stroking her head to keep her calm.

'I can't see her hind legs,' Bernard said with his forehead creased as he loosened the rocks under the animal and threw them aside.

A short while later he stood upright and removed the belt around his waist and looping it around Betty's stomach, threaded it back through its buckle to form a lasso.

'We'll try and hoist her up,' Bernard said, giving the end of the belt to his son and going to bend over Betty with his arm around her torso.

Thoko braced himself, and when Bernard grunted, 'Go!' they both strained their muscles and dug their heels in the dirt. 'Again!' Bernard cried and again they tensed their bodies.

The earth shifted gradually around the bony limbs and then without warning it opened up and sent them all scuttling into the dirt. Their cries of surprise cut through the quiet and unsettled a covey of quail nesting in the trees close by. Bernard, still holding on tight to his prize, gave the goat a thorough examination, and finding no broken bones, released her with a playful slap. The goat tottered about as she regained her senses, before darting off towards the waiting flock. Some of her companions rushed forward to welcome her back into their fold.

'Carry on, young man,' Bernard said, saluting his son with a playful smile before wandering off.

After trekking in the woods for half an hour he walked purposefully to a spot, crawled through the undergrowth and retrieved a snare. He removed the rabbit caught in it and reset the trap, and then with the rabbit slung over his shoulder, set off again. He had walked only a short distance when he stopped suddenly to cock his head to the sky. A drumbeat came echoing back to him. He stood listening to it for a bit and then after some inner turmoil, he made his mind up and changed his course.

The sound of the drum grew louder with each step and not long after he spotted a cluster of huts further ahead. He was about to turn around and walk back the way he'd come when just then, a woman with a baby strapped to her back left the bushes she'd been sitting under and went to linger at the compound's entrance. Bernard quickly took cover behind a cedar tree.

A bulky man with a shaved head who appeared to have been watching the woman left his seat and stood at attention in front of the gate with his legs astride. The woman muttered under her breath and the man responded with gestures that appeared to be driving her back to her previous seat. The woman, refusing to be ordered around, turned her head away from him defiantly, and at that moment, Bernard recognised her as Tariro, one of their church members.

'I know you're in there!' Tariro shouted suddenly, raising her voice high so that it rose above the guard's head and made its way to the huts behind him.

The man opened the gate and made a threatening movement towards her. Tariro took a step back and eyed him uncertainly.

'Get up, you piece of rubbish!' another voice swore harshly from inside one of the huts in the compound before going to prod the body asleep on a reed mat with her foot. 'This is not Tariro's house! Come on, out with you! Go and find someone else's time to waste!'

Tariro, hearing the woman's muffled speech, resumed her shouting. The woman inside the hut gave a loud sigh. Then she waddled over to a small table with a mirror and began twirling a long scarf elegantly around her head. Next, she turned to a colourful array of wood and glass bangles and began to slip them through her hands mechanically. Then she placed a string of brightly coloured beads around her neck and after patting them down against her chest, stooped down to slip on similarly coloured anklets.

She smiled at the bright trinkets hanging from her ears in the mirror and remembering the still half-asleep man, went to lean over him and yelled, 'Out! Out!' angrily. She pulled him upright with ease and then handling him roughly shoved him through the doorway.

The still inebriated man stumbled across the courtyard and was met by the verbal abuse coming from outside the gate which immediately intensified with his sudden undignified appearance.

'Quiet!' the obstinate woman in the doorway of her hut rallied back aggressively, stepping out to stand defiantly in the face of the torrent of insults being hurled out. 'Don't blame me if you can't take care of your man!'

Cursing loudly, the woman marched purposefully towards the gate, before stopping short of it, and unknowingly revealing her face to Bernard who was hidden from view only a short distance away.

Bernard gave a sudden start and ran his hand over his head, before turning back to scrutinise the face now turned fully in his direction.

'Lindiwe?' Bernard muttered with confusion, at the memory of a young girl who had not only been his friend at school but his first crush. Then she had disappeared one day, left for the city, he had heard. 'And if it is her, what happened to her voice?' Bernard wondered, 'How did it become so hard and so reckless?' He leaned back against the tree as he fought to recover from his shock.

The half-dressed man stumbled into the courtyard and staggering from side to side, squinted through a thick veil of drunkenness and seeing his wife standing outside the compound with their child on her back, suddenly baulked.

The gateman, after assessing the situation on both sides of his post, dropped his fierce stance and then, chuckling loudly, swung the gate wide open.

Garai, not fully recovered from his all-night debauchery, hesitated for a second biding his time. Then, pawing the ground to gain speed, bolted out of the compound through the gateway.

His wife, who had anticipated his move, let out a cry of frustration and pounced on him. Garai gave himself up to her and stood by submissively as she grabbed at his pockets roughly and began turning them inside out.

Finding nothing in them she began to yell out with despair, 'Are you telling me that you drank all the money? What is wrong with you? How will I feed the children?'

Garai dropped his head in shame, and in that instant, his wife began punching him, before seizing his collar, to the gate-man's delight. Then the family, with Garai cowering from the punches coming down on him and the screeches of betrayal surrounding them, proceeded down the path.

Bernard waited until the baby, bobbing up and down on its mother's back and seemingly unfazed by the whole ordeal, had disappeared in a bend in the road before he stepped back on the path.

19

A visit to the beer garden

Bernard was just beginning to congratulate himself for not being discovered near the beer garden when he heard footsteps coming up the road he had just left.

'Ah, Bernard!' a stout bald man with a bushy beard exclaimed. 'What are you doing here so far from home?' Then, noticing the rabbit slung over Bernard's shoulder, he said, 'Hunting, of course!'

Bernard looked up at his neighbour with genuine surprise and cried out, 'Samuel my friend!'

The men shook hands and stood talking for a while before Samuel said unexpectedly, 'I'm off to the shebeen. You must've heard the drums beating, right?'

'Oh,' Bernard replied, trying to hide his discomfort, 'Is that what that was all about?'

'Why don't you join me? You may just change your mind about our beer garden,' Samuel told him, laughing good-naturedly. 'Come on, whatever needs to be done at home can be done later,' he insisted, dispelling the indecisive look on Bernard's face.

'Why not?' Bernard agreed with a smile, now more eager than ever to set eyes again on the woman he believed was Lindiwe. He

75

stepped off the road, and pulling out ivy vines growing on the ground, returned wrapping them around the rabbit.

Not far off, the asbestos mine's gong rang, signalling the end of the night shift for its workers.

'Come,' Samuel urged, looking keen to get moving as quickly as possible, and Bernard with his game now neatly parcelled in the vines, marched briskly alongside his friend.

After the earlier excitement, the beer garden had grown quiet again. Only one patron, who appeared to have been there from the night before, sat on a stool with his head resting on the table in front of him. And at his feet was a clay pot lying empty on its side. Samuel gave an exasperated sigh when a group of mine workers came round a bend and entered the beer garden noisily just ahead of them. Hearing their loud chatter the drunk man roused himself from his sleep and then, as if in a hurry to be somewhere else, pushed past the workers on his way out.

Samuel, who had the confidence of someone who had visited the beer garden many times, led Bernard past the mine workers who were now seated around two tables on an assortment of makeshift chairs made from wooden stumps, metal drums and even moulded bricks. They turned to a discreet corner of the yard, and after gesturing to a chair, Samuel sat down and placed the hat in his hand on the table in front of him.

'Nice and quiet here,' Samuel said, as Bernard leaned back to survey the garden.

'Yes, it is,' Bernard replied with relief on noticing that though their seats were not visible to anyone in the garden they still commanded an excellent view of it.

A short distance from them three tall drums and a mbira rested on a raised platform under a thatched roof which was supported by four sturdy mopane poles.

Samuel signalled, and a woman elegantly draped in a printed caftan with a matching turban twisted high above her head ran up to him eagerly. On close inspection, Bernard realised that the woman was a lot younger than he'd first thought, probably just entering her teens.

The girl lingered beside Samuel and when he tilted his head up to whisper something in her ear, she smiled at him coyly. Samuel murmured again and the girl gave him a broad, shameless grin. Then, moving closer to Samuel, she laughed suggestively while rubbing her hips invitingly against him. Bernard squirmed in his seat.

'Don't worry,' Samuel said when they were on their own, sensing Bernard's unease, 'no one can see us from here.'

After a short pause, the girl returned with a clay pot and curtsied before the men. Samuel took a small sip of the home-brewed beer, and finding it to his satisfaction, nodded at the girl and then tipped the pot over his mouth.

He passed the pot to his companion and Bernard, suddenly feeling parched, drank from it eagerly. He placed the pot on the table carefully and feeling an immediate sense of calm, grinned sheepishly at his neighbour.

A few minutes later, the girl returned with a wooden bowl filled with water. She was accompanied by another young girl similarly dressed and carrying two plates heaped with sadza, relish and braised meat.

'What are you waiting for? Tuck in,' Samuel said when they had both washed their hands and dried them on the sides of their trousers.

Bernard waited until the young waitresses had laughingly skipped off to take an order from another paying guest, before turning to the plate in front of him.

As they dined, a steady stream of customers came flowing in through the gates and the garden hummed with pleasant chatter. Bernard stared through the hedge they were sitting behind as he chewed on a bone and was not surprised to see a few familiar Christian faces in the crowd.

Just then three men dressed in long printed shirts ambled onto the stage and took their positions behind the musical instruments there, while a fourth man carrying a guitar and with his hair twisted in small plaits around his head made idle chatter as he tuned his guitar.

Samuel pushed his empty plate back and sat up in his chair, just as a roar broke out from the crowd. A string of waitresses, whose dresses matched the shirts of the band players, came running through the crowd ululating and with the gourds tied around their ankles rattling enthusiastically.

The drummers welcomed them by smashing their mallets against the thick hides wrapped tight around birch drum shells.

A loud shrill rose to the sky as the dancers mounted the stage. The band members pounded their instruments and the music rang out, picking up speed and reaching a feverish frenzy.

The dancers turned their backs to the crowd and began to roll their buttocks seductively, the orange calabash rattles in their hands ringing out merrily. The guests whistled and applauded appreciatively.

The dancers swivelled back around and began to sway their bodies gracefully and the music slowed down with them, allowing the air to fill now with the sound of their angelic chords.

Their voices faded gently into the background and a raspy voice accompanied by the strumming of a guitar rose in their place to mesmerize and dazzle the audience into tranquillity. Bernard and Samuel exchanged glances, and Bernard shook his head in awe.

The song came to an end and the audience went wild again. The lead singer pranced about on the stage before taking up his guitar again. His fingers began to first pick at the fine strings and then they rushed back and forth and the music galloped with them.

The dancers kept up the pace as the music sped on, their bare feet pumping lightly against the floor and their sultry chorus soothing the singer's throaty chords, and now and then delighting their audience with a quick flash of forbidden flesh.

Bernard shifted in his seat to slow down his racing heart and some revellers unable to contain themselves any longer ripped themselves from their seats and began to work out their adrenalin in front of the stage.

'What did you think?' Samuel asked after the applause had died out and the backup singers had gone back to their waitress chores.

Bernard took a deep breath and then he said, 'Different,' in a pleased tone.

'I'd say,' Samuel agreed with evident enjoyment. 'This is how our ancestors entertained themselves, Bernard. 'Where's the harm in that?'

20

The reunion

Bernard was preparing to leave when the two men he had seen watching him earlier, approached their table.

'Ah!' Samuel said, looking up before rising to his feet hastily. He shook hands with the men and then, grinning at his companion, said, 'Bernard, I want you to meet Lucus and Dickson.' Bernard stood up and stretched an arm out to each man in turn as Samuel was saying, 'This here is my friend Bernard. This is his first visit to the establishment.' The men burst out laughing as if at some private joke and Bernard joined in good-humouredly.

Lucus, a heavy-set man, sat down slowly and then said as he rolled a cigarette, 'I've heard many stories about your father, Bernard. He was a fair man, hard but fair. I know how important his people were to him. He wanted the best for them. And now we have a chief we know nothing about, not even the tribe he belongs to. An imposter with no knowledge of our customs or beliefs, and brought in by those with an agenda of their own. You are the rightful heir to the throne that he holds, and from what we hear, you are your father's son in many ways.'

'I am flattered by your kind words,' Bernard, who had listened with

80

surprise, replied after a short pause. 'But you must've heard of my failed attempt to win back my father's legacy. Many would have put their mark next to my name, but when it is a question of survival, you cannot blame a man for going with the person, devil or not, with clout. My father found that out the hard way.'

'We want to change that,' Dickson, who'd been assessing Bernard as he spoke and finding him to his satisfaction, said. 'Yes, being a chief is admirable, but for real change to take place, we need to aim higher than that. Parliament is what we should be looking at. Putting our people there. That is the only way forward.'

'You mean ministers in parliament? People like us?' Bernard asked incredulously.

'Why not?' Dickson countered, looking at the men seated with him in turn. 'We have educated men, men who have studied abroad and who understand this sort of thing. Men who are lobbying right now for these changes to take place but who can't get the job done without the people it concerns saying this is what we want!'

'It is people like you, Bernard, men who are respected by their community who can help get the word around,' Lucus asserted. 'And it is in places like this that we can galvanize support for our cause.'

Bernard nodded absentmindedly. This was a new concept for him, something he hadn't thought of before. 'Imagine that,' he thought to himself. 'Making our own decisions, doing what is best for us, like we used to do, in the old days.'

Bernard who had been engrossed in his thoughts, hadn't noticed the two men leaving and it was only when the hum around him had died down that he looked up and saw both men now standing on the stage.

'Gentlemen,' Lucus began, in a buttery soft chord that captured every ear present. Heads turned and Lucas smiled back at them indulgently. In a little more than a whisper that aroused and caressed their senses, he said, 'Gentlemen, today we witnessed life as it used to be, our young people reminding us of who we are as a people. We are not just mine labourers and farm hands. We are not just servants waiting to be told what to do. We are men, husbands, fathers, grandfathers and sons. Each one of you here, regardless of your clan, belongs to the great empire of Monomotapa. We are descendants of a sovereign nation. People with kings and queens. People who believed in one God. People with a culture, a way of life. People with rules, our rules, set by our ancestors, and which we once followed. People with a heritage.'

The chatter in the garden dried up and food and drink lay forgotten as the crowd transfixed by the speech now feasted on Lucus's words and allowed themselves to be transported back in time. Bernard sat upright with a creased brow and marvelled at the orator's eloquence.

'This, what we have here, is not freedom,' Lucus continued, pausing to wet his lips. 'All of us here have forgotten what it means to be truly free. To be proud of who we are as a nation and not to be made to feel ashamed or allow ourselves to be marginalised because of the colour of our skin.'

Here and there a few assenting murmurs were audible.

'You are the wealth of this country,' Lucus told them. 'It is you holding the picks in the mines, and it is you toiling, come rain or sunshine, in the fields. There was a time when your grandparents worked for themselves and when every man's wealth depended on the amount of effort he put in. A time when every man was the master of his kingdom, no matter how humble that kingdom was. When grown men were respected and not called 'boys.' A time when we depended on each other as a community. And we were strong then, because of that. That is freedom, my friends. Freedom!'

Men who had, earlier on, slouched drunkenly, now held their heads up high, as the pride stirring in their breasts flowed over and lit up every face in the crowd. Bernard, who had at times blamed his father for their poverty, now saw that it was not stubbornness that led his father but wisdom and insight into how much his people were giving up to this new way of life.

The woman Bernard had watched secretly on his earlier visit glided up to the platform carrying a tray of refreshments. She left the tray at the edge of the platform and retreated as silently as she had come. Lucus picked up a mug and drinking from it, quietly receded into the background.

'You heard what the man with the sweet tongue had to say, and we should give him a round of applause,' Dickson's loud voice rang out as he walked cheerfully to the centre of the stage, chuckling appreciatively at the sound of hands clapping and cheering. 'I am not one for speeches,' he said as the applause died away. 'That I leave to my colleague and friend here. I will get straight to the point. We want change in the way the country is being governed. We want the rules to be the same for everyone. Equal pay and equal opportunity. Why should it be about colour, the one thing no one can change? We want a voice in the way things are done. And you ask, how can we achieve all these things when we have been refused even those things that don't amount to much? And I say to you, by lobbying those in power to allow us to govern with them. To give us enough seats in parliament so that we have a voice that holds weight. They say five black men to one vote, and we say we want the same as the white man. One man to one vote. We say give us more power and only then can we expect meaningful change. Soon you will see officials, sent by those who want to retain power, who will ask you if it is more seats you want, but be careful because they will say it in such a way that it will make little sense to you. They will try and trick you into accepting seats with less value. Don't put your mark down on anything you don't understand. Speak to your community leaders. Let them guide you. I say, don't let them buy your vote with free grain or cheap talk of land. Don't let them buy you by saying we brought civilisation to you because that civilization they talk about has come at a great cost. It has enslaved us to it. Broken up our families and forced us to leave our homes in search of a livelihood because the one we once enjoyed had been taken from us. This civilisation has dictated where we can live, what we can grow, and how many cattle we can keep. It has taxed every hut you have in your compound, and it has taken every able-bodied person from those same huts to work for it with a sjambok on their back.'

The two men on the stage were unalike, both in appearance and speech, and they capitalised on this difference to work the crowd. Lucus was the smooth charmer, drawing in the crowds, and it was Dickson, small and energetic, who drove the message home.

'I look around me and I see mine workers, farm hands and house servants, and only Bernard over there lucky enough to be a land owner,' Dickson said, wrapping up his speech with a smile. 'And every day we sit helpless as we allow our land to be eaten up by those we welcomed as visitors and who repaid us with servitude. Now I say to you all, let us band together and fight for what is ours. Our land and our customs.'

The air erupted in a deafening roar and others, including Samuel, ran up to congratulate the men as they left the stage. Bernard, still overcome with the emotions brought on by the speeches, remained in his seat and followed the two politicians with his eyes as they mingled with the crowd, laughing and chatting.

'It's not just our men, but our women too, working for change,' Samuel said in an inebriated voice, making Bernard look up abruptly at suddenly finding him back at the table. Then seeing the woman standing next to Samuel, Bernard started and stumbled up to his feet clumsily.

'Bernard,' Samuel said, by a way of introduction. The woman curtsied and then seeing the stunned look on Bernard's face, took his hand which was lying limp at his side and shook it. 'Lindiwe here,' Samuel continued, 'And her late husband are our long-standing heroes too. He was a trade unionist, and for many years they campaigned together for better pay and better conditions for our mine workers. Lindiwe's husband lost his life doing what he believed in, and we are lucky to have her carrying on where her late husband left off,' Samuel oblivious to his friend's dilemma finished off as he took his seat. And then as an afterthought and remembering his manners, he turned his head up to the pair still standing and said, 'Lindiwe is the owner of this establishment and Bernard is the late Chief Gumpo's son.'

'Please excuse me,' Lindiwe said to Samuel after a short pause, 'I have some urgent business to attend to.' Then turning to leave, she looked at his companion and said, 'I hope to see more of you, Bernard. We could do much with good men like you.'

The irony was not lost to Bernard who still had the image of Garai and Tariro fresh in his mind. He looked down quickly with embarrassment and Samuel, who had been watching them both, gave him a wink and then laughed out loud.

21

A visit from special friends

The wheels of a bicycle rattled erratically over gravel. Bernard looked up quickly and saw Mr Ndlovu sitting high on his seat and behind him was his wife with a basket hanging from one hand. Bernard replaced the reel he'd been untangling on the table next to his box of fishing tackle and then strolled casually to the front gate with a wide grin on his face.

Mr Ndlovu swung off his bicycle and held it steady as his wife disembarked with a neat jump. Then he swooped down with a practised movement and removed the washing peg tapering down his trouser leg to his ankle. He leaned the bicycle against himself and brushing the sleeves of his jacket with his free hand, noticed with regret how frayed his collar and sleeves had become. His eye turned briefly to his wife as a reprimand for the years of flogging his clothes had endured against the rocks on the banks of the creek that flowed just below the school.

His once white shirt now had a greyish tinge to it and most of the black in his suit had followed the stream on its downward tumble, leaving it pale and discoloured. It had been a good suit a long time ago but was now jaded and worn out like himself. Life was not easy on a headmaster's salary.

Mrs Ndlovu's plump, walnut-coloured face creased with concentration as she hunched herself over to pat down the voluminous skirt strapped around her waist. Then, using her headscarf, she dusted off the grains of sand that persisted in clinging on to her pleasantly stout legs gleaming with petroleum jelly. She scooped the basket off the ground and with her brightly coloured beads and trinkets brightening up her faded outfit and swaying gaily around her, she approached the gate. Her self-assured swagger befitting her role as a schoolteacher and the wife of a much-esteemed school principal.

'Good morning, good people,' Bernard called as he went to unlatch the gate for his friends.

Mr Ndlovu's hand flipped the rusted bell which had a habit of slipping under the handlebar of his bicycle back into position and clicked it. A dull and hollow shrill spilt out from it, and they all burst out laughing.

At the sound, Esther, who had been pounding corn in a tall wooden mortar, stopped suddenly and looked over to the mango tree where she'd last seen Bernard sitting. Noticing the abandoned fishing reel, she peered curiously towards the gate and gave a loud chuckle on seeing their guests.

'Clara!' she called out as she waded through the brood of chickens pecking the ground around the grinding mill. 'Come, carry on here,' she called out gaily.

Clara emerged from behind a hut, and Esther handed the long-handed pestle to her before rushing towards their guests. Mrs Ndlovu saw Esther and dropped the basket in her hand to the ground and amid squeals of excitement, the women ran towards each other and embraced noisily. The men looked on with bemused expressions on their faces.

'Clara!' Esther called out as the happy chatter entered the large hut, 'put the kettle on!'

After some time had passed, and refreshed with tea and sweet potatoes, the friends enticed outdoors by the warm sunshine and cool breeze, left the lounge room and made themselves comfortable under the mango tree.

'You haven't come out fishing in a long time,' Bernard commented with his eyes on Mr Ndlovu, as he packed away his reels, 'Shall we set a date?'

The Ndlovu's exchanged a glance and then taking that as his cue, Mr Ndlovu stood up from his stool and speaking in the voice he used at school said, 'My dear friends, we have come with good news today.'

He paused to take a handkerchief from his trouser pocket, wiped his spectacles with it, and returned it to its place absentmindedly. Then he straightened up and cleared his throat. Just then the air erupted with loud squawks as a fat hen darted past them, with Thoko in high pursuit of it. Mr Ndlovu dropped his hands to his sides and waited patiently for the racket to die down. Once the two were out of sight, he cleared his throat again and resumed his speech.

'I am very pleased to tell you both that my application for a farm has finally been accepted. As you can imagine, we won't be wasting any time, and we've decided to relocate before the end of this month.'

Bernard and Esther turned their shocked faces on the speaker and as if for confirmation turned to look at his wife. Mrs Ndlovu nodded her head, her eyes bright with joy. Mr Ndlovu slipped back onto his stool, and with his head bent, carefully removed an envelope from the inside pocket of his jacket. He paused with it in his hand before holding it out to Bernard.

Bernard accepted the brown envelope with red stamps and stared mutely at Mr Ndlovu's name typed on it. Then he gave his companion a long look and Mr Ndlovu tipped his head back at him. Bernard pulled out the contents of the envelope slowly as if afraid to damage them. And Esther, anxious to know what the two letters now lying on her husband's lap contained, sprang off the reed mat she was sitting on and went to stand behind him.

The first letter was from the Rhodesian Agricultural Institute. It listed all the examinations Mr Ndlovu had completed successfully and below that was a statement that the student had now been upgraded to the status of a master farmer.

The second document, which was much thicker than the first, was from the Ministry of Agriculture. It detailed an offer to Mr Ndlovu to purchase a 25-acre state-allocated farm in the Lumbibi district from the native commissioner on a moderate mortgage plan.

'It shows that you are an excellent student and soon to become a prosperous farmer,' Bernard announced with a happy chuckle as the men stood up and shook hands.

Esther tipped her head up to the heavens and ululated, her voice rising in a joyful crescendo and bringing Mrs Ndlovu to her feet. Then, laughing gaily, the women began to sing and dance, pounding their feet and twisting their arms. The men joined in, swaying their bodies and chuckling merrily as they clapped their hands encouragingly.

Meanwhile, the hen, still under attack, mounted a pile of wood at full speed. It launched itself up in the air and began to flap its wings wildly, shedding a few of its feathers in its futile attempt to avoid capture. Thoko watched in stunned silence as it sailed past him, and then oblivious to the world around him except the prey in his sights, lunged forward.

The hen and its pursuer came crashing down in the middle of the celebration, putting an end to the gruelling chase and turning the adults' earlier cries of joy into shrieks of surprise.

22

Puberty rites

When calm had been restored, Thoko returned to where the adults were seated, with the captured hen under his arm and a kitchen knife in his hand.

'Never mind that,' Bernard said to his son with a smile. Then turning to his guests he said, 'Today calls for more than just a hen. We must celebrate! Come, Ndlovu, I'll let you pick a good goat for our lunch today!'

Thoko released his captive, and the traumatised bird rushed to hide under a shrub, where it sat with its heart beating wildly.

'The school is going to miss you both,' Esther said fanning the fire with a flat basket and then bending over a black three-legged pot to stir the pieces of mutton braising in it.

'I'll miss teaching,' Mrs Ndlovu replied as she pushed aside a dish of sliced pumpkin leaves and dragged a platter of tomatoes towards her. 'But it's always been Ndlovu's dream to own a farm. As you've often heard, his father worked on a farm and that's where he got his love for farming. And I'm not too bad myself. You saw the ground nuts that I brought. What do you think?'

'All those from that little patch you have outside your kitchen door?'

Esther said in an incredulous tone. 'There's no doubt, you'll both make excellent farmers. It will be different from living at the mission compound, you'll have so much more land, all to yourself.'

'A little like what you have here, Esther. You don't know just how lucky you've been. I remember how stubborn Bernard was at first, refusing to let you use your money to buy the land. But it worked out in the end. Now you have cattle and goats and sheep. Imagine that!' she said with a laugh. 'Who would have thought, after what you'd been through.'

Sometime later the women left the pots to simmer beside the hearth and went and sat on a reed mat outside the kitchen and began to shell the groundnuts Mrs Ndlovu had brought.

'Clara,' Esther murmured ten minutes later, 'It's your turn in the kitchen,' and Clara dropped the nuts in her hand back in the basket and stood up. 'And Clara,' Esther added as Clara was about to enter the kitchen, 'use the big pot that's under the table.'

'Is Isaac back?' Esther asked Thoko sometime later as he approached them.

'They still have a week to go,' Thoko replied, tossing some nuts in his mouth.

'Thoko!' Clara admonished with a laugh as she rejoined them, 'You want to finish the nuts even before we start!'

'It will be your turn next,' Mrs Ndlovu said, looking at Thoko. 'Are you afraid?'

Thoko shook his head.

'Thoko is only ten, there's still plenty of time before he becomes a teen,' Esther said. 'And Bernard was asked to join the elders next year, so he'll be on camp to teach the boys everything they need to know about being grown men.'

'Huh!' Mrs Ndlovu laughed. 'That's why you say you're not afraid Thoko, your father will be there with you!'

'That doesn't mean he won't be initiated,' Esther said looking pointedly at her friend. 'Bernard can't save him from that.'

Thoko gave his mother a frightened look and asked, 'What about Clara?'

'It's different for Clara because she's a girl and girls don't have to leave home to be taught about women things because they are learning them all the time,' Esther told him with a smile.

Esther and Mrs Ndlovu's eyes met as they both remembered when almost a year ago, womanhood had imposed itself on the thirteen-year-old Clara and Esther had sent for Mrs Ndlovu.

'A man wants a woman who can take care of him,' Mrs Ndlovu had said kindly to the still bewildered child when the lesson of womanhood and cleanliness had been dispensed with.

Clara's frightened eyes had darted towards her mother, and Esther had placed a reassuring hand over her shoulder. And when Clara was ready for her next lesson, she went and knelt beside Mrs. Ndlovu in front of the hearth.

'Food is the key to a man's soul,' the esteemed teacher told her student. 'Sadza is not just maize meal and water but love and passion too.'

She drew the bucket of ground maize towards her and threw a handful of it in a big black pot. Then she sat back and watched, as Clara stirred the meal and cold water with a long-handled spoon into a thin watery paste.

'Your caresses must be gentle at first,' Mrs Ndlovu murmured as she helped Clara to carefully tip boiling water into the pot with one hand while using the ladle in her other hand to gently swirl it.

'Keep your hand firm but tender,' Mrs Ndlovu told the child encouragingly as the contents of the pot gently heated up.

The wood crackled, and orange flames curled around the hearth. The pot hummed merrily and when it began to bubble, Clara, under instruction, turned to the smouldering logs under it. She pulled one aside to lower the heat and brought the pot down to a steady boil. Then the teacher and her student withdrew outdoors and left the pot to bubble for a while under a partially closed lid.

'Don't move like an elephant when you approach the fire. The fire is your groom, move your body gracefully to arouse his senses, even before he has a chance to touch you,' Mrs. Ndlovu told Clara when they were back in front of the pot.

The pair shuffled erotically towards the burning logs and Clara was shown how to move sensually as she emptied a cup of maize meal over the bubbling mass.

'Turn up the heat so your young man does not fall asleep,' Mrs Ndlovu instructed, gaily, and Clara drew a log from the stack close by and the flames in the hearth strayed towards it.

The log blackened, and then ignited and the porridge foamed and gurgled as it heated up. Gradually the thin paste became soft and creamy as it thickened and filled the kitchen with its sweet aroma.

'More heat!' the teacher ordered, and in went another log, and the pot stepped up one notch and the porridge began to spit and hiss.

'The man is not your master, no matter what he may think,' Mrs Ndlovu told Clara. 'When his anger flares up, it's your job to tame him down.'

Clara dropped a handful of maize meal over the bristling cauldron and the porridge swooped around it. She dug her knees into the ground as her spoon plunged back and forth, catching the lumps that had formed and smoothing them out. The buttery white mass heaved and fell and then began to swell and subside in unison with the spoon.

'Very good,' Mrs Ndlovu said coyly. 'Now you've shown him who's really in charge!'

Then leaning towards the pot, the tutor scooped out a bit of sadza with her finger and after tasting it said, 'Nectar, not just for the body, but for the soul too.'

Then standing up she said, 'Come, leave him to rest and regain his strength.'

Clara smiled with relief.

She replaced the lid over the pot, and its contents sighed with satisfaction.

<h1 style="text-align:center">23</h1>

A Sunday banquet

The men scraped the fat off the goat's skin, and when they had lathered it with salt, they took it to the back of Bernard's shed. They suspended the hide on a string of wire which ran between two poles and left it to dry out in the sun. Then feeling ravenous after their morning chore, they returned to the shade of the mango tree, where they sat with their faces turned to the kitchen.

Esther read the sign, and collecting the bowls and plates drying off on a log of an outside scullery, took them with her to the kitchen. She dragged the chunks of smouldering wood to the side of the hearth and doused them with water. A cloud of smoke billowed out from the blackened wood and swirled around the hut. Mrs Ndlovu and Clara waited for it to pour out through the doorway before joining her.

The men stood up briskly, even before Thoko, who had been sent to call them, had a chance to open his mouth.

'I see you have a feast spread out for us,' Mr Ndlovu said grinning happily at the banquet of stewed and roasted mutton, spinach in a peanut butter sauce, fried cabbage and tomato relish.

He bent down and washed his hands in a bowl Thoko held up to him and then slipped behind a table that was squeezed against the kitchen wall.

'If we'd known about the news of your new adventure beforehand, we would've slaughtered an ox for you,' Bernard said laughing and taking a seat opposite his guest. Then he turned to the women seated on a cowhide spread on the floor beside him, and added, 'We must of course thank the chefs for their hard work.'

The women laughed appreciatively.

'What happened to your chicken, Thoko? I don't see it in front of us, did it outrun you?' Mr Ndlovu asked mischievously while rolling a ball of sadza in his palm and dipping it into a vegetable relish.

'I caught it, didn't you see?' Thoko replied defensively, guarding every village boy's honour of being the most efficient chicken catcher in the family for the traditional Sunday meal.

'But not after a long chase,' Esther countered. 'I was beginning to think you'd never catch it.'

'I don't know if my eyes were deceiving me, but did it actually fly?' Mrs Ndlovu asked with a puzzled look before chewing on a piece of steak.

'It did, right over Thoko's head!' Clara said laughing. 'Thoko only caught it because it fell, otherwise, he'd still be out there, chasing it!'

'Well, it fought gallantly and deserved its freedom,' Bernard said, joining in the laughter.

'Thoko,' Esther said to the boy. 'You haven't touched the yoghurt; you need to eat it if you want to be strong.'

'Yoghurts for women,' Bernard said. 'Let him have as much meat as he wants.'

24

Disturbing revelations

After an afternoon spent chatting and laughing, Esther and Mrs Ndlovu returned to the kitchen to cut up the rest of the goat. Thoko whistled, and the teacher watched as he left the courtyard with the dogs racing in front of him. Then she glanced back to the homestead and found Clara, who had been washing pots earlier, seated with her back against the granary and braiding her hair. Not far from her were the men, who having followed the sun all afternoon while nursing a clay pot of beer, now lounged under the shade of an avocado tree.

Having assured herself of not being overheard, the kind-hearted woman placed her knife back on the cutting board and turning to face her friend said, 'Esther, do you remember that in our last church meeting, the business of the shebeen came up?' Esther nodded absentmindedly. 'And we all agreed that we would do everything in our power to get it closed.'

'Yes, of course,' Esther replied, pulling a paper bag from the rafters and filling it up with meat for the Ndlovu's to take home with them. 'It's something I'm very much against, especially after hearing about how poor Tariro has been reduced to begging with all her husband's

97

money going to pay his debt there.'

'So, you can understand why I find it so difficult to understand why you'd allow the father of your children to spend so much of his time there,' Mrs. Ndlovu said with her full gaze on Esther.

'You must be mistaken,' Esther insisted, trying to hide her shock behind a flickering smile. 'Bernard has no time to go there, especially now that he is the chairman of the church council. You know how much he does for the community on top of all that. He despises the shebeen, he would never set foot there.'

The older woman opened her mouth to contradict her friend, but when she saw the look on Esther's face, she decided against it, and said instead, 'I'm glad to hear that you still stand with us on this problem. It's not just drink they sell there, but women's bodies too.'

Then, to lighten the mood that had now understandably turned bleak, she said in a bright tone, 'About the baptism. I want Thoko to try on his trousers before I go. That child is growing so fast. I may have to take the hem down a little. I can't tell you how upset I am that I won't be there to see him receiving his first sacrament, and Clara her confirmation.'

'I'm going to miss you,' Esther said with a sad smile. 'How will I even cope in your absence? You took me into your home when you knew nothing about me, and you took care of Clara and me. How could I even begin to thank you?'

"We'd known Bernard a long time then. He and Mr Ndlovu grew up together. And you were so young!" Mrs Ndlovu told her with moist eyes.

25

A confrontation

Esther had planned to wait a few days before confronting Bernard with the accusation, but as she had never kept anything from him before, she found the weight of the information now in her possession impossible to bear on her own.

The very next day, when the children were at school and they were alone, Esther took a deep breath and with her heart thumping, crossed the courtyard and went to where Bernard was hunched over a bicycle wheel. She watched him quietly as he carefully pried the inner tube from the tyre with a metal prong. He turned to look up at her briefly before tugging at the black tube and pulling it out. He shook his head ruefully at the patches already riddling it.

Normally Esther would chuckle softly or make some comment and hearing only silence and sensing a change in her, Bernard asked, 'What's the matter?' with his eyes still on his work.

'You've been spending a lot of time away from home,' Esther replied, her voice full of misery. And then trembling slightly, she asked, 'Where do you go, Bernard, each time you dress up and leave me working here in the fields alone?'

'And where is this coming from?' Bernard asked in a surprised but even tone.

'Please answer me, Bernard. I want you to tell me what you are doing with your time when you're not at home.'

'Have I not always been a good husband to you? Is it so bad that I would want to sometimes spend time with my friends and share a drink with them?'

'But that's not all you've been doing, from what I hear,' she said, her words heavy with the implication in them.

'So, you're listening to gossip now. Believing lies, lies that anyone cares to bring to you.'

'Lies about the amount of time you spend with Lindiwe?'

'Lindiwe and I are just friends. There's nothing between us.'

'I don't believe you,' Esther said shaking her head. 'I know it in my heart now that what you are telling me is not true.'

'Are you calling me a liar? Is that what you think of me, that I would do such a thing? Have I ever given you any reason to doubt my word?'

'Stop it! Stop it!' Esther yelled, 'You need to stop lying to me!'

'Esther!' Bernard snapped, rising to his feet quickly. 'Can you hear yourself?'

'There is no smoke without fire!' Esther yelled out again.

'You are overstepping yourself, Esther!' Bernard told her, with feigned anger to hide his guilt. 'If you don't watch yourself, you may find yourself in deep water!'

'Deeper than you are in already?' Esther retorted sarcastically.

'I'm your husband, Esther, my word should be good enough for you, but as it is clearly not, then maybe it is time for us to go our separate ways.'

'You don't think that you've already done that, Bernard? You're keeping things from me. We never had secrets between us before, not until this shebeen business started.'

'Believe what you want,' Bernard sighed, sinking back onto his stool.

'I suppose you'll go running to the church for sympathy and you will all drag my name through the dirt, guilty or not.'

He picked up the bicycle pump and began to drive the plastic handle back and forth with short bursts of pent-up energy, and the tube attached to it began to slowly inflate.

Esther dropped to her knees with both her arms around his waist and began to sob bitterly and Bernard stopped what he was doing and held her close to him.

'We can't go on like this,' he said to her gently, after she had calmed down. 'I will always love you, but I can't live with someone who doesn't trust me. We need time apart.'

'What are you saying, Bernard,' Esther gasped. 'Is she worth all the years we've spent together? Our children's heartache when they find out? You want to throw all that away for her?'

'Leave Lindiwe out of this. It is you who doesn't trust me!' Bernard snapped, pulling away from her. 'You won't be alone. You have the children, and you can have everything we build here. It's all yours.'

'The least you owe me is the truth. Be honest with me, Bernard. Tell me that you are not seeing Lindiwe and that she means nothing to you. Tell me that I'm wrong!' she implored, searching his face for the truth with eyes brimming with tears.

'You didn't believe me the first time, why should the second time be different?' he growled, avoiding her glance.

He picked up the small bowl of water at his feet and leaving Esther standing there forlornly, took it to another shady part of the courtyard.

Much later, he watched as Esther carried a flat reed basket to the vegetable garden and went to crouch beside a bed of green beans. Then he dropped his head in his cupped hands and wept for the hurt he was causing her and the dilemma that engulfed his soul.

III

Part 3 – Unfavourable times

26

Building a new hut

There had always been enough room to build another hut beside the one Bernard and Esther shared, but as the need for it had never risen, until now, that space had remained empty.

The couple started by paying a visit to the quarry not far from their homestead with their hearts full of sorrow. And when they returned, the wheelbarrow they had taken with them squeaked under its taxing load of clay. They paused for a few days to give themselves time to come to terms with what all this meant to them.

And when their short reprieve had come to an end, their footsteps led them to a forest, that lay just half an hour away from their home.

Bernard's sharp axe chose its branches well, biting only into those that were straight and slender before shaving off their leaves. And the scythe in Esther's hand, a few paces away, swung out at the long grass and left a path behind it where one didn't exist before.

Husband and wife worked in silence, wrapped up in their thoughts, dropping a word now and then to drive away the panic that silence brought.

'The sun is low,' Bernard observed, with his head turned up to the sky.

'The day is almost over,' Esther agreed, the scythe now hanging loose in one hand as she followed his gaze.

The breeze sighed as it sailed through the trees and Bernard's axe eagerly stripped the bark of a trunk. Esther standing quietly beside him twisted it into a rope to secure the bundles at their feet.

Then with Esther's body swaying gracefully to balance the bale of hay on her head, and Bernard's body hunched under the weight of wattle heavy over his shoulders, they made their way back to the shifting foundations of their home.

The sun lingered not long after before it dipped out of sight.

They cut a circle in the ground and pinned down a neatly crafted pole in its ridges. Two pairs of hands moved seamlessly, just as they did in the old days, as pole after pole was hammered down. But when a murmur or laughter came out of habit, it was somehow subdued and not quite the same as it had been before.

They thrust mud to cover the gap between each pole, and as the walls of the hut went up, they both knew that these were not the only walls, their hands were building.

They threw bundles of grass around the edges of the roof, then spread the thatch evenly over the straggly rafters. Their hands worked ruthlessly, tearing at the strands of hay that strayed over the boundaries that they too, were trying so rigorously to maintain.

Then they downed their tools and gave themselves a short break for the mud walls, like their hearts, to harden and to turn to stone.

The cattle snorted irritably as they were shoved out of their kraal before the break of dawn and fresh dung was removed from under their hooves.

Tired hands dug into the soft mash and threw, however much they could grab, over the floor and walls of the new hut. Open palms lathered down the plaster to shield the hut, but not their hearts, from the corrosive world outside.

Then they smoothed out the ripples, smothering balm to their battered emotions and soothing their bruised souls.

The building of the new hut came to an end, and it stood imposingly beside the one next to it.

And when the inevitable could no longer be delayed, Bernard announced, 'It's done,' with a bittersweet smile and Esther concluded, 'Yes it's over!'

And when Bernard moved into his very own hut, this then became the beginning of the end of what had been, for them.

27

A friend intervenes

Mr Ndlovu felt a sense of dread as the beer garden loomed ahead, and the repugnance he felt increased as he drew closer to its gate. He was annoyed with Bernard for putting him in this position and with his wife for insisting on him coming here, for what he knew was none of his business.

Just at that instant, a cry rang out, and a drunkard stumbled out through the gate. The woman staggered from side to side and then continued down the road in front of him. Mr Ndlovu hesitated at the entrance debating what was worse, entering this den of iniquity which was against his Christian upbringing, or the stony silence that awaited him at home if he shirked from doing his duty. Deciding the latter to be more intolerable, he pulled himself up to his full height, which was an impressive head taller than most men, before strutting through the gates.

He stood at the edge of the beer garden, and his eyes darted past the men sprawled on makeshift chairs and benches and the young women with their loose ways talking in voices that were too loud and too suggestive.

A look of disgust showed itself on his face for a moment. And when he saw no sign of Bernard, he gave a great sigh of relief, glad to be let off lightly with a good enough excuse to take back home with him.

But just as he was about to leave, a slight movement made him stop and squint towards a spot hidden behind a hydrangea bush. He walked purposefully towards it and there, seated on a bench and in the company of five other men, was the man he'd been sent to pay a visit.

'How much longer are we going to sit back and accept this kind of treatment?' Mr Ndlovu heard one of the men sitting with Bernard say, as he approached them.

'We should be prepared to take up arms because talking has brought us nothing so far,' another voice chipped in.

'Fighting is not the answer …' Bernard started speaking and as he was turning his glance to the man who had spoken last, his eyes fell on an unexpected figure that had materialised in front of him.

'Ndlovu!' he exclaimed in surprise. 'I'm very pleased to see you! Come take a seat with us!'

The man sitting opposite Bernard mumbled something under his breath and all the others including Bernard responded with laughter before the speaker left his seat and wandered off.

'Take a load off your feet,' Bernard said to Mr Ndlovu, indicating the now vacant seat.

Mr Ndlovu swept a condescending glance over Bernard's companions and remained standing.

'What's the matter?' Bernard demanded, with a sneer and his eyes gleaming with anger. 'Surely it's not because you think that the company is not good enough for you?'

Mr Ndlovu gave Bernard a pointed look before taking him up on his invitation and sitting down.

'What can I get for you, Headmaster? If you're not buying then I must ask you to leave,' Lindiwe, who Mr Ndlovu hadn't noticed, said in a careless tone.

Mr Ndlovu turned his head towards her sharply before reaching for some coins in his trouser pocket and dropping them on the table in front of him.

Lindiwe gave him a sideways look as she picked up the coins in a deliberate way, before turning around and walking away.

'Strikes are the way forward,' continued the man who had been speaking earlier. 'The men must refuse to work in the fields or go down their mines. We did that in Johannesburg. In the end, they had to give in to some of our demands. It wasn't much, but it was something. Talking did nothing there, and it will do nothing here!'

'You're talking war!' Bernard said with a stern look at the man. 'Are you forgetting the uprising? If we take that path, then we lose everything. All the groundwork we've accomplished so far. We're not looking for a fight, we want a peaceful resolution. We want to work hand in hand with the government, not against it.'

'What have you got yourself into, Bernard,' Mr Ndlovu snarled, giving him a hostile glance. 'All this talk about boycotting taxes and refusing to go to work will bring, not only those of you sitting around this table but the rest of us, nothing but grief.'

'You want us to carry on as we are, Ndlovu? To be nothing but servants? For our children to sit three at a desk, and to share one pencil between them? And these are the lucky few. The ones whose parents spend their days digging underground tunnels and who only come out of that dark at night. And for what? And what about Nyoni, who can't afford to send his children to school? Don't you think that the taxes that are collected from us, the hut taxes, the dog taxes, the dipping fees, and all of that? Do you not think that with all those taxes they collect as well as the labour we throw in, that some of that income could be given back to us in the way of better schools and education for all?'

'I don't know anything about those taxes you're talking about,' Mr Ndlovu replied. 'I keep away from politics and so should you.'

'Tell me, Ndlovu,' Bernard said, quivering with suppressed anger. 'How long has it taken you to finally achieve your dream of owning a farm, which of course comes with a noose of its own?'

Mr Ndlovu looked down at his feet.

'You forget what our fathers went through, what our mothers had to endure?'

Mr Ndlovu recalled his father's passing from some mishap on his master's farm. He was only a boy then and didn't know anything beyond that. Except that the family was evicted from their home not long after and he'd ended up on the mission as an orphan, as his mother hadn't been so lucky.

But he knew there was no point in holding onto the past and had buried those memories deep. And he wished Bernard would do the same. But Bernard was his father's son, and he'd always known that one day he'd be involved in politics just as his father had.

'Ndlovu,' Bernard said with less hostility, 'Tomorrow you'll be in your scotch cart and gone from this place. Spare a thought for those of us who will remain behind with nothing to look forward to.'

'How can you say that you have nothing to look forward to, Bernard? You have a wife, a son, and a daughter. And you have a home. You hear me? A home. Not borrowed land. It's what I've always wanted for my own family,' Ndlovu replied heatedly, forgetting for a moment why his wife had sent him there in the first place.

'Well, you have that now, your home, 25 acres of it!'

'Are you jealous of me, Bernard?' Mr Ndlovu asked. 'Does my 25 acres change me in your eyes?'

'That's where you're wrong, Ndlovu,' Bernard told him soberly. 'My fight is not with you. I am very happy that you are now a master farmer and that you have a farm. But look how hard you've had to work just to get your foot in the door. You didn't need that certificate to tell you that you are a master farmer. You grew up on a farm, like me. We learned everything about farming by working the land. This land belongs to us. It's our birthright.'

'That is reckless talk, Bernard. That sort of talk will bring you nothing but trouble.'

'You know what I say is true, the only difference is that you are too afraid to say it out loud. I was too, until I started coming here.'

'About that,' Mr Ndlovu said. 'Is that all that brings you here? Are you forgetting that you are a Christian and a married man? Forget this place and go home. Esther is there, waiting for you.'

At the mention of Esther's name, the men seated rose quietly and dispersed unobtrusively, leaving Bernard and Mr Ndlovu alone.

'Did Esther send you, is that why you are here?' Bernard demanded his eyes holding those of his opponents in a steel grasp.

'Esther has nothing to do with my visit here,' Mr Ndlovu replied without flinching.

'Oh, so it was Mrs Ndlovu then,' murmured Bernard, who had been leaning towards Ndlovu, as he now eased himself on his backrest.

Mr Ndlovu's glance dropped, confirming Bernard's suspicion.

The noise in the beer garden rose and two men staggered up, clutching each other around the throat and several others rushed over to separate them. One managed to swing his fist, and his victim fell flat on his side.

'Can't you see what you are doing, man? What kind of life is this?' Mr Ndlovu said, turning away from the fracas and back to Bernard. 'You want to give up everything you have for this?'

'Go home and tell Mrs Ndlovu that you have done what she asked you to do. But go now and let us part as friends. Travel well tomorrow and God willing I will have the honour of visiting you in your new home.'

'Your family needs you!' Mr Ndlovu told him urgently as he got off his seat and reached for his hat.

'You should leave now,' Bernard told him, this time gesturing his arm dismissively at his old friend.

Mr Ndlovu held Bernard's glance for a moment longer than necessary, before turning around abruptly and striding briskly towards the gate, grateful to have gotten over the whole unpleasant business and eager to get started on his new life.

Bernard's glance followed the retreating figure, and when he turned from it, his eyes fell on the untouched pot of beer Mr Ndlovu had paid for.

He tipped it over and then sat back and watched as the ground gurgled greedily as it gulped it down, and did not turn his eyes away until only a wet patch remained in the dirt.

28

Making amends

A clay pot sat on a table in Esther and Bernard's lounge, its sides etched with the story of their life. There were smooth bits which were those happy days when the two of them made a loving home for Clara. Thoko had come along after, Bernard's flesh and blood, and their happiness was complete. And between that were the humps and bumps which although appearing big at the time, had only served to strengthen the inseparable bond between them. And now that love, that treasured pot of clay, that they had both guarded so fiercely, lay shattered on the ground through a careless stroke of Bernard's hand.

'I've always loved you and I will always love you and support you in every way that I can,' Bernard told Esther, picking up each shard of clay and placing it meticulously where it once belonged.

'But you hurt me deeply, Bernard,' Esther murmured, looking at the pot that he was so painstakingly trying to restore.

'I can't change what happened,' he told her. 'People make mistakes. I made a mistake. But if you're not willing to move forward, then there's no hope for us.'

'I gave you everything,' her heart cried out to him silently. 'All you had to do in return was to be true to me.' This, he could've possibly understood and would've tried to right it, if only she could have put it into words.

He held the mended clay pot up to her, and to any other eye, it looked as perfect as it once was. But Esther saw only the weblike cracks in it, and the soul of their love haemorrhaging out through each. So, she said to him instead, 'If you want to leave you can leave,' her old insecurities seeping in to push him away. 'I won't hold you back.'

As the days went by, and Esther refused to bend, Bernard found himself shunning his marital vows blatantly and doing everything he could to turn the knife already in her breast in the hope that somehow it would thaw the block of ice that now sat there.

Back from his usual escapade, but this time treating himself to a few more drags of the hot stuff in his water pouch to give himself the courage required for the task, he staggered to where Esther was laying out strips of venison to dry out under the sun.

'It's all your fault!' he spurted out, with his chest pushed out, fighting to keep his balance. 'The problem with you is that you're too much with that church of yours! I should've never agreed to join it! It turned me into a shell, always looking inwards, not seeing the world as it really is!'

'Is that what you came back for?' Esther asked with one hand over the rack holding the tray. 'To tell me that? Don't blame me, Bernard, for straying away from our home. I didn't force you to join the church. You could've left it at any time you wanted, but this is what you chose,' she finished, gesturing at his drunken state.

'You can say what you want,' he mumbled between hiccups, 'but as far as I'm concerned, this is all your fault.'

He managed to turn himself back around and staggered to his hut to sleep off his troubles.

Impulsive behaviour

It was one of those rare occasions when the need to break the silence arose and when that necessary word sounded like a deafening echo in the widening chasm between husband and wife.

"We have the baptism today." Esther's reminder came crashing out and made Bernard start at the sound of her voice.

After a short pause in which he battled the guilt that her presence always seemed to cast over him, he replied reassuringly, 'Yes, I remember. I'll be there.'

Anger followed guilt and he cursed her inwardly for making him feel that way. 'Haven't I made every effort to put things right with you and haven't you rebuffed my every effort?' he said to himself.

Defiance came on the back of anger, and when Esther was safely out of sight, Bernard gave in to his earthly urges, and his legs, those treacherous limbs of his, addicted to their wayward ways, ferried him away from their home with swift impatience.

It had been weeks since his last visit there, and he expected to find his lover laid up in bed, pining for him, when Lindiwe's loud and careless laughter jolted him out of his romantic reverie. He redirected his footsteps towards the brash tones and harsh laughter and found her lounging with some other privileged guest. Startled by the sound of his footsteps she looked up quickly, her face brightening, when she recognised the man walking towards her.

'Bernard!' she called out, her voice trumpeting out happily for all to hear.

'I'm not staying long,' Bernard replied by way of greeting, upset that he hadn't been missed the way he had imagined. 'I have a baptism to attend to.'

Lindiwe opened her mouth and released a volley of laughter, and then seeing the hurt on his face, recovered from her mirth quickly. Teasing him playfully she said, 'When did you become so churchy, Bernard? You were always such a rebel when we were kids!'

He grinned at her sheepishly.

'Don't worry, I'll let you get there on time,' she promised as she cuddled up to him, before turning up to cup his face in her hands and planting a passionate kiss on his waiting lips.

Bernard smiled at her contentedly with his arm around her as the warmth of her body melted away the icy cold atmosphere he was forced to endure at home.

30

The Baptism

A boy dressed in a blue T-shirt, unlike the rest of the boys in their freshly pressed white cotton shirts, and not much older than Thoko, looked around uneasily. Then he approached a stern-looking man, in a faded black suit, hesitantly.

Esther's eyes swept past the man who was now in earnest conversation with the boy, before scouring the room again for some sign of her husband who had yet to arrive. She felt a wave of annoyance at Bernard, for yet another broken promise and the embarrassment of him being the only father, not present at his son's baptism.

As the minutes ticked on, a feeling of dread slowly overcame Esther. It wasn't like Bernard, despite everything, not to be there for Thoko and Clara without a good reason.

'Mrs Dube,' Mr Chaparira whispered, breaking into her thoughts. Esther turned her head abruptly, her hand clasping her throat. 'It's nothing to be concerned about,' the gentleman said quickly, attempting to dispel the anxious look on her face. Then leaning in closer so that what he had to say would be for her ears only, he said, 'I've just received word that Bernard has been delayed, and that he may not be able to make it for the ceremony.'

'Why? Is he hurt? Has there been an accident?' Esther asked with a palpitating heart.

'No, none of those things,' the man replied.

'That boy you were talking to,' Esther said, remembering the boy with the blue T-shirt and looking around for him, 'Is he the one who brought the news? Where is he now?'

'Yes he's the one, but he's gone now,' Mr Chaparira replied. 'I believe that's Lindiwe's son. I thought you knew who he was.'

'And you're sure it was him who brought the message?' Esther murmured.

Mr Chaparira nodded his head solemnly, and Esther's heart sank.

Inside the church, an aisle divided the rows of chairs in two. The front seats closest to the chancel were usually designated for the prominent members of the church, and Esther would normally sit in the third row on either side of the aisle. But because today was a special occasion, the priest had arranged that all prominent members give up their seats to those parents whose children were being baptised.

Esther could see that the priest's wish did not apply to Mrs Gara, who sat next to the only vacant seat in that row.

'Are you okay?' Mrs Gara asked as Esther lowered herself next to the eminent church leader.

'Just a little nervous,' Esther replied with her eyes on the children seated on a long bench and facing them.

'We are all nervous,' Mrs Gara agreed, chuckling softly. 'Imagine something going wrong now, after all those rehearsals!' Then she added as an afterthought, 'Is Bernard here? I don't think I saw him.'

'He's been delayed,' Esther told her lightly, 'But he should be here any minute now.'

Mrs Gara peered at her intently, and to Esther's relief, the entrance hymn commenced, and all the parishioners scraped back their wooden chairs and stood up to join the choir.

Four young girls with pumpkins and watermelons in their arms came dancing up the aisle and deposited their gifts at the altar. Behind them came two altar boys walking a little ahead of the priest.

When the priest reached the pulpit he raised his arms and made the sign of the cross before starting his sermon on the sacraments of baptism. And all the while Esther thought how odd it was that Bernard would prefer to be somewhere else on a day like today.

'Wasn't that beautiful?' Mrs Gara sighed as the priest anointed the last child's forehead with holy water, bringing Esther back to the present.

Not long after, the congregation filed solemnly into the courtyard where an amicable chatter commenced immediately as they congratulated each other. Then they made their way slowly to the old marula tree where a feast had been laid out by the church ladies.

'Pity about Bernard,' the priest said, helping himself to a slice of watermelon Esther had just cut up. 'Is he okay?'

'Yes, he is fine, thank you, Father,' Esther assured him with a quivering smile.

'You don't look well,' Mrs Gara said with a worried look coming on the pretext to help. 'Are you sure you're, okay?'

'Just a bit tired,' Esther conceded, with the tears threatening to spill out.

'Well, don't worry about tidying up, there are plenty of us here to do that. Go home and have a rest,' Mrs Gara insisted, knowing more than she cared to reveal.

Esther looked out for Bernard's bicycle as they turned into their driveway. And seeing no sign of it, she leapt out of the cart even before Thoko had time to bring it to a standstill.

With hurried instructions to the children to unharness the donkeys and provide them with water, she sped off to what had in recent months come to be known as 'Bernard's hut.' She pushed the door open slowly, half hoping to find him there, waiting for them.

The shirt she'd left out for him on his bed was gone, and in its place was his old work shirt. She picked it up in both hands and held it close to her face, drinking in the smell of him, her body aching with her longing for him.

Then, with it still in her hands and struggling to keep her composure, she rushed off to her bedroom. There, behind the locked door, she sank to her knees.

'How did it all start? What went wrong between us?' she asked herself. 'Did he just get up one morning and decide that he didn't want us anymore? Not a single hint from you, Bernard, nothing, nothing. You could've said something,' she moaned, and that on its own was more distressing to her than the act of betrayal itself.

The walls of the hut closed in, squeezing tight around her.

Her fingers tugged at the turban twirled around her head and it fell heedlessly on the floor. Then they peeled off the layers of cloth and beads adorning her body. And when she had stripped herself naked, she stretched herself flat against the cold floor, and her body shuddered with bitter sobs.

Outside the sun went down and the room darkened, and she slowly became conscious of her children's voices on the other side of her door. She pulled on her old work tunic and tied a tattered scarf around her head, then brushed the tears still clinging to her eyelashes.

Fixing a gash for a smile on her face, she opened her door, and the children threw themselves at her.

31

A fatal snake bite

After enduring a few days of heavy drinking, and with the stench of alcohol still in his pores, Bernard felt a great desire to put some distance between himself and Lindiwe's den of iniquity. He zigzagged homeward on his bicycle until he reached the creek that lay halfway between his home and the beer garden. He disembarked clumsily, and feeling thankful that the creek was dry at this time of the year, pushed his bicycle across the sandy bed.

Then overcome with a need to relieve himself, he shoved the handlebar away from himself and watched with satisfaction as the bicycle clattered down to the ground. He pointed at it as if commanding it to stay put before stumbling off the path and going towards some bushes.

Just as he was about to reach his desired spot, he lost his footing and after rolling helplessly downwards, landed in a hollow. Chuckling loudly to himself, and still lying on his side from the fall, he unzipped his trousers. He exhaled with satisfaction afterward, then snatched at some vegetation within his reach, and using this as leverage, pulled himself upright.

He staggered around on his feet, looking for a way out of the ditch when he suddenly stood still and looked down.

There, not more than a foot away from where he stood, was a brown cobra with the hood around its head fanned out and ready to strike. He watched as its tongue flickered in and out of its mouth threateningly while its beady eyes stared blindly in front of it.

Bernard gave a short cry, his feet leaving the ground instinctively before landing heavily just as the reptile's head darted toward him. He felt the sharp pain tear through his body and looking down saw its body coiled around his leg.

He kicked at it vigorously with his free leg and watched in disbelief as the monster dropped to the ground with a loud thud before slipping silently into the undergrowth.

Dragging himself through the bushes and now fully sober, he made the painful trip to the place he felt most safe.

Esther looked up from the chicken coop and with a loud shriek dropped the eggs in her hands and sprang towards the hunched figure making slow progress towards the homestead.

'Bernard! What happened? What's wrong?' she cried, as she dropped to her knees, her arms reaching out to him possessively.

Bernard groaned. He raised his head and sighed with relief at the sight of Esther. He murmured, 'A cobra, my leg!'

Esther pulled back and saw the puncture marks and the droplets of blood on the leg of his trousers. Choking back the tears, she cried out, 'Clara! Thoko!' hysterically, as she ripped the stained fabric apart.

Clara rushed out of the kitchen, wild-eyed at the panic in her mother's voice.

'Hurry, Clara! Tell Thoko to harness the donkeys, quick, your father has been bitten by a snake!'

Clara sped through the bushes, yelling out Thoko's name at the top of her lungs.

Esther tore off the hem of her dress and split it in two. Her hands moved frantically as she tightened one bandage above the bite marks on Bernard's leg and another below it.

Then leaning over, she urged him to his feet. Bernard shut his eyes tight to summon all his strength and then with a low moan and with his arm over her shoulder, he slowly lifted himself from the ground.

'We're almost there,' Esther reassured him as they edged forward.

They made their way slowly to the courtyard and Bernard lowered himself onto a stool. Esther rushed indoors and returned with a blanket which she wrapped around Bernard. Then she rushed to the edge of the courtyard and yelled out, 'Clara! Thoko!' her eyes searching the bush, 'What is taking you so long!' she sobbed.

She then raced off to the kitchen and came rushing back with a water gourd. Her hands trembled uncontrollably, as she held it against Bernard's lips. Bernard tilted his head back and gulped the water out of it.

Not long after Esther heard the loud crack of a whip followed by a rumble of wheels.

32

Down memory lane

Isaac helped the family to get Bernard into the back of the cart, then he stepped back and held his hand up to his playmate. Thoko nodded back at him. Then he cracked his whip and the wheels of the cart rumbled over the gravel.

'Isaac, if we're not back in time, could you bring the livestock back and lock them up?' Esther said from the back of the cart where she sat with an arm around Bernard.

Isaac looked up quickly to meet the glance directed at him and nodded his head.

'And if we're not back in the morning, can you let them out?'

Isaac nodded again, his eyes following the cart as it made its way gingerly through the driveway and then onto the road. He stood watching it until it was out of sight and then led the Dube's dogs back into their homestead. A few moments later he secured the gate and then with his dog walking beside him set off to find his father to tell him the unfortunate news.

'Are you certain it was a cobra?' Samuel asked, brushing his beard with his hand for the second time.

'It was a cobra,' Isaac confirmed.

The Dube family sat quietly in the cart as it raced up the road, and between short intervals, Esther put her hand on Bernard's chest to feel his heartbeat.

'Do you remember that tree?' Bernard, who had not spoken since being helped into the cart, now said weakly as they glided past an ancient mopane tree standing wearily on the roadside.

Bernard and Esther looked at each other first before laughing spontaneously. Then Esther turned her face down so that he could look in her face and said with a smile, 'How could I not?'

'That's where I tried to teach you to ride a bicycle,' Bernard said with a grin, 'And I ended up with crooked handlebars!'

'I was always happier sitting on the carrier behind you,' Esther told him. 'I still don't know how only two wheels can keep anyone upright.'

'It's the speed, you have to get it just right,' he told her.

They grinned at the memory of her very first bicycle ride and then he said with a smile, 'That's what did it for me. That's how I won you over!'

'That's where you're wrong,' Esther informed him, caressing his cheek with her palm. 'I knew what I wanted, even before you did.'

As the cart rushed ahead, Bernard tilted his head toward a crossroad and said, 'That's where I found you and Clara that day.' He shook his head and the tears welled up in his eyes and Esther grasped the arm around him tighter. 'I couldn't believe my eyes. I didn't think I'd ever see you again!' he told her.

'You saved my life, Bernard, and Clara's. What would've become of her if you hadn't come along that road, at just that time? And on a horse too. Pity I couldn't remember the ride, but Clara did, and I think she still does even though she was so young. And the Ndlovu's, how good they were to us,' Esther reminisced.

Bernard shook his head with a smile at the memory. Then, recalling his last meeting with Mr Ndlovu, he shook his head again, but this time with regret. And when Esther saw the sadness clouding his face, she held up his hand and kissed it.

'Esther, you know my heart was always yours, despite everything, it was always you,' he whispered, his voice broken.

Esther, not trusting her emotions, nodded quietly and pressed his hand. He opened his mouth again and Esther put her free hand over it and said, 'You don't have to say anymore, Bernard.' Bernard bent his head and dropped his glance.

After a short ride in silence, Bernard started up and muttered, 'Stop! stop!' with his chest heaving.

Esther yelled out to Thoko and Clara, and when the cart was stationary, she helped Bernard to the edge of the carriage. Bernard, just managing to lean over the side panel, parted his lips and emptied his stomach on the roadside, before slumping back into the cart with exhaustion. Esther wiped his mouth with the end of the cloth wrapped around her waist before giving him a drink of water from a gourd she had brought with her. And when he was again propped up against her with his head on her shoulder, she yelled out, and the donkeys took off with a quick trot.

'Can you see the clinic yet?' Esther yelled out after some time had passed, and Bernard's breathing had become more irregular.

'Yes, we're almost there,' Clara assured her mother as they sped ahead.

The cart slid off the main road and rushed towards a thatched square whitewashed building and Clara leapt off the cart and raced towards the clinic doors. A few minutes later two men came running out carrying a stretcher. A woman wearing a white coat raced behind them and before Esther knew what was happening the stretcher was gone and Bernard with it. She climbed out of the cart wearily and entered the clinic.

'Wait outside,' they told her. 'We'll take over from here.'

33

The long ride home

Esther looked up at the dark sky, laced with a shimmer of bright stars. Then she spread a blanket for the children in the back of the cart and when they had fallen asleep she went and sat outside the clinic doors with her back resting against the wall.

Sleep came unbeckoned only a few minutes after, taking her back home. Bernard and the children were sitting in the backyard, and when he sensed her watching them, he turned his head up to her with that gentle smile of his, and everything was as it was before.

Some time passed before two nurses came to find Esther, and they found her sound asleep, with a peaceful look on her face.

'Mama! Mama!' A voice called out softly, and the warm feeling disappeared and Esther's eyes blinked open.

She found one of the nurses crouched next to her and in that flash, reality thrust itself back on her. She struggled to her feet and asked, 'Can I see him now?'

The nurses looked at each other and then one of them began to speak.

'No! No!' Esther muttered as she shook her head determinedly, refusing to listen to the serious-faced person in his white uniform.

'You carried him indoors, telling me that everything would be fine!' she cried, as she tried to make sense of what they were trying to tell her.

'Where are the children?' the woman with the stethoscope around her neck asked from the edge of the veranda. A man guarding the premises pointed to a cart parked under some trees and the doctor walked briskly in that direction, before calling out.

The children crawled out of the cart and went to stand in front of her, rubbing the sleep from their eyes. The woman spoke in measured tones and then a loud howl escaped Clara's lips before the doctor's soothing tones and the quick flick of her head to where Esther stood in a daze put a stop to it. The murmur died down and the children nodded their heads with their eyes on the doctor, occasionally raising a hand to wipe the tears, now streaming down their cheeks. At the crack of dawn, a drum began to beat, a slow and solemn thumping from behind the clinic.

'Can you hear that?' Samuel asked, turning away from the cow he was milking and looking around.

He went and stood at the edge of his compound with a worried look on his face. His wife, who was kneeling over a slab of granite and grinding roasted ground nuts with a flat stone, paused in her labour and sat alert on her haunches. The drum rang out again and Samuel's wife covered the grinder with an open basket and flicked a hand at the chickens milling around her. They skipped out of the way as she got to her feet. Rubbing the dirt off her knees, she went to join her husband at the boundary of their compound.

'It's over,' Samuel whispered harshly. 'A life gone, just like that,' and they clung to each other for a moment, his wife's tears soaking his shirt.

In the village, the chief dressed in his purple robe and seated on his tall chair held his sceptre up to his drummer. And from the humble palace, the sound of the royal drum passed on the message they had just received to the villagers. Back at the clinic, the drummer nodded his head in acknowledgement when the sound reached them.

Samuel called out to his son and when his bicycle was brought to him, he turned it towards the farm compound where Nkosazane lived with her two sons. Riding alone down the rocky path, he succumbed to the grief that he'd been working hard to hold off and the tears poured out of his eyes unheeded.

Thoko and Clara stared in front of them as the stretcher that had carried their father through the clinic doors was brought out again, only this time around, it had a white sheet thrown over it.

The doctor held her arm out to keep Esther back as the stretcher was lifted into the cart. And it was only after the body was carefully shifted off it and the men were back on the ground, that she lowered her hand.

Esther, seizing the moment, scrambled in after it, shaking off the hands that reached out to help her up. She pulled the sheet off Bernard's body and laid her head over his chest.

'My soul mate,' she whimpered as she yearned for those strong arms to wrap themselves around her. She brushed her face over his mouth, eager for one more taste of his lips. And then, with a low moan, she pulled the sheet back over him and sat beside him, her face stiff with grief.

The doctor nodded at Esther before going to murmur to the children sitting quietly in front. Thoko leaned forward and tapped the donkey closest to him with his rod and the cart creaked into motion. With their heads bowed mournfully, and the wheels of the cart dragging laboriously through the dirt, they slipped back onto the road they had travelled only a few hours earlier, leaving behind them, the three health professionals standing crowded together, their hearts heavy with grief for them.

34

The vigil

A sorrowful wail started up as the cart carrying Bernard's body turned into the driveway, and some of the mourners came running up to meet it. They converged on the hearse, with the women tearing the scarfs from their heads and sobbing loudly while the men, with stoic faces, followed at a slower pace. Esther, seated with her head tilted to one side and with her grief shrouded by silence, was oblivious to the sounds around her.

An elderly man pointed out directions and Thoko guided the sombre procession towards Bernard's hut where Nkosazane, dressed in black and assisted by three other women, was waiting.

A loud piercing howl poured out of her as the cart reached her and her helpers scrambled to keep her upright. Then she began to sob loudly as she was led back into Bernard's hut.

Bernard's two brothers, Shepherd and Phineas, climbed into the cart as kind hands helped Esther out, and the body was conveyed indoors. Bernard's body was placed on a sand bed sprinkled with water. And when the door was shut behind them, Nkosazane and her trusted companions stripped Bernard of his clothes and washed his body in warm water. Then they lathered fat all over him before wrapping him up in the skins of a zebra to honour his ancestral clan. In the courtyard, the mourners talked in low tones and sipped beer out of clay pots.

'This is indeed a shock,' Lucus whispered as he shook the hand of an elderly man before taking a seat beside him. 'It was only a fortnight ago when I was with Bernard. What happened?'

The elderly man who had already narrated the story numerous times throughout the day paused for effect and then repeated the circumstances surrounding Bernard's death in a grief-stricken tone.

A goat had been slaughtered and behind the kitchen, several women hovered over three-legged pots that sat staunchly over blazing logs.

Esther entered her lounge room with its happy memories with dread. Several elderly women holding their vigil there sat in a circle with their backs against the wall and their legs tucked to one side. There had been a quiet hum as Esther came through the doorway, but the voices dropped away as she began searching in the dull light for her mother-in-law. A sombre air engulfed Esther as she padded past the small paraffin lantern burning in the centre of the room, its light flickering on the drawn faces of the women around it.

She found Nkosazane seated on a mat at the far end of the room with her legs stretched out in front of her. She knelt beside her and placed the dinner tray in her hands on the floor next to her. Nkosazane glared first at Esther and then at the tray before turning away from both abruptly. Several gasps flittered through the room.

'I don't want anything from you,' Nkosazane muttered in a hard tone, with her back to her daughter-in-law.

Esther straightened up slowly with a puzzled look on her face.

Nkosazane peered at the doorway and then seeing a small child loitering nearby called out, 'Come here, child!' in a commanding voice. Small feet carrying a frightened face pattered up to her. 'Take this tray away!' she snapped at the child. 'And tell the women in the kitchen that I won't eat anything prepared by this woman,' she continued, gesturing at Esther.

A few dissenting voices wavered unconvincingly as the child carried the tray out, before being silenced by the staunch look on the grieving mother's face.

Esther stumbled blindly out of the hut with her heart beating violently and was met by a muffled lowing. She stared into the dark and saw an outline of an animal standing under the acacia tree near the granary. Then with her eyes adjusting to the dark, she noticed how its head, which was suspended in the air, sat at an awkward angle. She edged closer just in time to see a long silver blade plunging deep into the animal's flesh. The arm holding the knife jerked consecutively, and then with another quick movement the blade emerged red and bloody.

Esther let out a cry of shock as her treasured bull, the one she and Bernard had bought as a calf and which had fathered many calves in the years that followed, slumped downwards. It lay there facing her with blood running out of its mouth and nostrils and with its neck straining from a thick rope tethered to the tree. And even before its body had run cold, she watched as a group of men descended on it with their knives drawn. And then it became all too much for her. She rushed off into the dark, not quite knowing where she was going.

When Bernard's mother heard of the slaughter, a satisfied smile broke on her face. 'This is a dinner in honour of Bernard, to celebrate his memory and to remind the village that he was the son of a chief,' she told her sons.

But to herself, she said, 'I want it to be the biggest wake any of them has ever attended. Am I not a king's daughter and of royal blood after all, and accustomed to living a life of privilege? I'll show them, you'll see, that poverty has not made me forget who I am.'

35

A Chief's burial

As the evening closed in, four fires were lit in the courtyard and when the embers were smouldering, metal racks were laid over them. A wheelbarrow filled with flesh dripping with blood went round supplying chunks of steak to the grills that had been set up.

The mourners muttered appreciatively to each other and drew their seats to the fire closest to them as a sweet aroma of roasting meat reached them.

Not long after, women carried bowls of rice, stewed lamb, and roasted vegetables and a host of delicacies, to several long tables set up near the light coming from the kitchen window.

The reigning chief and his entourage, suitably impressed by the elaborate banquet, filled their plates and chatted amicably as if forgetting the reason, they were there. And when they had withdrawn to a hut to eat their meal, the rest of the guests were invited to tuck in.

Nkosazane who had kept herself in the shadows monitoring the proceedings to ensure everything went as she'd planned, was pleased to hear her guests commenting on the feast and admitting to having never seen a spread such as the one before them.

Much later and drunk with food and drink, the mourners curled up wherever they could and despite their best efforts, fell asleep. And in the still of the night, four men crept to Bernard's hut and came out again huffing under the weight of the burden over their shoulders.

Using the stars and the woman leading them to guide them they tramped through the bushes and when they reached a river, they followed it downstream. They came to shallow waters and after crossing the river trekked through the wilderness. After an hour of swift walking, they reached the sacred hills of Bernard's ancestors.

The woman tore at rocks and brambles shrouding one side of the hill and the men, after depositing their load on the ground, went to assist her, clawing at rocks and vines. Boulder after boulder came undone when at last the hill opened and revealed its secret entrance.

The woman gathered dried foliage and when she had a sizeable mound, the men came and stood in a circle around it. She crouched down and lit a match and the mound flared up. When it was burning brightly, she emptied a handful of seeds over it.

The fire laboured under their weight, churning out a great cloud of smoke which the men scooped up in their open palms and rubbed themselves with until they were completely immersed in smoke fumes.

The woman leaned towards the fire and began chanting, while the men grabbed the lantern and squeezed their way through the narrow opening and then down a passage that opened into a chamber.

The light from the lantern rose and fell on small rectangular compartments built of stone. Inside each one lay the skeletal remains of a chief surrounded by his personal belongings, Bernard's father and his father before him among them.

The men found the compartment they were looking for and leaving behind the lantern to guide them, they exited the cave and returned carrying Bernard's body. They laid his head over a wooden headrest and drew the skins he was draped in neatly around him.

After placing his weapons and water gourd beside him, they scattered the compartment with gifts of wild oranges and figs for his journey to his afterlife.

Back outside, the woman asked, 'Is it done?' and the men replied, 'Yes, Nkosi,' and the woman nodded.

They returned the rocks to their original place before pulling the vines and brambles back over them and leaving the hill looking the way it had when they first arrived.

Back home, a rooster crowed to herald the new day, and the mourners stirred. Someone stood up to stoke the fire and keep it ablaze, before retiring to their seat. A few hours later, everyone was awake, except for those recovering from their night's journey.

And Esther, lying in her hut with her children beside her, told herself this was just a nightmare and that when she stepped outside the door, Bernard would be there, on his favourite stool in the courtyard, with his hands busy, and with that look on his face that he had just for her.

36

A Christian burial

It is bad luck for a coffin to leave a home through the front gate, so an opening had been made through the hedge at the back of the compound. And it was through this opening that the pallbearers, unaware that a log now replaced the body in the casket, filed out. They were followed closely by Nkosazane and her two sons and behind them was Esther and her children.

Inside the family graveyard, the coffin was lowered beside a newly dug hole and a man dressed in a black cassock and carrying a bible stepped out from the crowd and went to stand at the head of the grave.

'What is the meaning of this, this is supposed to be a traditional burial!' Bernard's mother hissed angrily as she turned to glare at Esther.

The priest, who had already been warned about the woman's reluctance to have a Christian burial for her son, waited patiently for the murmurs that followed to peter out.

Nkosazane on the other hand, encouraged by the whispers, began to remonstrate. An elderly woman, after listening to her, cursed and then pushed her way to the front, and confronted the protesting woman in a low terse tone. Nkosazane stopped her bawling prematurely and allowed herself to be led away by the women comforting her.

But after covering a short distance, she turned back and pointing a finger at Esther yelled, 'This is all your doing. You put your church between my son and me, and today it is you who put him in that box!'

The priest waited until Nkosazane was safely out of earshot and order was restored before he resumed his sermon. Then he walked around the grave sprinkling holy water over it before going to pick up a censer, and holding it over the open hole, swung the chain attached to it back and forth. The smoke from the burning incense flowed out into the grave.

A hymn started up, and some of the people around the grave began to sing as the coffin was lowered into the hole. Then the priest gathered up his possessions quickly and, making the sign of the cross, disappeared as discreetly as he had come.

'Mama, we're ready for you,' a young man said, bowing to the woman perched on the edge of a rock. Bernard's mother turned her head up arrogantly and together with her aides returned to the graveside.

Taking her place between Shepherd and Phineas at the head of the grave, she resumed her role of the bereaved mother.

After the speeches commemorating Bernard's life had been made, an elderly man grabbed a shovel, dug it deep into the small mound of fresh soil beside the grave, and threw the earth over the hole. After throwing several shovels of earth, a second man stepped up and took the shovel from him. A line of men formed as each waited their turn with the shovel.

When the casket was completely covered and only a small mound of soil remained beside the grave, Clara and Thoko turned away and buried their faces against their mother's body. And Esther standing stiffly beside them, with an arm around each and with her gaze in the distance, was aware only of the emptiness inside of her.

37

An accusation of sorcery

A hinge and several nails Bernard had planned to use to repair the kitchen door on the day of the baptism now lay half-buried in the sand, beside it. The door hanging awkwardly on one hinge, creaked noisily as Esther emerged from the kitchen carrying a tea tray.

She walked briskly to the lounge room where her guests were seated and placed the mugs of tea on a small table within easy reach of each. Then she sat on a mat facing them.

'Do you know why we are here, Mrs Dube?' the elder asked, leaning towards her. Esther shook her head with her face downcast. 'We are here because of an accusation that has been made against you,' the man told her with his gaze on her.

'My son is dead because of you!' Nkosazane rallied with fury. 'Did you think I'd just sit back and let you get away with it?'

'Now, now,' the elder intervened, 'we are not here to cause a disturbance.' Bernard's mother leaned back in her chair; her face flushed with anger. 'As I was saying,' the man continued with his neck bent again towards Esther, 'these are serious accusations.'

'What do you mean?' Esther asked. 'How am I responsible for

Bernard's death?'

'You may think you are not responsible because sometimes a person can do something without being aware of what they're doing,' the elder explained.

'Witchcraft!' Nkosazane yelled, her dark eyes flashing. 'That was not a real snake that bit Bernard. It was you. We have consulted three different spirit mediums, and they all say you did it!'

'How? Why?' Esther asked, her voice raised high with disbelief.

'Because he left you for someone else,' Nkosazane retorted. 'I told Bernard you were not good for him and now see what has happened. Bernard would've never married you in the first place if you hadn't bewitched him. I've never trusted you from the very first time I set eyes on you.'

'Bernard and I loved each other, and even with everything else that was going on, I would have given my life up for him.'

'You expect us to believe that?' Nkosazane retorted with an incredulous laugh, turning to the three men with her. The men indulged her by chuckling and shifting in their seats. Phineas folded his arms in front of him and Nkosazane grew serious again. 'You spend your time in the bush foraging for roots, don't deny it, all the villagers know you are a witch!'

'I find medicinal plants,' Esther said. 'Plants to cure people's ailments, not harm them.'

'Mr Shoko died after drinking your medicine,' Bernard's mother insisted. 'How do we know how many other people you've poisoned?'

The elder who had been watching Esther withdrew his eyes and, grunting quietly, stretched his legs out in front of him.

'Mr. Shoko was kicked by his bull, Mother,' Shepherd said, 'But that doesn't take away the fact that three witch doctors have confirmed that she's a witch.'

'Esther,' the elder said after a long pause, 'the chief has held many meetings concerning this issue. He has consulted with all the prominent members of our community and even his independent spirit medium. They have all reached the same conclusion. I am here on behalf of the chief and as such, it is my duty to inform you that a charge of sorcery has been found against you.'

He gave a heavy sigh and holding his hands together sat with them between his legs.

'How can this be?' Esther implored with a look of disbelief on her face. 'I am a Christian; I do not believe in witchcraft.'

'All the same,' the elder concluded, 'my visit here is not to argue with you but to pass on the chief's verdict. You know our customs. You will take only what you can carry, everything else stays behind.'

'What about my children?' Esther implored. 'Will you allow me to take them with me?'

'The children belong to your husband and in his absence, everything he owned passes on to his mother as the head of his family,' he said, looking at her sternly.

Esther shook her head miserably and then with a sigh of resignation, she folded her hands together on her lap and bowed her head.

The reed chair rustled briskly and Nkosazane sprang to her feet energetically. She picked up the tray Esther had brought in with her and took it outside with her. And then, calling out to Clara to make a fresh pot of tea, she tipped out the tea from the untouched mugs with a small shudder.

'I am sorry for your troubles,' the elder said, trying to be heard above the loud clucking of one of Esther's hens Nkosazane had given him, as he clamped it in the back carrier of his bicycle.

Then he swung his leg over the bar of his bicycle. And with the hen sitting crouched behind him with its mouth half open and its chest palpitating with fear, he rode off without a backward glance.

38

A widow is banished

A bag was hastily prepared for Esther, and she told herself that, when the time came, she would leave her home and everything in it with her head held high. A hand prodded her, telling her that the time was now, and Esther's heart stopped beating.

Phineas had sent Thoko to the next village on an errand, and Clara was howling behind a locked door. And Esther felt like a log had landed on her chest, taking all the wind out of her.

'Are you going to let a woman get the better of you? Two grown men and you stand there powerless. Lift her if you must!' Nkosazane snapped angrily, looking at her sons with disdain.

Shepherd and Phineas lunged forward and threw themselves on Esther, and all three bodies came crashing down before the men sprang up to their feet and dragged her across the courtyard. Esther's hand reached out and she held the gate post tight. The men shifted their positions. Shepherd used his fists to prise her fingers from their hold before she was thrust roughly through the gate.

'Go on. Get!' Phineas, the younger of the two, said as he stood threateningly over her, gesturing towards the forest. 'Don't you have any shame? No one wants you here. Not even your children!'

Esther's glance leapt to the locked hut, where she could hear her daughter's loud sobs.

'I said go!' the man repeated, shoving her with his foot.

'Where do you expect me to go?' Esther challenged him, ' This is my home', her voice hoarse with crying.

'That's not for me to say, but you must go, or I will set the dogs on you.'

Esther picked up the bundle at her feet and turned towards the forest, and the men remained standing until she was out of sight.

But when the dark and the night sounds started to engulf her, Esther turned back determinedly and retraced her footsteps. Reaching her homestead, she pushed the gate aside and let herself through. A dog unknown to her barked viciously and raised the alarm and without warning she found herself pinned to the ground.

The air filled with curt orders issued in low tones and men grunting and above all that was the commanding voice of Nkosazane. Again, the men dragged her out of her home and dumped her in the bushes. Too exhausted to protest, she crawled to a nearby tree and spent her first night there.

'Phineas, Shepherd!' Nkosazane's voice cut through Esther's numbed senses at the crack of dawn. Phineas stumbled out of a hut, and moments later Shepherd emerged from another. Their mother pointed in the direction of the gate with her jaw set.

'Get up, get up!' the men howled, angry at being woken up and making use of their fists and bare feet to probe Esther into action.

Esther raised her head, and the nightmare continued where it had left off. This time her hands were bound behind her back and a cloth was tied around her eyes before they bundled her up and threw her into a scotch cart. One of the men climbed in after her and shoved her to lie face down, with his full weight over her.

The cart rattled and heaved over rocks and stumps of coarse grass and every movement for Esther pressed against the chassis of the cart, was like a punch ramming into her.

On and on it went, through thick bushes and bare pastures and then the sun came out and the weight over her was relaxed. The man looked down at his captive and then with a dry chuckle, climbed into the front seat of the moving cart. Esther dragged herself upright and the cart carried on at its leisurely pace accompanied by a steady hum of voices coming from the front.

'Mary! Joe!' the driver shouted after much time had passed.

The animals stopped abruptly, their third stop since the start of this long journey. Esther was ordered out of the cart. She stumbled blindly to the ground where the men were waiting for her.

And then, sandwiched between them and with her heart beating frantically and her legs trembling with fear, they led her through the forest, now and then throwing a punch at her to quicken her step.

'Stop!' one of them yelled, and her feet stopped moving. The blindfold was ripped off, and then Shepherd shouted, 'Ah, ah ah, don't turn around. What do you want to see? Look straight ahead and don't move!'

'This is it,' Esther thought as she held her breath and closed her eyes. 'This is the end of my life.'

Accepting her fate, she bowed her head, and her lips trembled in silent prayer. A sharp pain exploded through her senses, and she sank lifelessly to the ground.

39

A grandfather's visit

Overhead, a flock of southern masked weavers voiced their uproar at the setting sun as they made their homeward dash across the silvery grey sky. And below a lizard crawled out of a crevice and climbed over some rocks before picking its way over the woven cotton and soft flesh obstructing its way.

Esther's eyes flickered open and a bolt of pain forced a low groan through her parched lips as she tried to raise her head slowly off the ground. The lizard scrambled off her hastily and disappeared into the nearby rocks.

Esther pulled herself painfully into a sitting position and one hand went instinctively to the back of her head which was caked with blood. She let her gaze roam over the unfamiliar landscape before a cacophony of a child sobbing and adults screaming came rushing back to her, and a pain different from the one of bruised limbs, and even more severe than the first, forced her to curl up into a little ball.

The wilderness welcomed her back again into its fold, and she smiled serenely as warm arms reached out and wrapped themselves around her.

The years peeled away, and she was a young child again, standing with her hands behind her back and the soft contours of her face glowing with anticipation because her grandfather had brought her here to show her something special.

He pointed to a belly-shaped tree that looked like it had been pulled out of the earth and then stuck back into it again with its roots sticking out on top of it. And when her grandfather, who towered over almost everyone in their village, went to stand next to it, he looked as small as she did when she stood next to him.

The little axe in his hand swung back and forth, its blade chipping into the trunk of the tree. And when it was safe for her to come closer, he showed her all the bark he had collected and how to coax out the fine fibres hidden just under the hard exterior.

Then her grandfather climbed high up into the stunted branches above, while she remained under the tree, bouncing back and forth to gather the velvety orange pods he threw down to her.

Back home, her grandmother made a spinach relish from the leaves of the upside-down tree they'd brought back with them, while the sound of her grandfather's hammer resounded through their homestead.

And when the sun went down and the sound of the hammer died with it, her grandfather held up a blanket he had made from the fibres he had so carefully peeled off that majestic being.

'Something to remember me with,' he told her, with a smile spread out on his face, even though she knew that he didn't need to give her anything for her to remember him.

'You have to keep moving,' he whispered, leaning so close to her that the diamond-shaped patch of white hair just above his forehead and nestled comfortably in a sea of black almost touched her.

A mist swooped in gradually, growing thicker as it swirled around him until he was no longer visible. And when her eyes flicked open, she found that she was alone with darkness around her.

With her grandfather's words fresh in her ear, she fought the impulse to remain where she was and pushed on, on all fours. Only a short distance from where she was, the baobab tree whose secrets her grandfather had come to remind her of, loomed large in front of her.

Just then, the sun popped out from the other side of the universe and Esther snuggled up to its belly-shaped trunk.

She grabbed the fallen leaves and crunched them between her teeth.

Then she smashed a cream of tartar pod against a rock and when the seeds popped out, she sucked on them, and her strength seeped slowly back to her.

40

A hunter to the rescue

The sun came up slowly and when it was high above, it hovered there for a bit, before it began its descent, elongating the shadows on the ground. A short distance away, a man with a quiver strapped to his back and a bow swinging loosely in one hand crept through the long blades of grass. He crouched low and trained his eye to the sound of scratching in the undergrowth. His arrow hissed through the air and a flock of grey and white speckled feathers scooted out of hiding.

The hunter watched them as they raced through the khaki veld, before strolling casually to his target and crouching beside it. He pulled the arrow from the still-warm body and wiped it clean with tufts of grass before returning it to its leather pouch. Then he grabbed the guinea fowl by its legs and with his face tilted towards it, examined the purple-blue bald head hanging lifelessly at the end of its scraggly neck, before dropping it unceremoniously in the bag tied to his belt.

He rose to his feet with an unhurried movement, aware of everything around him. His eyes raced to the giant tree standing staunchly on its own. A slight movement, that would have gone unnoticed by anyone else, but which sounded to his trained ear, like the thunder of ten galloping horses, made him drop his glance to the ground below its twisted branches.

With narrowed eyes, he saw the miniature figure swathed in black mourning clothes and seated on the ground. He melted back into the foliage and using it as cover, raced stealthily towards the gigantic trunk. It was only when he was ready that he showed himself to her. Esther looked up suddenly, cupping her hand to her mouth and stifling the cry of terror behind it.

'How are you, Mama,' the man murmured, clapping his hands in greeting and going to squat a short distance from her.

Esther recoiled from the sound of his voice.

'Why are you here?' he asked, looking at her searchingly with his head held to one side.

Esther could feel his gaze on her as he attempted to peel off the barriers shielding the vacant eyes. But all he could see was the swelling on the side of her head and the dried blood over one of her eyelids.

'I don't want to seem inquisitive, but can you tell me what happened to you?' he asked in a gentle tone after a moment's reflection.

Esther turned her eyes down and the wind rustled the leaves above them.

'Do you come from around here? Is your home nearby?' he persisted, scraping at the walls shielding her. 'What about your family and children? Do they know you are here?' he queried in a soothing tone and her eyes fluttered with interest. The hunter saw the opening, and he used comforting words to melt down the barrier.

At first, Esther's grief and heartache came out in a gush of tears. Then, all the emotions of betrayal and grief and anger she had so expertly concealed came bursting out in a gut-wrenching shrill that made the hunter step back in fright. With her face contorted with trauma, she flung her head back and dashed it against the hard ground, as she screamed out her anger and frustration. She thrashed the ground with her arms and legs and the dust leapt around her.

Embarrassed, the man looked away. Then she gradually quietened down and a heavy sigh slipped through her lips. She dragged her bruised body off the ground and crawled back wearily to the tree and sat with her eyes turned away from the horrified ones turned toward her. The wilderness pulsed on, and then the man sidled closer, but not too close, and sat on his haunches with his face hidden away from her. Esther adjusted the scarf on her head and stretched an arm out to retrieve a shoe lying in the dirt.

The man's sharp eye spotted a button torn from her dress. Picking it up, he brushed it clean with the back of his hand before holding it out to her. Esther made him keep his hand out before turning red swollen eyes and a face streaked with defiance towards the scrutinising glance fixed on her.

'Can you walk?' the man enquired kindly, stooping down to help her up.

Esther's eyes filled up with tears again at the memory of those similar words she'd uttered to Bernard not so long ago, unaware at the time of how drastically things would change for her.

The man walked a little ahead and she followed slowly behind him. A short while later, the sound of water splashing and children laughing reached them. The man murmured to her quietly and left her behind. He walked up to where several women seated on flat rocks protruding from a running stream were doing their laundry. The children stopped their splashing, and waving their hands, called out to the man gaily. The man's laughter trickled back to them.

The hunter had his head tilted to the ground and he spoke in a low tone, and when his voice grew quiet, one of the women clapped her hands together as if shocked by what the man had just told them. Then she waded through the water and together with the man, went to where Esther was waiting.

IV

Part 4 – Thoko and Sonia

41

News of a British Colony

Sonia stood in the doorway of the living room, listening to her mother reciting a poem in her strong French accent despite her many years in England. The audience was an odd bunch of painters, writers, and dancers, most of whom were unknown to her, which was nothing unusual for Sonia. She remembered, even as a small child, waking up in the morning to find their large country mansion filled with an assortment of strangers, drawn in by her parents' artistic and bohemian lifestyle.

She spotted her father, Lord Crawley, an author by profession, who had scandalised the family name by marrying a relatively unknown actress, sprawled on a cushion among their quirky friends.

Her mother came to the end of her recital, dropped her hand holding the book dramatically, and paused. And then with a big smile, she bowed to her audience, who responded appropriately by clapping their hands enthusiastically.

'What did you think, darling?' her mother called out to her.

'Outstanding!' Sonia replied, before turning around to stroll through the rest of the house.

'If a lion didn't exist, which animal do you think would be crowned the king of the jungle?' a voice asked from behind an easel.

Sonia looked around to see who the person was talking to and, seeing no one, was about to stroll on when a face peeped out from behind a canvas and pointed a paintbrush at her saying, 'Now that I have caught your attention, what if I told you that in a British colony called Rhodesia, wild animals are being squeezed out from their natural habitat and if nothing is done about them they will soon become extinct?'

Intrigued, she edged to where the man sat and he stood up and together they strolled out into the garden, where the man had plenty more to tell her.

'But you're not an activist,' Ellie wailed, 'And you want to join a group of activists.'

'Not join them, Ellie, help them. Look at this,' Sonia said, spreading out a file on her writing desk. 'This is a copy of their report.'

'I thought you said, they'd lost their case,' Ellie commented, peering at the sheaf of papers in a non-committal way.

'They are appealing the decision, and this is where you come in. You're the lawyer. But look at this. This is a more personal account. See how beautifully it's been written about the place. We can help them.'

The notes talked about the people and the animals and how they had for centuries co-existed without conflict, and how building a resort, no matter how it looked, would cause more harm than good to both animals and natives.

'The more I read them,' Sonia said, watching Ellie as she slipped the sheets of paper methodically back into the file and then appealing to her with a serious face, 'The more I am convinced that this is an effort worth supporting and fighting for.'

'I don't know,' Ellie said. 'This could take time.'

'If we present our case now, the Supreme Court has agreed that it will come to a decision soon.'

'How long?' Ellie asked.

'Three months max. That's not much, Ellie, you must admit, and I've even done most of the groundwork. I just want you to pore over my notes and make changes where you feel necessary. Come on, you must be curious at least to see what this new country is like, instead of what you read in the papers.'

'Well then, let's get started, we don't have much time!' Ellie conceded, knowing how stubborn her friend could be.

Sonia squealed with excitement and rushed over to hug her friend.

42

A Pro Bono case

Less than a fortnight after this conversation Sonia and Ellie left Heathrow Airport. They arrived in Cape Town, South Africa, on Imperial Airways where they spent a few days. They then boarded a light aircraft that landed in a thriving town in Rhodesia called Bulawayo.

There they were met by Thokozani Dube, a young lawyer whose notes Sonia had in her possession. Thoko, who like Ellie had taken time off to work pro bono on the case, had arranged office space for them with a leading local law firm.

Sonia stood up from her desk and looked around the small law firm she had occupied in the last six weeks and marvelled at how comfortable she felt here in a continent she knew so little about and in a country that was so far away from home.

'Well, this is it,' Ellie said, tapping her briefcase as Sonia came up to meet her.

'It's all up to you now. Good luck,' Sonia said, with her arms around Ellie. 'It doesn't matter if we lose, fingers crossed we don't, but at least we can say that we've given it everything we had.'

'Giving up already!' Ellie squealed. 'Don't you have any faith in me?'

'Of course I have.' Sonia laughed. 'Now go on, or you'll be late!'

Ellie saluted her friend, turned around, and strode briskly through a doorway, her high heels ringing out on the cement floor.

Sonia found a bench in the wide corridor and sat down. Not long after, Thoko, dressed in a suit and carrying a briefcase, arrived saying, 'Any news yet?' with a worried look on his face. Sonia shook her head, and he went to stand a short distance away from her.

The loud click of heels resounded again sometime later as Ellie rushed over to where her two friends waited for her nervously.

'They've ruled in our favour,' she called out excitedly, even before she reached them.

'They did?' Thoko and Sonia chorused and rushed to throw their arms around her.

'Yes! It says here essentially that the Native Commission is barred from parcelling up the native reserve and making it available to incoming settlers. And this is coming from the Supreme Court!' she said, holding up the papers in her hand.

'I knew you could do it,' Sonia asserted with a triumphant grin.

'Well, sense had to prevail in the end,' Ellie replied, 'And we did it together, the three of us!'

'Send them a congratulatory message,' the mayor said, with a glance at his secretary despite the verdict not going his way.

'I'm holding a banquet in your honour,' he shouted to Sonia over the telephone, when she called to thank him. 'I've invited the local newspaper to attend too!'

'It's good for publicity,' the mayor told his secretary as he replaced the receiver. 'It shows us in good light.'

And when the invitations arrived, Sonia and Ellie both received an extra one, 'For whoever you choose to bring,' the mayor's secretary said in a follow-up call.

'Are you sure about this?' Thoko asked with a puzzled look at Sonia when she handed him an invitation with his name on it.

'Of course,' she replied gaily. 'You were the one who carried out the ecological assessments that turned them around. So, will you come?' she asked with a disarming smile, arching her eyebrows at him.

'Most definitely,' Thoko replied, tapping the card in his hand on his wrist.

43

An unwelcome guest

Sonia and Ellie found the mayor in the reception area welcoming his guests, when they arrived.

'Ladies, welcome!' he called out to his guests of honour as he left his post.

He led them proudly through a broad foyer whose walls were lined with portraits of hunters staring into the distance. Men wearing broad-brimmed hats and with moustaches twirled, holding rifles in various positions while towering majestically over their trophies. And on the ground lay rhinos, lions, leopards, elephants, and many more, beasts that had succumbed to the predator, and now lying lifeless and silenced forever.

They stepped through a doorway, and the mayor turned to them and asked proudly, 'What do you think?' with his arms spread out towards an opulently decorated room furnished with elegant Victorian-style furniture that sparkled under the light pouring down from the ornate chandeliers hanging from the ceiling.

'Not bad, hey?' he laughed. 'For a club in the middle of nowhere!'

He led them to the main table which, like the others, had an array of fine bone crockery, polished silverware, and crystal glassware nestled in luxurious satin tablecloths.

Several young men dressed in their dinner jackets and bow ties and with their hair oiled and brushed down jumped out of their seats as they approached and bowed their heads to the two women graciously.

The room filled up and the chatter rose, and bar staff were kept busy off-loading drinks in crystal glasses before loading their silver trays again with those that had been emptied.

Meanwhile, in the reception area, a young waiter cowered under the wrath of the head waiter for being inattentive and delivering the wrong beverage to a guest. Another waiter, the informer who had dobbed the unfortunate fellow in, hovered nearby, eager to witness the punishment to be meted out.

The head waiter stopped talking suddenly, and the other two followed his gaze to the doorway where a man stood uncertainly. The man looked at the card in his hand again as if to reassure himself, before making up his mind and striding in.

The head waiter quickly waved off his staff and slipped back behind his pulpit. A light titter from the guests sitting in the dining area opposite the reception area accompanied the handsome man to the reception counter.

'I am here to attend the banquet,' the man said in a quiet and courteous tone as he placed his invitation on the counter.

The head waiter flicked his head in the direction of the banquet and then turning to his list announced triumphantly, 'I'm sorry, sir, your name is not on the list!'

Thoko could feel the eyes on his back as the murmur of voices behind him grew louder.

'Could you check your list again please?' he suggested in a light tone.

A clatter rang out as an irate patron threw his cutlery down and, folding his arms angrily, glared at Thoko's back with a look of revulsion on his face.

The head waiter bowed his head and tapped the counter with his fingers as his eyes ran through the list a second time, before coming back with the same answer.

'What are we to do then?' Thoko enquired politely. 'I have here a written invitation that states that I can attend, but you say your list does not have my name on it, so which of the two is correct?'

The head waiter shook his head and then beamed a smile at the enquirer to make up for his dilemma, and when Thoko showed no sign of leaving without an answer, he said in a courteous tone, 'Please wait here, sir, and I will find out from the chairman what to do.'

Thoko nodded, and then with his body turned to the door and with one hand resting on the counter, waited.

'There's a gentleman with an invitation to attend the dinner, but his name is not on the list. I explained this to him, and he insists that there must be an error with the list,' the head waiter told his master in a low tone.

'If he has an invitation, then why the bloody hell won't you let him in?' the chairman demanded, annoyed at having his night spoilt with trivialities.

The waiter leaned in further and whispered in his ear.

'What?' the chairman snapped, turning his ear away from the speaker abruptly to stare at him in disbelief. 'How the bloody hell did that happen?'

The chairman banged his beer glass back on the table and sprang off his seat energetically. The head waiter rushed ahead and gestured to another waiter and after dispensing a few words in his ear, watched silently as his message was delivered to the six-foot doorman sitting unobtrusively in the bar area.

The doorman acknowledged the message with a nod and moved his stool close to the reception counter.

The chairman stormed down the foyer purposely intending to throw out the impertinent soul by his collar, when he found himself staring at a dignified young man with a compelling presence.

'Are you a member?' the chairman asked as he tried to put a genial smile on his face.

'I'm afraid not,' Thoko replied, wondering why that would matter when some of the guests attending the celebration were not members themselves.

'Sorry, old boy,' the chairman responded, 'It's members only.'

Thoko looked at the chairman with disbelief, and then realising the real reason he was being refused admission, dropped his eyes quickly with embarrassment. Recovering from his blunder, he mumbled his thanks and then left promptly as he fought hard to maintain his dignity.

The chairman shared a joke with his indignant fellowmen and then, shaking his head with amusement, rejoined the celebration just in time to hear the first speaker.

After the speeches, a troop of waiters came rushing in with entrees of fresh oysters, prawn cocktails, and smoked trout. Music streamed out of speakers around the room and accompanied the plates of beef, mutton, and poultry and a pleasant presentation of a variety of vegetables and salads.

As the evening wore on, women stopped to fan themselves delicately and the men discarded their jackets and loosened their ties. A long pause of drink and chatter followed before trolleys with a mixture of savoury and sweet delicacies were rolled in.

Sonia looked at her wristwatch once more before glancing around the room. Then she crept out of the room unnoticed.

'There was dancing and oh so much fun, Sonia,' Ellie said after. 'What happened to you? Where did you disappear to?'

'I came back here, I couldn't take it any longer,' Sonia replied. And then turning a stern look at Ellie, she asked, 'Why was Thoko's name left off the list?'

'Who said his name was taken off?' Ellie replied with genuine surprise.

'Did you even notice that he wasn't there?' Sonia grumbled. 'He helped us with all that work, and they wouldn't even allow him in.'

'They have their way of doing things here, Sonia. We shouldn't interfere with their laws,' Ellie told her friend kindly.

'Yes, I know,' Sonia replied, 'But it all sounds a little silly.'

44

A train ride

A taxi drove down the wide streets of Bulawayo, its passengers rushing past colonial-style villas with shaded verandas.

'Are you sure you don't want me to come with you for company?' Ellie asked.

'I'm sure,' Sonia replied. 'I'll be fine. And I've already taken too much of your time.'

'It's been exhilarating,' Ellie admitted. 'I am glad I came. But it is time to return home.' After a short pause, and speaking urgently she added, 'You don't have to do this, you know, Sonia. You can abandon this crusade of yours and catch the plane back with me.'

'I would never forgive myself, Ellie. And you know me, I don't leave business unfinished!'

'I do know that about you.' Ellie laughed, and then with her tone serious she added, 'I admire your courage, Sonia, I do, really.' Sonia gave her a small hug and then settled back in her seat.

'Place of slaughter,' Ellie murmured. 'What?' Sonia asked with alarm. 'Bulawayo. It means a place of slaughter in the Ndebele language,' Ellie told her.

'Mmmm,' Sonia acknowledged with a faint smile. Then she said,

'And Peter?'

Ellie smiled at her friend and asked coyly, 'What about him?'

Peter was a young Australian who had just returned from a hunting trip. He was a friend of the journalist who had covered the event at the banquet where Ellie had met him.

'I like him,' Ellie confided. 'We'll be travelling back to England together before he returns to Australia. And who knows what will happen from there on?'

The smile on Ellie's face was enough to tell Sonia that her friend was more smitten with her new beau than she was letting on.

'No need to come out,' Sonia said, declining Ellie's company when they reached the train station, before bounding after the taxi driver with her luggage.

After purchasing her ticket, Sonia pushed her way through a crowded part of the platform alongside which, was a stationary train with its doors opened wide. She watched the passengers shoving and haggling as they tried to squeeze themselves into the long compartments fitted with wooden benches and already filled to their full capacity.

Further ahead, a conductor who seemed to have been looking for something frantically stopped suddenly at the sight of her. He raised his hand and approached her briskly, all the while apologising to her profusely.

He led her attentively away from the crowds and took her towards the head of the train where only one or two passengers were waiting on the platform. He hovered around her protectively as she climbed up the iron steps into the train before whipping ahead of her and opening the door to her carriage where she was again reunited with her luggage.

'You'll be safe here, miss,' he assured her, 'And just ahead of you is the dining car, if you care for some refreshments.'

After warning Sonia to lock her carriage door and showing her how the conductor jumped back on the platform and tipped his hat to someone who had suddenly appeared there.

A guard's whistle shrilled and the train jerked into motion, hissing angrily and releasing a cloud of smoke that enveloped the tracks and spilled out on either side of it. Sonia leaned out of the window and listened to the wheels chugging on furiously and when the station was out of sight the train steamed ahead. Sonia leaned back in her seat and allowed it to carry her away with it.

Many hours later, the wheels began to squeal and spark, rousing Sonia out of her slumber before the train came to a decisive stop. She pressed her forehead against the window and at the tail end of the train, a guard holding two small flags jumped out of the caboose. Villagers carrying baskets of fruit and freshly cooked produce poured out from the plains and rushed to the carriages near the guard's van and a brisk exchange of goods and coins commenced.

A short while later the guard consulted his wristwatch and when the long hand had reached the required number, he blew a whistle hanging from a cord around his neck. The whistle belted out a second time and the guard held up his green flag, prompting the train driver to sound his horn. Laughing and shouting the villagers withdrew from the tracks as the train shuddered and then dragged itself forward reluctantly. The guard popped back into his van and the train charged through the khaki landscape its rhythmic motion sending Sonia back to sleep.

Three loud raps on her carriage door woke Sonia.

'Bedding, madam,' a broad smiling porter announced carrying neatly folded dark blue blankets and crisp white sheets embroidered with an 'RR' logo on the corner of their hems.

Sonia stood in the corridor as a bed was made for her on the top bunk of her generously sized compartment. Then the porter rushed off, his face beaming happily, and returned soon after carrying a tray with a sturdy porcelain tea set with Rhodesia Railways etched on its side. Sonia thanked him, then she leaned back in the soft leather of her seat, and with a teacup cushioned in her hands, watched the orange glow of the setting sun. Night crept up slowly and when the black expanse above was covered in a myriad of sparkling jewels, Sonia joined the handful of passengers in the dining car for a glass of wine and dinner.

Outside, the train chugged on relentlessly over the tracks. The next day, exhausted from its long all-night journey, it drifted gently through a stretch of dusty bush that was broken now and then by a cluster of round mud huts with thatched roofs and pockets of grazing livestock. Then it crawled into the little village of Umvuma, which meant, 'he who admits,' and it felt to Sonia, an appropriate place for her to deliver her apology.

A conductor, different from the one who had shown Sonia into her compartment in Bulawayo, was there to escort her out of her carriage. 'This is Aaron, your driver!' he told Sonia in his thick Afrikaans accent, gesturing to the man standing respectfully a little behind him with his head bowed, after taking great care to guide her back onto the platform. Then he turned to the driver and issued an instruction in terse tones, with his face twisted in an angry scowl. The driver nodded his head several times before scrambling into the carriage and emerging again with Sonia's luggage.

'I don't want to hear of any trouble on the way,' the conductor ordered, his eyes throwing the driver a threat. Then he turned to Sonia and said, 'You need to be firm with them, show them who's boss. Insist on obedience and remember, never to show fear!'

He paused with his stern eyes on her, before reaching out for her hand and bidding her farewell with a cheerful smile.

45

A goodwill errand

Aaron parked the car beside a picket fence before rushing to open the back passenger door for Sonia.

'Is this the place?' she asked, looking at a small building with throngs of people sitting outside it.

The driver nodded with a bright smile on his face.

'How did you know where to find me?' Thoko inquired curiously when the shock of seeing her had subsided.

'Ellie had your address on her file. And your itinerary. She's very efficient, as you know, and she wanted to make sure that you would arrive safely.'

'And I did, as you can see,' he reminded her.

Sonia turned her face down with embarrassment.

'You put me in a very difficult situation,' he told her with suppressed anger. 'I fooled myself into thinking that for the first time, things had started to change for the better. And that a person like myself would be seen for what they've made of themselves and not by some ridiculous branding.'

'That was never my intention, and I should've known better,' Sonia admitted. 'I just wanted you to know how much I appreciated your help.'

'I'm glad to hear that,' he replied, smiling for the first time. 'You've helped my people keep the fences out. It was something my father felt strongly about.'

'Conservation is not my thing really,' Sonia confessed when the animosity had been pushed aside and they were talking as the friends they'd become. 'Now, flowers and plants, that's where my heart is.'

'I don't see the difference,' Thoko told her. 'They're pretty much the same to me.'

'You're right, of course,' Sonia agreed with a laugh when she had given that information further thought, 'but I didn't want to give you the wrong impression.'

'I understand,' he responded with a chuckle.

'I'm here for a week, in my capacity as a botanist. You know the area and I'd hoped that you could spare me some of your time and show me around.'

'I don't think it's advisable,' Thoko said stiffening, 'You, coming here, and us being seen together.'

'Why not?' she wanted to know, and he replied, 'You know why.'

'You're playing with fire,' Ellie warned the next time Sonia called her on the phone.

Sonia knew Ellie was right.

'But I can't help myself,' she said to herself.

The weeks turned into months, and as they found one excuse after another for her not to return to England, Sonia knew that she couldn't live without Thoko, and nor could he, without her.

'I have to go now,' Thoko said as he tried to pull himself away.

Sonia's grip on him tightened, refusing to let him go. 'Not like this,' he told her in answer to the longing in her eyes. 'I won't let them cheapen what we have by hiding away as if what we have is something to be ashamed of, just because the world we live in says it is.'

'Then marry me,' Sonia asserted. 'There I said it, marry me.'

He dropped to his knees, and clasping her hands in his, asked, 'Are you sure? Are you willing to give up everything you have now, to be with me?'

'Yes,' she murmured.

'You have to be certain,' Thoko told her firmly. 'It won't be easy for either of us, but more so for you than for me.'

'Being away from you is harder,' Sonia replied. 'And my answer is still yes.'

Men of the cloth preached about equality and acceptance, but being equal in God's eyes was not always enough, it seemed.

'It's against the laws of the country,' the pastor they visited told them. 'Think of your children. They'll be neither white nor black. And what future would they have in a place like this?'

'What is wrong with your own kind, are we not good enough for you?' Thoko's trusted friend demanded.

'It may not seem right, but it feels right here,' Thoko replied with his palm pressed against his heart.

'Well, if that is the case,' his friend conceded with a knowing grin, 'Then I'll put you in touch with someone who might be able to help you with your little problem.'

Sonia wore a white veil that flowed from the top of her head to her white lace dress below and Thoko was dressed in a shiny blue suit with a frilled white shirt and a high collar.

'Say cheese!' the photographer said when the Catholic priest officiating their marriage pronounced them man and wife and a light flash followed to capture the moment.

46

Anniversary wishes

Thoko had brought home a small box, the size of Sonia's open palm to commemorate their first year of marriage. She opened her eyes wide because she had something for him too, but nowhere near as extravagant as his gift appeared to be.

Her gift to him was a bouquet of flowers made from coloured paper, delicate and yet enduring and he held them up lovingly to his face, making up for all the time she'd spent making them.

She stared at the box still unopened in her hand and he said, 'Go on, go on,' urging her to open it.

And when she did, she found that the box was lined with white satin and lying snug inside was a heart-shaped gold locket with their wedding photo in it.

'Do you like it?' he asked as he wiped the tears from her eyes, even though he knew that she did.

'I'll always treasure it,' she replied, as she held her hair up, and he stood close behind her as he fastened the gold chain circling her throat.

Behind the trees was the shopping centre where the protocol of 'who goes where' was strictly adhered to. And Thoko had agreed to accompany her reluctantly, 'But only up to the trees,' he told her with a warm smile.

Sonia leaned her head against his shoulder and nodded her head.

'You go on, I'll be fine with my friends over there,' he reassured her and pointed towards the men loading crates on a lorry parked on the side of the road.

She gave him a glum look and already she could hear him calling out to the men.

Sonia saw the young couple before they saw her, chatting happily and walking arm-in-arm and she looked at them wistfully. They turned towards her, their faces friendly, and Sonia was about to reach out to them when they suddenly recognised who she was because even though she did not know them, they knew of her.

Their feet faltered and their faces twisted with contempt. The man held his arm up protectively as if shielding his young companion from her, as he guided her as far away from Sonia as he could.

A safe distance away, they resumed their chatter, but it had a sting in it now, and Sonia was quick to catch a quick flick of their heads as they snuck a look her way.

The hum of voices died as Sonia entered the general store. She held her chin up all the same and took a stroll among the merchandise displayed on wooden benches. One shopper nudged another and they both stared in her direction.

This was a tight community that took good care of each other but not those who broke the rules.

No pleasantries were exchanged as Sonia went about her business, eager to escape the looks of disgust that followed her.

The storekeeper was caught between being a gentleman and his loyalty to his other customers, but despite his views, the woman was still one of them.

He sent his 'boy' to make himself useful and walk behind her with a shopping basket.

'Will that be all,' he muttered as he tallied up her purchases, avoiding her glance.

Sonia nodded in reply, too angry to utter a word.

'Did you see that? Strutting around the shop like she has nothing to be ashamed of! The government shouldn't be allowing this sort of thing to happen. It's bad for the country,' a woman gossiped as she walked up to the counter and turned around to draw in the other customers to her conversation with encouraging looks.

'I say we sign a petition, expel them by force,' her male companion added decisively.

'No woman is safe if this sort of thing is allowed. They'll get it into their heads that we're all here for the taking!' another chipped in.

'It's the children that I worry about. Can you imagine, the countryside overrun by little mongrels? And do you know children like that are born mentally deficient?'

'You mean with a screw missing,' the male companion snorted before roaring with laughter at his own joke. The others joined in.

'Do you agree with all that business about mixed couples and half-caste children,' Mr Upton, a retired Cambridge professor, quizzed his wife when they were safely out of earshot.

'Of course not,' his wife replied. 'What utter nonsense. It's attitudes like that that create the problem. People are people, no matter what society thinks, and who's to say that there's been no mixing in our so-called pure race.'

'Precisely!' her husband asserted, putting the subject to rest.

'It's not right that there is a set of rules for you and another for me. What harm is there in you entering any shop you choose, or for us to have a meal together in a restaurant? What makes me acceptable and you not?' Sonia asked in hurt confusion after she tipped the 'boy' for carrying her purchases and she and Thoko were alone.

'It's just how it is,' Thoko replied with a smile. 'Look at us, see how different we look. My nose is broader than yours, my hair is kinky. Look at my lips, so different from yours.'

'I love your nose, and your hair, and especially your lips,' Sonia murmured.

'As I do yours.' Thoko laughed. 'But most people are not like us. They have a deep fear of anything that they are not familiar with. We knew, you and I, what to expect. What we were signing up for. Remember?'

'Yes we did,' Sonia murmured, her eyes melting into his, 'But it still doesn't make it right.'

47

A cottage at the edge of a village

One day Sonia and Thoko's rambles in the veld took them to a part of the countryside they had not ventured to before. Sonia leaned down and patted her horse's shoulder, and the animal stood still.

She placed the field glasses hanging around her neck over her eyes and twisted around slowly in her saddle as she surveyed the valley below.

'Can you see that?' she murmured after a moment's hesitation and with the field glasses still over her eyes.

Thoko held up his binoculars and strained his eyes in the direction she had pointed and said, 'It must be an abandoned building.'

'No, it's not. I can see a woman carrying a pail and walking across the courtyard,' she mused. 'And a dog, there under a tree. And cattle and goats, but just her. It's so isolated, there's no other homes around.'

'Yes, I see that,' Thoko commented.

'We should take a ride over and make friends,' Sonia suggested.

'It's quite a long way off,' he replied absentmindedly, 'And there's not much light left in the day, if you want to photograph those aloes you've been going on about.'

'Yes I must do that,' she replied, her face lighting up. Then, digging into her stirrups and already in a gallop, she shouted, 'I'll race you to the end of the veld!'

And he was left to catch her up.

'I've never spoken to you about my life before going to live in South Africa,' Thoko said the following day, 'And you've never asked.'

Sonia looked across the room to the couch where Thoko was seated. That was his side of the study and dedicated to his leather-bound law books that were lined up on shelves against the wall.

The other side, much bigger than the first, was Sonia's and it was filled with plants flowering in pots on the floor. The wall behind her had coloured charts and diagrams showing various growth patterns of the plants she was studying. And there was a file cabinet where she kept finely detailed notes and a register listing each new species she found.

She left the table with an aloe under the microscope and went to circle his neck with her arm and he put the notebook and pen in his hand down on the coffee table in front of him.

'No, I didn't. You weren't ready to talk about it and I didn't want to pry,' Sonia replied, slipping down beside him and clasping the hand reaching out to her.

'The house we saw today, the one with all the animals and the woman on her own. There was something about the way the woman walked, that reminded me of my mother,' Thoko said, his voice muffled with emotion.

Sonia gasped and moved closer so that each could feel the even heartbeat of the other.

'They banished her, you know, threw her in a cart and drove her away. I wasn't there, I didn't see what happened. I returned home from an errand and all I heard was that she'd left, and I didn't think anything of it, even though I didn't remember her ever leaving us on our own before. At first, I thought she'd be gone for a short while, but the days went by and when she still hadn't returned, I asked about her and my uncle just laughed in my face. Afterward, when we were alone, Clara told me, so I left without telling anyone, not even Clara. I was ten years old. I jumped on a cattle train and didn't get off until I reached Cape Town. The rest you know.'

The tears welled up in Sonia's eyes and they comforted each other in the silence that followed with the warmth of their bodies because the pain of knowing, was not just felt by the one whose secret it was, but equally so by the one who it was entrusted to.

'Let's go and visit the house,' Sonia whispered when their tears were spent, and she could trust herself to speak. 'She may not be your mother, and you must be prepared for that, but even if she isn't, at least you'll know. And who knows, maybe she could tell you something that may help us to find your mother.'

Thoko leaned towards her with his arm protectively around her waist and knowing her fear of the dark said to her with a playful smile, 'You mean right now, at night, with all the owls screeching out their vengeance?'

'Maybe not tonight,' she conceded, touching his nose with her lips, before making herself comfortable on his lap.

48

Arrival of a messenger

The young man scanned the homestead and then alighting from the scotch cart, patted each of the two donkeys in turn before ambling towards the gate. Inside the compound, Esther bent over a pile of firewood, picked out two chunks of wood, and with Jacob trailing faithfully behind her, carried them back with her to the kitchen.

'Mama!' a voice called out.

'Who is it?' Esther whispered to herself with her glance at the gate.

'I've come with a message,' the young man called out.

'The gate is not locked,' Esther yelled back after a short pause.

'Does your dog bite?' the man asked looking at Jacob's pricked ears.

'Only bad people,' Esther replied with a light chuckle, and then murmuring to Jacob to stand down she continued to the kitchen and left the lad to enter cautiously under Jacob's stern surveillance.

She returned to the courtyard wiping her hands on the cloth wrapped around her waist.

The youth pulled the stalk of grass he'd been chewing from his mouth and said, 'Good morning, Mama,' with his head bowed, rubbing his hands together.

Esther received the youth with the same respect and when the formalities of greeting had been completed, they went and sat under the shade of a hut.

'Mama, I don't know if you know who I am. My name is Robson, and I am Phineas's eldest son,' the young man began.

'I could see the resemblance in your face,' Esther admitted.

'I've been sent by Big Granny. She requested that you come and see her,' Robson told Esther.

Esther had not had any contact with Bernard's family in many years. Shepherd had arrived unexpectedly at her doorstep a year after they had thrown her out of her home. She didn't know how he had found her, and she hadn't bothered to ask him. But he'd come, his head bowed and his eyes darting everywhere as they avoided hers. It was then that he told her of her son's disappearance.

She looked at Robson now and wondered if his coming today had anything to do with Thoko. And then, refusing to hear anything worse than what she'd been told that day, she scrambled up hastily, with her heart pounding.

'You've travelled a long way, you must be hungry,' she uttered to Robson hurriedly as if having just remembered her manners, before rushing off.

In the safety of the kitchen, she hovered over the hearth and rekindled the fire, her hands moving mechanically as they laid bits of wood over coals while her mind worked on other matters.

A log smoked and crackled and then ignited and when the pot over the fire began to bubble and Esther was now in control of her emotions, she called out to Robson.

'Why does she want to see me? Has something happened to Thoko?' Esther asked with her lips trembling.

Robson shook his head and then said, 'She didn't say.'

Esther stared at him hard, and when she was satisfied that he was telling her the truth, she turned back to the fire to prepare their lunch.

'How is Clara?' Robson asked suddenly after they'd eaten.

'She is well,' Esther replied, smiling for the first time. 'She has a son, Temba. He lives with me most of the time, but he's with his parents today. You'll meet him tonight.'

'Temba,' Esther said, later that evening, 'This is your mother's cousin, Robson. I'll be accompanying him back to his grandmother's house early tomorrow. After you've taken the cattle out to graze, I want you to tell your mother where I am going. Do you hear me?'

'When will you be back?' Temba asked.

'I'm not sure. It depends on how long it will take me to get there and back.'

'Can I come with you?'

'And who will take care of this place if we are all gone?' Esther asked, looking at him for an answer.

The boy turned his glance down.

49

A neighbourly visit

A day after Esther and Robson left on their trip, a man and a woman arrived at Esther's home on horseback. A dog barked and a boy went running to the gate.

'Is your mother here?' Thoko asked the boy from his saddle.

The boy shook his head at the man with his gaze on the strange pale-skinned woman with green eyes, sitting on a horse beside him.

Thoko and Sonia left their horses at the gate and when they were in the courtyard Thoko said to the boy, 'Will she be back soon?' Again, a shake of the head from the boy.

Thoko stood hesitantly outside the main hut, too afraid to open the door and not find what he was looking for. Then, taking a deep breath, he stepped forward and pushed the door open.

His eyes darted over the narrow bed and rested on a wooden suitcase at the far end of the hut. He compared the suitcase with the image he had buried in his mind, and he couldn't be sure, not with absolute certainty, that that suitcase belonged to his mother.

A slight tremor ran down his spine and he shut his eyes briefly.

Then he closed the door gently and went to inspect the rest of the homestead. He approached a triangular silo and standing on his toes tipped his gaze down to the cobs of maize inside it before turning to examine some pumpkin leaves drying out in the sun on a wire rack.

He picked up a leaf and held it to his nose, breathing in the memories that came swarming back to him with pleasant nostalgia.

Then he went to lean over a rickety fence where a hen sat on a bed of hay. He prodded the warm feathers gently with his fingers and peeped at the eggs under them.

Some moments later he went to join Sonia in the backyard where he found her hunched over a flowering succulent.

'Do you know this plant?' Sonia asked, turning away from it for a moment.

'A type of aloe vera, a healing plant,' Thoko replied, with his brow creased. 'We had a few of those growing in our backyard before my father died.'

Sonia stood back and took a photograph of it.

'It's her,' Thoko whispered with his warm breath on the back of his wife's neck. 'I can feel her presence.'

Sonia turned her head and looked back at him with her body still.

They went and sat under a camphor tree at the edge of the homestead until the sun began to set again.

'Never mind,' Sonia told him when they were back on their saddles and riding home, 'We know how to get to the house now, and we'll come back soon.'

Thoko waited a few more days before he came back on his own, but he found the homestead deserted this time.

50

A reluctant guest

Many miles away, and almost three days after leaving her home, Esther cupped a hand over her mouth when her old home appeared a short distance ahead. Robson steered the animals down her old driveway, erasing the last fifteen years of Esther's life.

A mental image of Bernard rose before her, his gentle eyes smiling and lighting up his face. And beside him were their children, Clara and Thoko, and all of them, untouched by age.

Robson pulled on the reins and popped off his seat with youthful agility. He held his arm out to help Esther out of the cart, but she had a distant look in her eyes and appeared not to have noticed.

He murmured to her softly, his voice awakening her from her daydream. She took the hand stretched out to her and disembarked. Robson turned the cart around, and Esther was left to take the last few painful steps down her old driveway now eaten up with weeds alone.

As she drew closer to the buildings, her glance was met with crumbling huts and ruefully strewn thatch roofs.

An overweight woman scrambled up from under a tree and waddled up to welcome her with a clumsy curtsy before holding out a grubby hand towards her. A look of recognition came to Esther's eyes, and despite the bleak memories that it brought with it, she offered Robson's mother a warm smile.

Robson's mother, who was known as Mai Robbie, called out and a young child went running to one of the huts and came out again carrying a brown and white cowhide.

Mai Robbie took the mat back with her to the tree she'd been sitting under earlier and then, heaving and puffing, spread it on the ground for Esther to sit on.

'Clara doesn't live here anymore. It's been many years since I last saw her. She left, not long after you did,' Mai Robbie said as she shifted about against the trunk of a stunted guava tree Esther remembered planting.

Esther wanted to remind Robson's mother that she hadn't left on her own accord and that she remembered her standing by passively, as her husband dragged her out of her home. But Esther knew that no good would come from dredging up the past. So instead, she clamped her jaw shut and left it to Robson to tell his mother what he knew about Clara.

A child, a girl, not much older than Thoko had been when she'd been forced to leave him, ran up to Mai Robbie and whispered in her ear and Mai Robbie turned to Esther and said, 'Come, I'll take you to Big Granny now, she's ready to see you.'

Esther was led to the hut she once shared with Bernard, and they both entered with their heads bowed respectfully and took their place behind the people already seated cross-legged on the floor there.

'Has she come yet?' a frail voice rasped through the gloomy room and when Esther's eyes had adjusted to the dark, she saw a wasted body lying on a high bed with a threadbare blanket thrown over it.

'Yes,' Mai Robbie replied, crawling to the front. 'She's sitting there behind the others.'

'I want to talk to her alone. Take everyone out,' the patient snapped, but the voice was weak and not as Esther remembered it.

Mai Robbie looked at the speaker long to make sure that she'd heard correctly and then seeing the old woman's jaw tighten, half rose to her feet and ushered everyone out of the hut.

'Come closer,' Nkosazane addressed Esther. 'You can't still be frightened of me after all these years, surely?'

Esther's stomach tightened, she wet her lips with her tongue and remained silent. After a short pause, she edged closer to the bed and waited with her eyes on the old woman.

Bernard's mother lifted her head and strained her eyes towards her son's widow and saw that the many years that had passed had taken little of her former beauty.

There were faint lines under Esther's eyes and around her mouth and her once oval features had become more angular, but overall, time had been kind to her.

Esther on the other hand tried to hide her shock at the withered face turned her way, erasing the image in her memory that she'd held onto for all those years.

The chiselled features that had once given the older woman an aristocratic look in her younger days now protruded almost grotesquely.

'How are you feeling?' Esther murmured for want of something to say.

Eyes that were once black and piercing now stared dull and listless back at her before turning to the wooden beams above.

Outside a child's laughter burst out in the open before an adult hissed and the child's gay chortle broke off prematurely.

'See for yourself,' the invalid replied weakly after the long pause, bringing Esther's mind back to the room.

She looked at the speaker and the aged eyes retreated into their hollows.

'When you look at me, do you not see that I will not be on this earth much longer?' her mother-in-law asked with a tired sigh.

Then the room filled up with a cackle of coughing and wheezing and Mai Robbie, hovering just outside the doorway dashed back in. Kneeling beside the bed and holding up the patient's head, she tilted a mug carefully to the waiting mouth.

'I know now that what I did to you was wrong,' Nkosazane said, pushing the back of her head against the thin mattress when they were alone again.

Esther dropped her eyes to the floor.

'My son was young when he died, and I was angry that he died when he did,' she said, her eyes flashing as they used to in the old days, but only briefly before the fire in them died out gradually. 'I received word about your son,' she continued.

Esther's heart quickened as a sharp tremor of terror passed through her. 'Is he alive?' she asked, her voice trembling. She tried to hold her tears back, but they fell bitterly down her face.

'I should have sent word to you then, but I was angry with you, and I wanted you to suffer just as I was suffering for the loss of my son. That is unforgivable. I know that now.'

'What do you know about my son,' Esther demanded, though she was terrified of the answer.

'Your son is doing well. He is somewhere in South Africa, but I don't know which town. I was told that is where he ended up when he ran away from us.'

'When did you find this out?' Esther asked.

'Ten years ago,' the old woman replied, 'But I haven't heard anything else since then.'

'Ten years,' Esther whispered aggrieved, 'Ten years.'

'And your daughter, she's well too, but you already know that about her. I heard she found you on her own. I wasn't sorry to see her go. She was lazy, you didn't train her well.'

'Why are you telling me this about Thoko now?' Esther asked.

'I'd like to think that I will live forever, but I've known for some time now that my days on this earth are numbered. And guilt is a terrible thing. It's like a worm. It bores into you. Eats at you. That is why I asked you to come. I can't leave this world without asking you for your forgiveness. I was wrong and now I ask if you will soften your heart and let me go to my grave with peace in my heart.'

Her voice trailed off in another bout of coughing, causing Mai Robbie to barrel in once more. Alone again, the old woman held a shrivelled and gnarled hand out to her son's widow, and for a moment Esther looked at it, not quite knowing what to do.

She recalled the many years of mental anguish she had endured under Nkosazane's hand and the bitterness she felt towards her. Then Clara had come to find her, and the animosity she had once harboured left her without her even knowing.

Her gaze now turned to the hand resting limply beside its owner, and taking it in both her hands she said, 'There is nothing to forgive. What happened, happened, just as it was supposed to.'

And a smile spread over the distorted face turned towards her.

51

The Intruders

Sonia parted the curtains and peered out of the window and then she stiffened.

'Thoko,' she said, with a puzzled look on her face, 'Those two shady characters we saw hanging around the brook, I think I may have just seen them again.'

'You can see them now?' Thoko asked, striding up to stand beside her.

'Over there,' Sonia said, pointing.

Thoko looked out through the glazed glass, before going to a drawer and pulling out a torch. He opened the back door and shone it towards the stables. Two figures crouched against the wall broke cover and scurried back to their horses before riding off briskly into the night.

'What do you think they're after?' Sonia asked with a frightened look.

'I'm not sure,' Thoko replied. 'I passed by the brook on my way home today, and I managed to have a chat with one of them. He said that they were just prospectors searching for gold. He showed me his claim. It looked legitimate. I wouldn't worry too much about them. They were probably out riding and didn't realise how close they were to our property,' he reassured her while making a mental note to make it his priority to find out more about the two strangers.

'I was thinking of going there tomorrow,' Thoko said, later that evening, meaning the compound they were both intrigued with. 'I'll hitch up the carriage now that you've grown so fat,' he told her teasingly, placing his hand over her belly.

Sonia, now in the last weeks of her pregnancy smiled at him warmly and waddled to a couch and he jumped up to his feet and hovered around her as she lowered herself down. When some time had passed, she eased her way to their bedroom where a bag sat open on the bed with miniature garments spread out around it.

The neutral-coloured clothes were the first she packed; fluffy white cotton nappies and baby-soft white vests. Then followed the yellow ones; matinee jackets, booties, and hats, colours suitable for both girls and boys. She slipped in a blue jersey set next, just in case Thoko got his way and it was a boy. The last outfit on the bed was pink. She held it close to her face and breathed in its fresh minty smell of lemongrass, because pink was for girls, and she knew that the baby she was carrying was a girl, without knowing how.

She tired easily these days, but the doctor assured them that it was nothing to worry about and was to be expected as her time was near.

An hour ticked on, and Sonia slipped into bed and lay there with her eyes open.

There was a knock on the door and they both thought how strange it was to have visitors at this time of the night.

Thoko left the study and went to the bedroom to check on Sonia saying, 'Stay here and rest, and I'll go and see who it is,' and Sonia smiled back at him gratefully.

She picked up the locket that Thoko had given her as a gift from the bedside table and opened the heart-shaped charm to look at the photograph of just the two of them inside. Then she slipped the chain over her head and held the pendant flat against her own heart with her palm and she smiled at the warm feeling that came over her.

It went quiet suddenly and Thoko had been gone longer than expected.

'The dogs didn't bark, why didn't the dogs bark?' Sonia asked herself, struggling out of bed.

She stood in the doorway and looked down the passage, and from the mirror on the wall adjacent to the front door, she could see Thoko's back and she could hear him talking through the crack in the doorway.

A voice answered from the other side of the door, a quiet murmur, and one that was not familiar to her.

Her heart began to thump loudly as a feeling of dread overcame her. She opened her mouth to call out a warning to Thoko when suddenly there was a sound of wood splintering, as a booted foot smashed its way through the door.

Two figures rushed into the hallway with their rifles trained on her husband. A shot rang out and then another, and then there were raised voices and movement, and she could no longer see her husband in the mirror because he'd fallen over and was lying crumpled on the cement floor.

The men gazed down on their victim for a moment. Then the butt of a rifle came down and blood gushed out of the skull of the fallen body.

Sonia's face went a deathly white and although her body was screaming out its outrage no sound came from her trembling lips. She backed away from the door and limped to the bedroom window, and it swung open on its own accord.

Then with her movements heavy and clumsy, she found herself outside with a frosty breeze on her face.

She crept stealthily along the brick wall until she reached the end of the house. And then with her back against the wall, she drew in her breath, before plunging into the open and dashing across the yard as quickly as her body would let her.

The thick woodland that surrounded their dwelling welcomed her into its sanctuary before it swallowed her up and she vanished out of sight.

Inside the house, a man dropped to one knee and felt his victim's pockets. Finding a small bunch of keys, he rushed off to the study with them. His companion stooped down casually and tugged at a gold chain sticking out of the dead man's waistcoat before going through his pockets. He found Thoko's gold watch and his wallet and he thrust them into his trouser pocket. Then he went to join his partner who was rifling through the treasures in the safe.

The ground beneath Sonia's feet moved rapidly as she tumbled ahead blindly with an arm stretched out in front of her to stop herself from running headfirst into bushes and trees.

'The forest is not your enemy,' Thoko's voice murmured gently in her ear, 'The trees are your friends. They lead you into the forest and they lead you out again. You just need to know how,' and she didn't ask how because he had already told her the secret.

She panted painfully and her fingers clutched the tree closest to her.

'Trees are no different from people, the older they are, the more they have to offer,' Thoko whispered, a mischievous grin playing on his face as he rubbed his palm gently over the bark of a red mahogany tree.

'Come,' he said, taking her hand and drawing circles on the tree trunk with it, 'Feel how much rougher this side of the bark is compared to the other sides.' He stepped towards a neighbouring tree still holding her hand and this time it was her hand that guided his, and when she turned her face up to him it was filled with astonishment at her discovery.

She pressed the side of her face lightly against the rough side of the trunk she was clinging to.

'Can you feel the breeze on your face?' Thoko asked, standing so close to her that their bodies almost melted into each other.

She acknowledged with a nod and he folded his arm around her and she nestled back into the familiar curves of his body. His free arm came up and he showed her the direction of the wind and then he touched the rough patch on the tree where the wind had left its mark.

'That's your compass,' he said, planting a kiss on her forehead. 'Follow the pattern left on the trees by the wind and it will lead you out of the forest.'

Sonia's head was throbbing, and her arms and legs were battered and bruised. She leaned her face against the rough patch of bark, her tears soaking her cheeks.

'You can't stop now,' Thoko urged her, 'For the baby's sake, and ours!'

Sonia mumbled under her breath about not being as strong as he made her out to be and he smiled at her encouragingly, confident that she wouldn't disappoint him.

'One step at a time,' he coaxed. 'There is no rush, take your time.'

Gradually, the dense forest began to thin out and although the world around her was still eclipsed in darkness, it was now a shade lighter than before.

Sonia emerged from the woods and found herself in an open grassy plain. She waded through the shoulder-high grass, fearful of what might be hidden in the undergrowth. The ground beneath her feet grew firmer and the grass dwindled to knee-high.

She perked her ears at any sound that broke the night protocol of silence and echoed in the deathly quiet air.

She stumbled onto the path quite unexpectedly and her heart began to beat rapidly at some sign of humanity. She pushed herself along it, one step at a time, until finally, it led her, hunched over herself, to open ground.

She lifted her head wearily and squinted ahead, and there, just a short distance away, a barrier of white thorn bushes defied the night and showed themselves.

She sank to her knees and dragged herself towards them until her body finally gave in. Her eyes followed the sound of barking, and she saw hidden behind the thorn branches a shadowy outline of what was unmistakably a dwelling of some sort.

52

Unexpected company

The sound of barking drifted in and out of Esther's sleep effortlessly, reality merging with fantasy so that she could hardly tell one from the other. The persistent barking rattled open the blinds to consciousness, and she rubbed the sleep from her eyes and blinked in the darkness.

She stood behind the partially open door and peeped out at Jacob charging back and forth as he tried to find a way past the barrier of thorn bushes so that he could launch himself at the intruder.

'Jacob!' Esther hissed, 'what's all this noise you're making at this time of the night? Do you have no respect for those of us who must wake up early for the fields?'

The gatekeeper paused in his barking and turned his head to his mistress when he heard his name being spoken. But then, eager to impress the urgency of the situation on her, he turned back to the encroacher and drowned out whatever else Esther intended to say to him.

'You are going to be the death of me, bringing me out in the cold!' Esther muttered under her breath all the same.

She ventured out timidly, leaving the door half open, in case of a quick retreat, and went to stand beside Jacob where he now sat, panting with exhaustion. He welcomed her with a volley of barks.

Her eyes were not as good as they used to be, but gradually she made out a small mound lying on the ground. And as if sensing her presence, the mound stirred, and Esther clapped a hand to her mouth.

Summoning the little strength she had left in her, Sonia called out for help, inviting Jacob to commence his barking.

'Down, Jacob!' Esther snapped, recovering from her shock and rushing to drag two thorn bushes aside.

The dog stopped its wild scamper, and after a protesting whimper, grew silent.

'My husband, please!' Sonia sobbed, but Esther's arm was already around her waist and helping her to her feet.

They inched their way across the open ground and then through the gate. Sonia's legs suddenly gave way, forcing Esther to drag her down the driveway.

'Not far to go now, stay with me,' Thoko whispered to his wife as she fought to keep her eyes open.

They pushed their way through the doorway and then, with a heavy sigh, Sonia collapsed on the bed Esther had only just a few moments ago crept out of.

'My husband,' Sonia implored weakly, her icy cold fingers reaching out to Esther.

'Shoosh, shoosh,' Esther cooed in reply, now aware of the strange woman's condition, before bending down to light a lantern.

With the room now bathed in light, Esther quickly began unfastening the buttons of the mud-splattered cream skirt and then yanked out the printed blouse tucked neatly inside it. Then she smoothed out the wide pleats in the skirt and revealed the small bulge under it.

The woman moaned through blue lips and Esther noticed how pale the woman's face had become. She began to rub her arms vigorously, before doing the same to the bruised feet. The woman sighed softly and licked her lips, and the colour came back slowly to her face.

Then Esther rushed off to a smaller hut and holding the lantern above her called out, 'Temba! Temba!' as she shook the boy urgently with her free hand. Temba sat up in his bed abruptly and looked around the room wildly.

'It's Gogo, Temba,' Esther said, speaking in a rushed tone. 'Are you awake, child?'

He turned his eyes to his grandmother and smiled sheepishly.

'Listen to me! I want you to run as fast as you can to Clara. Tell her she must come immediately. Tell her it's very important. Do you hear me?'

The boy threw off his blanket and staggered to the door. She asked him to repeat her instruction, which he did in a dull tone muffled with sleep.

'Go now!' she said satisfied.

She watched him for a moment as he took off in a trot into the dark night, before rushing off to the kitchen. She rekindled the fire under the still-warm kettle. And then leaving it to boil, filled a mug with water and took it back with her to the bedroom.

She poured some water out of the mug into her palm, and then, lifting her patient's head a little with the other, held her cupped hand against the woman's mouth.

Droplets of water trickled out of her hand slowly and wet the woman's lips before slipping into her mouth. After a third handful of water, the woman's eyes fluttered languidly, and her lips parted slightly.

Then Esther pulled a stool from under her bed, placed it in line with the head of the bed, and leaning back against the wall, waited.

An hour passed and then came the sound of running feet. Esther stood up abruptly and went to the door.

'You've come at last!' she said, drawing back the door and holding it open for her daughter to enter. 'I was starting to think that Temba had lost his way.'

'What is it? What's the matter?' Clara asked frantically, giving her mother a worried look.

'Is Temba with you?' Esther asked.

'I told him to stay at the farm, and I ran the whole way in the dark,' Clara murmured, eyeing her mother curiously.

'Never mind that,' Esther said. 'Come quickly, we're running out of time.'

Clara hurried behind her mother, and when her eyes fell on the figure lying on her mother's small bed, she stopped suddenly, a small gasp escaping her lips.

'Quick! Put your arm around her back and try to hold her up,' Esther instructed, as she hitched the skirt up over the woman's stomach.

Its owner groaned feebly but remained quite still.

Clara, now quite recovered from her initial shock, took up her position as instructed, and the woman grabbed onto her arm instinctively, before letting out a blood-chilling scream.

53

A baby is born

A shadow stood in the doorway and peered into the room, where the light from a lantern sitting on a table, illuminated the face of a woman lying peacefully in a narrow bed.

'How is she?' the man hovering in the doorway asked in a harsh tone.

Esther and Clara, who hadn't heard him approach, looked up abruptly. The man took a step forward and Esther replied, 'The child is okay,' before turning down to a dish of water on the floor and dipping a cloth in it.

Esther paused for a moment and then dabbing the blood-soaked blouse with the cloth in her hand said, 'She wanted to hold her baby, but she didn't have the strength, so I lay the child on her chest, and I put her hands over its tiny body, and she smiled. A happy smile. That's why her blouse is so messed up.'

'Is she okay?' the man repeated, as if not hearing her.

Esther shook her head and then she flinched as the man's fist struck the twisted beam supporting the door.

Clara held up a small bundle wrapped in a colourful crocheted blanket to the man and he gave it a cursory glance before turning away from it. Just then another rider on horseback came dashing down the driveway and the man went to meet him.

The women could not make out what they were saying but the two men appeared angry with each other. Then, as if reaching some agreement, they marched back into the room together.

They shrugged their way past the two shocked women and paused in front of the bed as if trying to decide what to do next. Moving quickly, they lifted the still-warm body from the bed and took it to where their horses stood. A few moments later, the air exploded with the thunder of hooves.

When the baby had finished suckling the watered-down milk from Esther's palm and was now lying contentedly on a bed that was much too big for it, Clara turned to her mother and asked, 'How could they just take the mother and not the baby?'

Esther guessed the answer but brushed it away with a small shake of her head.

Then, bending over the baby, Esther let her finger trail around its face before hovering over its stubby but cute nose.

She held each of its perfectly formed hands and feet in hers and the baby squinched up its face and kicked its tiny legs and the room echoed with cheery laughter.

'I think she'll grow up to be very beautiful,' Clara said thoughtfully.

'Yes she will,' her mother replied with a smile playing on her face.

'Let's call her Peggy,' Clara said dropping a kiss on the baby's face.

54

A piece of jewellery

A few weeks later, Esther and Clara returned from the field with their hoes as they often did and went to rest under the shade of a mulberry tree.

'Temba, what's that in your hand?' Clara called out, looking curiously at her son who sat on a log where he was trying to prise open something in his hands.

Temba held up a piece of jewellery and Clara yelled out, 'Bring it here!'

'What is it?' Esther asked curiously.

'A necklace,' Clara replied, grabbing the chain from Temba and scrutinising it. Then, looking up at him she asked, 'Where did you get it from?'

Temba turned back and pointed towards the gate. Clara followed her son up the driveway. Then Temba stuck his finger at one of the gate posts.

'You found it here?' Clara asked. 'Are you sure?' The boy nodded.

Clara bent down to inspect the ground and found that the earth there had indeed been disturbed. And when Clara returned to her seat she exchanged looks with her mother.

'I saw the chain around the woman's neck,' Clara said to her mother a short while later. 'It must've fallen off her when they were carrying her out. See here,' Clara said, showing Esther the broken link.

'It has a picture inside,' Temba offered, and the women looked at him with puzzled expressions.

He took the locket from Clara and opened it, and Clara stared at the photograph dumbfounded before showing it to her mother. Esther gazed at the locket with little interest at first and then, noticing the white diamond patch of hair above the man's forehead, took it from Clara. She held the locket close to her and peered at the man smiling back at her, before cupping her mouth with her hand.

'It's a wedding photograph. She's wearing a white lace dress, and the man has a flower in his top pocket. It's Thoko, isn't it?' Clara whispered.

Esther stared at her daughter as if in a daze.

'They came here,' Temba told Clara and Esther.

'Who came here?' they asked in alarm.

'The man and the woman in the picture. They came together,' Temba replied. 'That time when Robson came. A day after you left with him.'

'Why didn't you tell me, Temba?' Esther asked. 'Did they say anything to you?'

'What did they want?' Clara demanded.

Temba shrugged his shoulders at the barrage of questions.

'The woman had green eyes, and she had a camera. She took pictures of those flowers,' he said, pointing at the aloes in the backyard.

'What about the man, was his name Thoko?' Clara asked with her voice raised.

Temba shrugged his shoulders again and said, 'He walked around the yard. And he opened all the doors and looked inside, then he went to the chicken run.'

'Did he say what he was looking for?' Esther asked, annoyed with

Temba for not having told her sooner.

Temba stared at his grandmother blankly. Then Esther remembered the woman who had given birth and died in her bedroom that night and she wondered who she had been running away from. And the awfulness of what that could mean made her block her mind to it all.

From one of the huts, a baby began to fuss. Clara stood up and returned cuddling Peggy in her arms.

V

Part 5 – Peggy and Kenny

55

The social welfare wardens

It was not long after Peggy had just reached her ninth year, that the countryside became abuzz with disturbing news.

'You have to remember to always stay alert!' Esther told Peggy urgently.

Esther had a plan. She took Peggy's hand and together, they followed a path that cut through the veld.

'Make sure that when the time comes, to run fast. And no matter what, don't look back, do you hear me?' Esther said stopping to look at the face turned up to her.

Peggy nodded her head, and they resumed their walk. And when the path faded out, there were landmarks to plot the way.

'You see that tree?' Esther said, pointing to a willow tree with clusters of creamy-white flowers weighing down its branches. 'That's where I want you to run,' and Peggy nodded her head.

When they reached the tree, they stopped in front of it and Esther lifted her right arm and told Peggy to do the same, and asked, 'Which arm is up?' and Peggy replied, 'The one I eat with.'

'Now follow the direction of your hand with your eye, what do you see?' Esther asked.

'Anthills,' Peggy replied.

Esther nodded and walked on and Peggy followed closely behind her. They passed the tall earthy chimneys with the white ants racing up and down them. Then, without losing their pace, they sped up a grassy slope that led them to an elevated platform with a panoramic view of the valley below. Esther drew the child to her and pointed to the ground below, where a silvery white stream cut the green meadow in two. Then she pointed at their homestead where dots of cattle and other livestock stood grazing.

'You see the road leading to our house from here?' Esther said, moving her finger across to a jagged track. 'That's the road they'll use. Make sure you don't come back down until you see the car driving back up that road. Do you understand?'

Peggy nodded with her eyes on Esther.

'What will they do to me if they catch me?' Peggy asked her grandmother when they were back home.

'Do you want them to catch you and take you away from here?' Esther returned.

Peggy shook her head vehemently, to show that she was opposed to the idea.

'And Chipo?' Peggy asked, referring to her playmate who was the same age as her and who lived at a compound close to theirs. 'Will they take her too?'

'No, they won't take Chipo,' Esther replied.

'Why not?' Peggy asked, and both Peggy and Chipo turned their bewildered faces at Esther.

'They just won't,' Esther told them stubbornly.

When Chipo had gone home and they were alone and Esther had had time to think of what to say, she sat Peggy down and told her why Chipo was safe, and she was not.

'What about Aunty Clara?' the child wanted to know. 'Why was she allowed to stay when she's the same colour as me?'

'Times were different then,' Esther told her simply. 'Now they have new ideas and different rules.'

Peggy's eyes filled with tears at this new knowledge of herself, and Esther grabbed her harshly and said, 'You are my granddaughter. I gave birth to your father. The colour of your skin does not change that. It is just a law made by people who think they know what is best for us without consulting us. It has no place in my home, and I will not let them take you away from me.'

But Peggy was curious about the school she'd be taken to if she was caught, and the other children that looked the way she did.

'If I go,' she said to her grandmother, 'Will you come with me?'

'And leave my home?' Esther retorted, with an incredulous look on her face. 'And Clara and Temba. You want to leave all this for a school and people you don't know?'

Peggy shook her head, and when Esther kept her eyes on her, she mumbled, 'No, Mama. I want to stay here with you.'

Esther was high up in the hills when she saw the car. There was no sound, just an intermittent glint of metal sparked by the sun's rays, that made her turn her head away from the mushrooms she was picking. She shaded her eyes from the sun with one hand and stared in its direction.

A lot had changed since she'd first arrived. There were no fences in those days, and now they were everywhere. And even today, she had to ease her way through several of them just to get to where she was. And the road was only a dirt track then. But it had grown broader, and it was like a river now, with tributaries rushing off in every direction.

The vehicle drew closer, ploughing its way through the veld, a cloud of dust chasing after it. It bumped through the ridges caused by the recent rains before swerving to dodge an aardvark hole and then tilting to one side as it manoeuvred around an anthill. A short while later it disappeared behind some bushes.

Esther spotted a plant she had been searching for and dismissed the car from her mind. She scraped the ground around the plant with her hoe before pulling it out whole with its roots. Back home, she intended to crush the roots and spread the poultice over an almost-healed boil on Peggy's arm, so that it wouldn't leave an ugly scar. She began to descend the hill with a satisfied smile on her face when something caught her attention.

She uttered a cry of surprise when she saw the vehicle she'd seen earlier now parked in her courtyard with a group of people crowded around it. The bundle of wood fell off her head and landed with a thud at her feet and the basket in her hand clattered carelessly to the ground and all she was aware of was her granddaughter standing in the centre of the group with nowhere to run.

She began to run wildly while screaming at the top of her voice at the darkness reaching out to swallow her up. But no one could hear her and even if they turned her way, all they would see would be grass and trees.

Her legs were weak, and her heart was beating much too fast. She had to stop and rest, even if for a little while.

The chief was there with them, although the elder's presence alone would have sufficed. But it pleased him to be seen in the presence of white people and to ride in a motor car.

Clara pleaded with the elder to wait, 'just a bit longer,' with her eyes on the social welfare officers who she knew to be the ones in charge.

'She could be gone a few minutes or the whole day. Time means nothing to these people,' the male officer said, heedless of the chief and the elder who understood him well, even though the chief pretended otherwise.

Then he rested his hands on his hips and stared at the hill Esther was now descending, before turning his glance back to his companions.

A gust of wind whipped up the woman's grey hair and pulled at it teasingly. She brushed it down with the back of her hand before tucking it back behind her ear. Then she pulled down the hem of her grey dress as she conversed with the elder who repeated it to the chief. The chief nodded back at her.

Esther fell into her daughter's arms as she raced through the gate, and the chief turned a stern look at her. The elder stepped up and cautioned her quietly to compose herself. Clara drew her mother away and they stood a little apart from the rest.

The woman consulted the book in her hand. It contained everything they knew about Peggy. It said that she was born in the year of the first rains after the drought that lasted two years and this had been translated to them to mean around September in 1939. It said that Peggy was probably Clara's daughter, even though no one could confirm that Clara had been pregnant, then. The father's name was missing as was often the case in matters like these. The record listed Peggy as being nine years old.

The woman now scribbled in the margin that the child was 'tall for her age.' She added, 'Fine features, slim built, hazel eyes, hair brown with soft curls.' Then, turning away from her writing and looking at Peggy's bandaged arm, she addressed Peggy in a curious tone and an unfamiliar language, asking, 'What happened to your arm?'

Peggy stared back at her blankly and the elder stepped in to translate. The woman wrote in her book, 'Appears ignorant, unable to communicate in English.'

Then turning to Clara, she asked, 'What is your husband's name?' and Clara murmured, 'Charie.'

The woman wrote Charles beside Peggy's name, and that day Peggy became Peggy Charles.

The group prepared to leave. The chief rushed to the back passenger door and opened it eagerly before bounding in and leaning back against his seat. Then with a huge smile on his face, he turned to look out through the window.

Peggy gave the elder a frightened look as he guided her to the other side of the car. She boarded the car awkwardly and shifted uncertainly to the centre seat when he slipped in after her.

The car shuddered and Peggy shut her eyes tight. Esther leapt toward it and Clara fought to hold her back. Then the monster rumbled into motion and Peggy pushed her hands down hard against its soft leather upholstery.

They bounced over the bumpy ground and Peggy swayed from side to side as they went around the mulberry tree. Then they drove through the gate, the blast of the car engine drowning out her grandmother's cries of sorrow.

The dust churned behind the car and its occupants chuckled with amusement as those sitting behind learnt how to operate the window mechanisms. Then the windows went up and shut out the dust, and with it, the fading sound of weeping outside.

The car sped off, leaving behind a lone figure writhing with despair on the ground. And huddled over it, were two more figures, doing what they could, to offer comfort to each other.

56

Bewildering revelations

The children drifted into groups, finding companionship with those who spoke the same dialect as their own before they were pulled together again, into one group.

'You are here because you are coloured,' the headmaster told them from his podium in the school hall.

The matrons mingled with the children and translated the unfamiliar words to them. Enlightened the children turned their startled eyes up to the man on the platform, unsure what that word, 'coloured,' meant and wondered why it made the headmaster's lips twist in a sneer when he said it.

'I will have nothing but English inside these walls,' he continued before glaring at them fiercely.

Inside the dormitory, there were rows of small beds with white sheets and quiet sobs when the lights went out.

'Count yourself lucky,' the matrons told them. 'You have clean clothes and more food than you can wish for.'

There was a hole in Peggy's chest now, that wasn't there before and as each day passed, that hole grew larger.

'Forget about your lives before you came here. This is your new life now. The people around you are your family now,' the headmaster told the children as their roots were slowly severed from under them.

Alone with her loneliness, Peggy struggled to remember the faces of her family that were slowly fading from her mind and to contain the sorrow that filled the hole that now sat where her heart used to be.

'Please, ma'am, can I go home now,' Peggy, who had been a good student and had done everything they'd asked her to do, pleaded with her innocent eyes turned up to the matron.

The matron looked at the child with horror, surprised at how much more work was needed to take the bush out of her.

Then, seeing the funny side of it all, she opened her mouth up wide, and laughter bellowed out of it.

57

The wooden suitcase

Esther made herself comfortable outside her hut and then called out to Chipo.

'Leave the child with me and go and fetch my suitcase,' she said when Chipo approached carrying an infant on her back.

Chipo knelt on the mat and loosened the strap over her shoulder and Esther lifted the boy off Chipo's back and began playing with him on her lap. Chipo returned a few moments later with a wooden box and Esther handed the child back to his mother.

'This used to be my mother's suitcase,' Esther said to Chipo as she opened the lid of the box.

She pulled out a thread of glass beads strung on a piece of bark string and holding them up said, 'My father gave these to my mother when she was younger than you are,' before laying them flat on the mat.

Picking up a set of copper bracelets and brass anklets and talking to Clara this time as she came up to join them, Esther said, 'She used to like to wear lots of jewellery, around her neck, on her wrists, and over her feet.'

She held up a blanket made from the fibres of a baobab tree, and

213

said, 'My grandfather made this, especially for me.'

There were other items in the suitcase, like the small red post office book, that held painful memories for Esther but which in the end became her saviour. And then there were those she had no wish to share with anyone. The tobacco pouch that once belonged to Bernard and the pipe he liked to smoke. Things he had kept close to him, and which now kept him close to her.

The child chuckled excitedly and stretched his chubby arms out in front of him. Temba swooped down and laughing gaily scooped his son up in his arms. He nuzzled the tiny body with his nose, and the child chortled happily much to the adult's amusement.

'I see you have your suitcase out. Are you going on a journey?' Chipo's mother, who had come to visit her daughter on a whim as she often did, asked as she reached out to shake Esther's hand.

'She likes to air her suitcase now and then,' Clara explained as Esther picked up the locket and began to play with it in her hand.

'That's a nice necklace,' commented Mai Chipo, who had managed to squeeze her generous bottom next to Esther.

'It's an old one,' Clara said, taking the locket from Esther. 'It belonged to Peggy's parents.'

'I know that necklace,' Mai Chipo asserted as her mind travelled back in time. 'I worked for a young couple once, and the woman wore a chain just like that around her neck, always.'

'You must be mistaken,' Clara explained and opened the locket. 'You see this woman in the picture, that's Peggy's mother. She gave birth to Peggy in my mother's bed.'

Mai Chipo stared at the pale-skinned woman with the straw-coloured hair and green eyes and then turned to the man with the patch of white above his forehead, and then she clapped her hands and sat for a moment with a perplexed look on her face. Turning back to Clara she asked, 'And you say these are Peggy's parents?'

'That's my son,' Esther told her proudly. 'My grandfather had that same white patch of hair, and he passed it on to my son.'

'I know those two people,' Mai Chipo exclaimed. 'I used to work for them and my husband, dead all these years, used to take care of their horses.'

'Are you sure about that?' Esther asked, her heart thumping in her chest.

'I am sure,' Mai Chipo replied and then added confidently, 'It was terrible what happened to them.'

Clara and Esther looked at her strangely.

'You mean you don't know?' Mai Chipo asked with a puzzled look on her face. 'It was a tragedy. Everyone talked about it for a long time.'

Clara and Esther shook their heads with confusion.

'I used to arrive for work early every morning to sweep the yard, and that day when I arrived the house was completely burned down. It was terrible. There were police and people everywhere. They brought out a burnt-out kerosene stove that they said caused the fire. The madam always cooked for her husband, but when she became heavily pregnant, I took over the cooking and I'd never seen that stove before. I even told the constable, and he said maybe it was a new one that they had just bought.'

'Did they both die in the fire?' Clara asked dubiously.

Mai Chipo nodded. 'Two bodies were recovered. I saw them with my own two eyes. A man and a woman.'

'The woman died giving birth to Peggy. Then two white men came to collect her body,' Clara insisted.

Mai Chipo mused, and then said, 'She didn't have any family in the country. She told me that herself. But now that you mention it, I remember the men you're talking about, prospectors from around there. They were the men who saw the house burning and went to report it to the authorities.'

'Thoko is dead,' Esther said, gasping for air. 'They killed him. That's who she was running away from.'

'They must've thrown her body in the burning house to cover themselves,' Clara concluded, and the others murmured their agreement.

'I'm sorry,' Chipo's mother said quietly. 'I had no idea that was your son. The madam said that the necklace had their names written on it, and she showed me the writing.'

Clara turned the locket to its side and looked closer at the two small leaves lying on either side of it. And there etched inside of each were Sonia and Thoko's names written in minute italics.

She leaned over to her mother and, running a finger over the letters, read the names out to her.

Esther wiped the tears staining her cheeks and smiled at the writing. Mai Chipo, happy to be proved right, chuckled lightly.

'I can show you where their home used to be,' Chipo's mother offered, 'But it is a long way from here and we'd have to leave early in the morning.'

'Don't worry, Mama, I'll get the cart ready, and at least Gogo can see where her son is buried,' Temba told his mother.

<h1 style="text-align:center">58</h1>

The blush of flamingos

Sue's skin was the colour of snow-capped mountains, and her lips were the warm pink blush of flamingos. Her eyes were the burst of spring leaves, and she looked nothing like Kenny or Peggy.

'Are you sure she's yours, Cuz?' Felix asked, staring at Kenny's almond-coloured face with a twinkle in his eye.

Kenny's hair was springy and if you held some of it with the tips of your fingers and stretched it out to its full length, as Peggy liked to do, it was much longer than it appeared to be. Kenny went to the crib where Sue was lying, and he bent down to pick her up.

'Don't wake her Kenny,' Peggy called out from the kitchen. 'You know how cranky she gets if you mess up her sleep.'

He picked her up all the same and held her under Felix's gaze. Then he peeled back the chubby folds around her neck to reveal a distinctive brown mole sitting in a sea of white.

'See that?' he said to Felix. Turning to pull down his collar with his free hand, he showed him a similar birthmark on his own neck. 'That's my proof,' he said.

'That's mischievous talk!' Sylvia yelled out at her husband from the back veranda. 'We're coloured with all kinds of blood running through our veins. Throwbacks happen. Look at Morris over there,' she said, and everyone's glance turned to the fair-skinned man sipping his whisky. 'Both parents black as night and look how he came out!'

They all burst out laughing and Sue woke up with a fright and began to cry.

'I told you to leave her to sleep,' Peggy complained, stepping out of the kitchen to take the child from him.

Kenny bought a pram for Sue from Mr Kashish on tick.

'Watch out he doesn't make you pay for it for the rest of your lives,' Felix warned.

The pram had big wheels, and its carriage almost reached the top of Peggy's chest.

'Something to show her off in,' Kenny told Peggy with a grin when they were on their own.

They took the pram for a stroll in town and pushed it over the dirt under the watchful eye of the man guarding the street pavements with his baton. They stopped occasionally to gaze through the glazed windows at the merchandise in the store from a distance.

'Choose whichever one you want,' Kenny told Peggy in front of a hatch, behind one of the stores.

And the man inside the shop stood aside, to allow Peggy to peer at the reams of colourful fabrics stacked on the shelves. She pointed to one of the shelves and after a few stabs in the dark, the man picked out the roll she wanted and brought it up close for her to inspect.

'What do you think?' she asked Kenny.

The material was a bright yellow colour, perfect for summer, and Kenny said he liked it, but only if she did too. The man on the other side of the hatch waited impatiently because a queue was forming slowly behind Kenny and Peggy and the pram was taking up more room than it should.

Kenny nodded at the storekeeper, who dropped the ream of fabric flat on a table put there for the purpose. Then he pulled and pushed at the roll of fabric until it lay stretched out alongside a metal measuring tape attached to the table. He picked up a large silver pair of scissors with black handles and asked, 'Two yards?' with the scissors poised.

Kenny and Peggy both yelled out, 'Two yards!'

Kenny had another shop to visit, but Sue was starting to fret. 'Go ahead,' Peggy told him as she turned the pram and pushed it to a shady patch where a few cars were parked haphazardly among the trees. Peggy took Sue out of the pram and finding a flat stone, sat down and held Sue to her breast.

'What do you think you're doing?' a woman snapped as she came dashing through the car park to glare at the baby suckling on Peggy's breast.

'She's hungry, madam,' Peggy told her, not understanding at first.

'Then take her to her mother!' another retorted, standing over her threateningly.

'I'm her mother, she's my daughter, madam,' Peggy told the women quietly.

'That's ridiculous!' one stormed, 'I'm going to call the police now!' the other added before they both rushed off on the errand.

'What are you doing, hiding here?' Kenny asked irritably when he found her by chance hidden among the trees.

Peggy shook her head, too rattled by the incident to say any more about it.

Angie came a year later, and to Peggy's relief, she looked every bit the child she and Kenny should bear. She had Kenny's tight curls and Peggy's colouring, and the sisters, although so different, were also so much alike. The family was on one of their town visits. Kenny was pushing Sue's pram, but Angie, who had taken possession of it, was asleep inside. Peggy held Sue's hand, and Sue, with her blond curls bobbing up and down and her turquoise eyes greedily taking in her surroundings, asked many questions. Now and then, she turned her face up to one parent or the other when the answer was, in her opinion, too slow in coming.

A woman dressed in a pink jacket and a pink skirt, and wearing a pink hat so that everything on her looked pink except for her shoes which were black, stopped suddenly. She waved her hand at the family, and they stopped walking and looked her way. She came down the wooden steps gingerly, the wood sighing with each step she took.

'My, how she's grown,' the woman said, appraising Sue before turning to the pram and peering inside.

Angie, who had been lying on her back with the hood of her sister's old pram up now, suddenly sat up at the sound of the foreign voice, giving the woman a clear view of what she'd been looking for.

'Well,' the woman said, screwing up her mouth with distaste and turning her head away quickly, 'They certainly don't look alike.'

The woman shot Peggy an accusing glance before turning back to the wooden steps. A man with a shiny brown leather belt around his waist and carrying a baton ran up to assist her. He held his arm out to her, his black face beaming. She said something to him, and they both turned to stare down at the family from the pavement.

'You want to walk now? Kenny asked, peeping into the pram, and Angie nodded her head.

He hauled her out of the pram and rested her on his shoulders. Then turning to look up at the pair staring down at them said, 'Wave to the lovely people up there, girls,' and the children held up their hands gaily.

The woman turned away abruptly and the security guard, after chasing behind her briefly, went back to guarding his walkway.

59

A business venture

Kenny's workshop was in the backyard of Mr Kashish's shop. It was a small, fenced patch of land squeezed between his landlord's business and living quarters.

'I've always told you that I will strike it rich and get you out of here,' Kenny told Peggy in their cramped rented cottage. 'This is it. This is my chance now. I've already spoken to Kashish and he's happy to give me a loan to buy the materials I need.'

'Another loan, Kenny, on top of the loan for Sue's pram, that we are still paying off, and the arrears on the rent for the workshop,' Peggy moaned.

'But we'll get it all back and more. As soon as we deliver the garden chairs, we'll get paid!'

'Why can't Caleb pay for the materials? If you're providing the labour, then he should at least buy the steel to make them. It's only fair he does that.'

'It doesn't work like that, Peggy, and anyway, I've already given him my word, and I can't go back on it.'

'You're sure about this Caleb bloke?' Felix asked, picking up a blow torch off Kenny's worktable and examining it.

There were tanned pieces of leather drying on the wire fence behind where Kenny sat on a low stool stripping a sisal palm leaf. Beside him were the pulpy strings he had already extracted and which he was now spinning into cords for the seat of a wooden bench he was making.

'He seems genuine,' Kenny replied, with his eyes on his hands. 'He's done all the marketing, the hard part, he tells me, and all I need to do is keep my side of the bargain and have the chairs ready.'

Peggy waited until they were alone, and the door to their bedroom was shut before she confronted Kenny, but it may as well have been open.

'What do you mean he's taken the money and split?' Peggy asked, her voice choked with tears. 'How are we going to pay for rent and food and all those loans you have with Kashish?'

Sue and Angie sat up in the narrow bed they shared and pressed their hands against their ears. They waited for the outside door to slam shut, and when it did the house grew quiet.

After a short pause, the silence was interspersed with the sound of muffled sobbing.

When Kenny returned home a few days later, looking sheepish and out of place, and Sue asked him where he'd been, he replied, 'Uncle Felix's and Aunty Sylvia's house,' before scooping her up in his arms and holding her close.

Angie didn't want to be left out, so she ran up to him, and he put Sue down and now it was her turn to be pampered.

'Why can't we come too, when you go and stay there?' Sue asked, with her head turned up to her father and Peggy stared hard at Kenny daring him to answer.

'Well, I'm back now, and it was only for a few nights,' he said, talking to Sue but looking at Peggy, before ruffling Sue's hair with his hand.

'That's Uncle Felix and Aunty Sylvia now,' Kenny said at the sound of a car stopping in the sanitary lane sometime later.

'You sure Peggy doesn't mind?' Sylvia asked Kenny through her open window when he took Sue and Angie to the waiting car.

'You know Peggy, she's easy,' Kenny replied with a smile as he opened the back door for the girls to jump into Felix's car, before shutting it again.

Felix drove them to the tavern and went to park at a discreet spot behind the bottle store attached to it.

Sylvia took Sue's hand, and when she hesitated beside the car, Felix said, 'Go on, we'll be fine here on our own,' before turning back to Angie sitting quietly in the back seat.

Sylvia and Sue looked like mother and daughter as they entered the whites-only tavern. They emerged not long after, accompanied by a man with orange hair carrying a clipboard, and stood outside the doors of the tavern.

Sylvia was in conversation with the man and Felix, sitting low in his seat, smiled as he listened to Sylvia as she spoke in her posh voice.

The quiet hum was shattered by the sound of rattling, and the three figures standing together, turned to watch as a man straining under the weight of bottled cartons approached pulling a trolley behind him.

The orange-haired man gave the trolley a perfunctory glance, before placing a tick on his clipboard. He clicked his fingers at the man with the blue overall and said, 'Okay, Meshack, take it to the madam's car,' before turning his attention back to Sylvia.

When the trolley reached the parked car Felix, dressed in old overalls, sprang out of his seat and rushed to open the back. The two men chatted gaily as they loaded the boxes of brandy and whisky into the boot of the car.

And when they were done, the orange-haired man bent down to say something to Sue before all three chuckled merrily. The rattling noise commenced as the trolley made its way back to the tavern.

Felix swung the passenger door open for Sylvia and gave her an elaborate bow as she stepped back in the car. Then he rushed to the back door Sue was attempting to open and cried out, 'No, no, my lady, you too need to be treated like royalty,' before swinging the door open and bowing to her.

'All good?' Kenny asked Felix when he brought the girls back home.

'All good!' Felix replied and patted the boot of his car.

When Sue and Angie rushed indoors to tell Peggy about their ride out, Peggy shook her head at Kenny.

60

A cricket match

Peggy popped into the kitchen where Sylvia was preparing snacks before going to join the women slouched on metal garden chairs and nursing their beverages on the back veranda.

Kenny stopped to listen to a jazz record spinning on a turntable and Felix said, 'Nina Simone,' from the dining room table where he was playing cards with the men seated there.

'What time is the game?' Kenny asked, after going round the table and shaking hands with the men.

'Four o'clock,' someone answered.

'Three forty-five now,' Felix offered, looking at his watch. 'We still have time yet.'

'I'll have a gin and tonic,' Kenny said to Tinashe, a dark-skinned girl and Sylvia's half-sister. He took out some notes from his pocket and nodding towards Peggy said, 'And ask the madam sitting outside what she wants.'

Tinashe put the notes in her apron pocket and went out to the veranda to take down Peggy's order.

'Attitudes need to change,' a balding man stated, resuming the conversation that had paused at the table on Kenny's arrival. Then he held his glass of whisky up to the light and studied it carefully before taking a small sip.

'The colour bar is the problem, Morris. You cannot expect the nation to pull together when the policies in place are there only for a handful of the population. What about the rest of us, do they not think that we too want to progress and be given the chance to hold our heads up with pride?' Alan asked, stroking down his long sideburns.

"We have everything working well for us now, a good economy. We just need social reforms, and the sky's the limit," Kenny said, slipping into a chair.

'That will never happen. Can any of you see that happening, white, black, and brown pulling together like one? These honkies have had it too good for too long, and I tell you what, they won't budge,' Felix warned.

'Why can't things just stay as they are?' Morris asked. 'Leave the people who know how to govern, govern. You're inviting trouble by allowing the hoety to take over. It will be a disaster!'

'Easy for you to say, bra, you can skip between the two camps as you choose, honkie today goffal tomorrow,' Tim said with a sour twist of his mouth.

'It's because of people like Sylvia and I who are allowed to go out and buy whisky that you get to taste it, and look how you've grown to like it,' Morris said with a laugh to diffuse the tension. The others joined in merrily.

'I know first-hand that there are a lot of angry people ready to pick up arms and fight for what they feel belongs to them,' Felix told them in a serious tone when the laughter had subsided. 'The whities get government handouts left, right, and centre. Schooling, sport, entertainment, you name it and poor Kenny over there is forced to deal with sharks just to get his business off the ground.'

'Well, it's all bust now, I'm back to square one,' Kenny said, dragging his long legs from under the table and resting them under his chair.

'What? You mean Caleb gave you the slip?' Felix asked, his face turned full on Kenny. 'I told you not to trust that oke, bra.'

'You have to move on, Kenny boy,' Morris advised. 'Pick yourself up, dust your pants, and count it as experience, bad experience.'

'Well,' Felix said, 'I'm telling you okes the bush war is escalating as we speak. And if things don't change soon, we'll have hondo at our doorsteps, mark my word!'

'Democracy is complicated, and we know as a fact that blacks are not yet ready to handle power,' Alan read out aloud, before folding the page from the *Bulawayo Chronicle* up and slipping it back in his pocket. 'That's the same bullshit they feed us at work. "Not capable," even when we are the ones producing the results. And how can anyone ever be ready if they're not given the opportunity?'

'That's my point too, bra, you hit the nail on the head. And if they keep holding the carrot out for too long, you can't blame the oke on the street for grabbing it now, can you?' Felix responded and slapped his lap with his hand.

'I'm out,' Kenny said, flicking the cards in his hand on the table.

Felix went to the lounge area and turned the radio on and then walked over to the gramophone and when he lifted the needle of the record, a loud protest rose from the women sitting on the veranda.

'I'm turning it off so that I can move the turntable closer to you ladies,' he explained to the dissenting voices from the doorway.

'Cricket's on!' someone shouted, and the men left their card game and went and sat in the lounge room to listen to the crackle on the radio.

Tinashe went to answer the knock on the front door. Then she went to the dining table where Sylvia was arranging sandwiches on a tray and whispered in her ear.

Sylvia looked at the door, then she went to a desk in the corner of the lounge room and unlocked a drawer. She pulled out a brown envelope and took it with her to the man standing outside the front door.

The man felt the envelope with his fingers and then secured it in the inside pocket of his jacket. Then he tipped his hat at Sylvia and slipped away.

'You're still paying those buggers?' Alan, who had left the lounge room to help himself to a peri peri drumstick, muttered to Sylvia.

Sylvia gave him a smile for an answer, and Felix said through the doorway, 'If we don't, then they'll find any excuse to raid us. This way means they'll leave us alone.'

'Bloody police!' Alan swore, 'They're all corrupt.'

Felix went to the couch where two youths were seated. He put his arm around his son's neck, gave him a squeeze and said, 'I want you to make something of yourself, you hear me?'

Ashley smiled up at his father.

'He knows,' Sylvia told Felix as she walked past carrying drink glasses in a tray.

'Come, both of you,' Felix said, and Alistair, Alan's son, stood up with Ashley, and they both followed him into the lounge room.

'Don't fill the children's heads with nonsense,' Sylvia snapped at him. 'You and your politics!'

'They're tomorrow's future,' Felix told her. 'They shouldn't stick their heads in the sand and pretend that everything is okay in this country.'

There was a murmur of agreement from the men seated.

'It's not right,' Lydia told Sylvia when she was back on the veranda. 'I saw you paying that man, you shouldn't have to. We are people too. We're not allowed to do this and not allowed to do that, but who stops them? They have their pubs and their restaurants and what do we have? And then when we try to make the most of our situation, they still come and fleece us.'

'I don't let them get me down,' Sylvia confided with a laugh, before turning to the room at large and asking, 'Anyone for a dorp?'

After dinner, there was more music and dancing, and it was after midnight when Kenny and his family made their way back home.

Late Sunday afternoon, when Peggy was on her way to collect the washing off the line, there was a knock at the door, and Kenny went to answer it reluctantly.

'Who was at the door?' Peggy asked, returning from the backyard with a basket full of clothing in her hands, and Kenny replied, 'Kashish.'

They waited until the girls were in bed before the blame erupted in a volley of raised voices that pierced the walls.

Angie whimpered with fear and Sue pulled a blanket over their heads. They lay in the dark with their arms wrapped around each other and waited out the storm threatening to break up their family.

'I want to see my children before I go!' Kenny thundered.

'You don't have children!' Peggy yelled back. 'Not until you're fit to be their father.'

One door slammed shut and then another, and then it was silent.

Sue and Angie rolled over in their bed and fell asleep not long after.

VI

Part 7 – Life without Kenny

61

Peggy's new friends

Sue and Angie were playing dolly house with the broken pieces of what had once been a blue and white porcelain cup on their front porch when Rachel arrived carrying a duffel bag.

'Hello, girls!' she called out as she hurried through the front door before yelling out, 'Peggy!' in the same breath. 'I'm not taking no for an answer. You're coming out with us tonight,' she continued in a firm tone, even before the door shut behind her.

She marched through to Peggy's bedroom, dropped the bag she was carrying on the bed, and unzipped it. She retrieved a black charcoal iron stuffed with newspapers and coal and placed it on a stone plate. Then she lit the paper inside it with a match.

The paper flared up and began to burn and when the coals were a red shimmering colour, she pushed a metal comb with a long wooden handle between them.

'Right sit,' she ordered Peggy, pointing to the stool in front of the dressing table.

She pulled the comb from the coal and stood behind Peggy and the children's eyes widened with horror.

'Keep still no matter what!' Rachel ordered as she ran the red-hot iron through Peggy's hair.

The iron teeth sparked dangerously, and the room filled up with the pungent smell of burning hair. The comb gradually lost its heat, and when the coals had died down, Rachel took the iron outdoors and rattled it. Bits of ash flew out and when the coals had revived their glow and were sparkling again, Rachel shoved the comb back between them.

'Your hair is straighter than Mildred's,' she told Peggy when she was again guiding the comb through Peggy's hair. 'I have to heat the iron more than four times just to get her hair looking like yours is now.'

Peggy smiled in the mirror at the compliment.

Outside, the sun disappeared and inside the house, someone turned the lights on. And when Rachel was finally done, Peggy's curls were all gone, and her hair lay long and stiff down to the middle of her back.

Rachel painted Peggy's lips with a bright red lipstick and smeared blue eye shadow above her eyes. Then she put a smudge of red on Peggy's cheeks and told Peggy to rub over it with her hands.

'Make sure the door is locked,' Peggy told Sue, as she closed the door behind them and the two women giggled like teenage girls as they left the house.

'I'm not going to sleep till Mummy comes back,' Angie told Sue.

But when she woke up, it was the next morning, and Peggy and Sue were sitting out on the veranda, sipping morning tea and chatting happily.

62

The taxi ride

It was a Saturday evening a few weeks later when Rachel returned to Peggy's house, but this time she'd brought three friends with her. They arrived blowing circles of smoke from their cigarettes in the air and laughing without restraint.

'We're late, and you're not even ready yet!' Rachel, who was leading the group, yelled as they burst in through the front door wearing housecoats and turbans tied over their heads.

'I can't come,' Peggy told her with a long face. 'I have a headache.'

'So, take an aspirin!' they chorused.

'I can't leave the children on their own,' Peggy uttered, using another tactic.

'Lock the door,' they insisted, 'like you did the last time!'

'They're big girls, older than my two at home, and they manage without me! Isn't that right?' another said, lifting Angie's chin, with scarlet-tipped fingers and looking at her.

They ushered Peggy to her bedroom and Rachel pulled out her heavy coal iron and began to get it ready. An hour later, they all piled back into the lounge room and continued their uproarious chatter there.

'Dutch courage!' Rachel called out before tipping her head back and drinking from a bottle. She wiped her mouth and shuddered as the alcohol took effect and then with her face turned down held the bottle out to her companions. A hand grabbed it, and down the liquid flowed into the waiting mouth, as it made its round. Peggy shook her head when it reached her.

'You think we like doing this?' Florence yelled out accusingly, 'Drink up!'

Peggy took the bottle and held it to her mouth, and Sue and Angie watched their mother curiously, surprised to see her drinking anything but a fruit drink.

'Come!' Rachel ordered, and Peggy followed her back to the bedroom.

They returned a short while later.

'What do you think, girls?' Rachel asked as she swivelled Peggy around.

Sue opened her mouth in surprise and smiled appreciatively at her mother. And Angie, who refused to recognise the woman in the dress that was much too short for her and whose face was plastered with all that makeup as her mother, crumpled up her face and sobbed.

Outside, a car hooted, and the women quickly removed their housecoats and turbans. They slipped on their high heels and tittered out through the front door noisily. A rough voice yelled out to the driver of the car.

'Don't forget to lock the door,' Peggy told Sue, as she hurried out behind her friends holding her heels in one hand.

63

A night out with friends

The taxi driver had brought alcohol with him and the women continued their drinking as he drove. The taxi turned off the main road and went to park at the back of the Midlands Hotel.

'How much?' a man dressed in black asked standing at the driver's window.

The driver muttered an amount, and the man paid the fare. The women, now intoxicated, left the empty bottles strewn on the floor of the cab and tumbled out of the taxi.

They followed the man through the back door of the hotel, and down a passageway. He stopped at the first door they came to and whispered to Rachel before swinging it open. Loud chatter and music poured out and accompanied them as they went further into the hotel.

A second door led them to a more discreet room that was dimly lit and smelt strongly of the tobacco smoke swirling thickly in the air.

Inside, male revellers with loosened collars and rolled-up shirt sleeves and with their faces flushed pink with alcohol mingled with their dark-skinned partners. A pair of white arms pulled at a brown body and its owner turned around smiling before sliding back against the man's lap.

The small group paused outside the door and when they marched in, the room erupted with raucous whistling and wild cheers and Peggy froze in the doorway.

Rachel turned back and grabbed her roughly by her shoulder. Caught between the black waiters rushing about delivering food and beverages and the patrons strutting noisily back and forth, Peggy found herself being swept into the room with the crowd.

An hour went by before Peggy, managing to wriggle out of a pair of sweaty arms, made her escape.

'Where're you off to?' Rachel asked, her voice harsh with alcohol.

'Toilet,' Peggy replied, her heart thumping.

She found the powder room and with the door locked behind her, stood on the toilet seat and fiddled with the window. Then she eased her way out through it, just as the lock of the door gave way, and Rachel's voice rang out.

Peggy moved swiftly, taking care to keep to the hedges and away from the main road, because at night she was her father's child and ran the risk of being arrested for wandering about the streets of the town after dark without a pass.

Back at the hotel, Florence said to Rachel angrily, 'She made a fool of us. You can't just let her get away with that.'

64

Ambushed in the alley

A few weeks later, Peggy was on her way home from work when a voice suddenly rang out causing her to stop.

'So, you think you're better than us!' a figure melting off the brick wall and blocking her path sneered.

Peggy, who had been caught off guard, looked up abruptly.

'Too hoity toity for us, hey?' Rachel hammered on as she jabbed Peggy's chest with her finger before giving her ribs a brutal shove.

Peggy cried out in pain and held her side. Suddenly three more figures rushed out of hiding. They descended on her and began punching her and issuing verbal insults under their breath. Peggy collapsed to the ground and a foot landed on her head and began to grind the side of her face into the dirt. She brought her arms up to try to pull the weight off her face and more punches came down on her from all directions.

'That's enough!' Rachel shouted, panting with exertion.

The women pulled back and used the hems of their skirts to wipe the sweat off their faces. Then they turned away and walked up the alley laughing and chatting.

Peggy groaned and dragged herself to the side of the lane where she sat for a moment with her back against the wall.

The front door burst open, and the children looked up, their eyes filled with fear. Then their mother appeared with blood running from a cut under her eye and with her work uniform ripped and covered in smudges of blood and dirt. She limped in through the doorway to a loud bout of wailing.

A few days later, Lily came to visit unexpectedly on her way home from the hospital where she worked as a ward aide.

'You should've sent for me,' Lily said from the bedside where she sat dressed in her peach-coloured uniform as she dabbed the wounds on Peggy's face.

Peggy tried to speak, but finding the pain unbearable, left her tears to flow instead.

The children began to whimper, and Lily stood up and ushered them out of the room saying, 'Come, you two, see what I've brought for you in the kitchen.'

She left the kettle on the two-plate electric stove to boil and began to line a saucer with the fairy cakes from the tin she'd brought with her. She placed the cakes, and the plastic mugs filled with tea on the table in front of the children and said, 'I want you both to drink up and let Mummy have a rest, so no noise, okay?'

She left the kitchen carrying a tea tray. A moment later Sue and Angie sprang out of their seats and went to crouch against the wall that divided the bedroom to the kitchen and pressed their ears against it. And Peggy, her voice frail with pain, told Lily everything she hadn't been able to tell anyone else until now.

'You're lucky you got back home safe,' Lily murmured. 'You have to be careful, Peggy, those girls are rough.'

65

Loss of wages

It had been more than a week since the attack, and although not fully recovered, Peggy limped towards Gwelo's upmarket suburb of Kopje. Breathing heavily after the steep climb to the grand house near the top of the little hill, she weaved her way through the neatly cut shrubs and went to the back door where the gardener had already left a morning paper for the master of the house.

'Toby,' a woman's voice murmured from inside, 'Go and see who's at the door.'

Toby dropped the satchel in his hand on the floor, and with the door half open, yelled back, 'It's Peggy, Mum!'

'Peggy?' his mother uttered with bewilderment. 'At this time of the morning?'

The boy looked at Peggy and his mother asked no one in particular, 'Where has she been all this time?' while walking towards the door.

She stood behind her son and then muttered, 'Yes?' while looking at the bruises on Peggy's face.

'I've come to work, madam,' Peggy informed her.

'You can't just go and come as you please,' the madam reminded her. 'You're no good to me if you can't be here when I need you.'

241

Peggy looked down at her feet.

'I'm sorry,' the madam asserted. 'You can't just disappear and then expect me to be waiting for you. I found someone else.'

'What about my pay?' Peggy enquired sullenly.

'Your pay?' the woman repeated. 'What about it? You haven't worked the whole month. That's the agreement. Now go!'

Toby, whose eyes had been following each speaker in turn, now turned his glance back to his mother. She gave him a small nod. He swung the door shut and left Peggy staring back at it.

'I feel a bit bad,' the madam said as she watched Peggy walking towards the gate through her bedroom window. 'She's been with us quite a while.'

'How long,' her husband asked, adjusting his tie in the mirror.

'Toby was five, I think when she first started working here, and he's almost ten now. Can you believe that long? I wonder if she has any children of her own.'

'Who knows,' her husband replied, going to stand briefly beside her. 'They're all the same, untrustworthy and lazy!'

'She was honest. I hope the new one won't give us too much trouble,' his wife said.

'If she does, then we'll get someone else,' he reassured her, bending forward to kiss her full on the lips before striding out of the room.

'Damn!' he swore irritably a few minutes later, swerving his car abruptly to avoid knocking over a woman limping on the edge of the road without recognising her as the woman his wife had just dismissed. Just as he had not recognised the woman dressed in a mini frock that night in the hotel lounge, even when he had pulled her down to sit on his lap.

But Peggy's eyes had picked him out the minute she entered that dreadful room. And it was because of him that she had summoned enough courage to escape the hotel as soon as she had.

66

The scavengers

Peggy stopped at several houses on her way back home, to offer her services to their owners through the gardeners, but with no success. She had just turned into the sanitary lane that would take her home when she was alerted by noisy chatter. Peering ahead, she saw a group of street urchins covered in dirt and rummaging through the garbage bins behind the shopping centre.

She watched as the scavengers tipped over a silver bin and then waded through the rubbish shouting out with glee whenever a treasure was discovered. Small brown arms tore boxes and packages apart and shook out whatever they still held in them. Brown hands tipped beer bottles over and eager lips caught the droplets of residue spilling out.

A cacophony of voices erupted suddenly, and a small brown figure rushed into the lane from the shops and bolted down it, pursued by a shopkeeper and his assistant. The stout owner covered a short distance, then stopped. Doubling over to catch his breath, he stared ahead at the offender who was quickly outpacing his employee.

Flicking his glance behind him, he locked eyes with the curious ones trained on him and their owners, all caught in various stances of pilferage, leapt out of the garbage bins they were in with a loud clatter and streaked in the opposite direction before disappearing into the walkways leading to the lane. A sigh of dismay escaped Peggy's lips before she scurried homeward.

Sue and Angie, with the excitement of their escapade still ringing in their ears, lifted the latch of the kitchen door and then stopped abruptly.

'Where have you been?' Peggy asked in a low tone from her seat at the kitchen table.

The girls looked at each other and then at the floor.

'I asked you a question,' Peggy repeated in her no-nonsense voice, and again their eyes rushed up to the speaker before dipping down again.

'I want you to come in and close the door,' Peggy ordered.

Angie, who was always the obedient one, pushed her way past Sue and went to stand in front of her mother. Sue turned to the door and closed it reluctantly.

'Come stand here,' Peggy said with her eyes on Sue and pointing to a spot next to Angie.

Sue dropped her head and took small steps towards her sister.

'Look at yourselves,' Peggy stormed.

The girls who would have normally cleaned themselves up before their mother returned home from work, now turned gloomy eyes on each other. They both had smudges of dirt on their face, arms, and legs. Angie's hair stood in a frizz around her face and one of her plaits had come undone. Sue's blond curls were matted with grime and the front of both their frocks were soiled, probably from the contents of a bottle they had unearthed at the bottom of a discarded box and which they had tipped over to discover what it contained, under the instructions of their leader.

Peggy had picked two thin long sticks from the peach tree in the backyard earlier and had grumbled quietly to herself as she ripped off their leaves. She now turned her glance to the green sticks lying naked on the table.

She turned to the children and asked in a quiet tone, 'Who gave you permission to roam the streets?' She stood up from her seat and yelled out, 'Answer me!' startling the children into escape mode.

'Stop right there!' Peggy yelled. She picked up one of the sticks with one hand and grabbed Sue's arm with the other. 'And you, stand over there,' she said firmly to Angie, pointing to the chair she had just vacated. Angie rushed to the chair and stood beside it. 'I don't want a sound out of you,' Peggy said, turning back to Sue.

Angie's face twisted with horror as Peggy hunched over Sue, and began to strike her with the stick. Sue took her punishment silently, screwing up her face in pain and prancing about to try and lessen the stick's impact on her. Angie was aware that the second stick was reserved for her, and began to whimper.

'Shut up! Shut up!' Peggy yelled. She threw the broken stick down and released Sue's arm. Then she grabbed Angie roughly. 'I said shut up!' she hissed at the terror-stricken child as she felt for the stick on the table with her free hand. Angie clamped her jaw shut as the stick cut across her upper body and legs. 'Go to the bathroom and wait for me there!' Peggy ordered when both sticks now lay broken on the floor.

'Don't use your hands on them,' Lily had said to Peggy once when she had walked in on her beating the girls for breaking one of her rules. 'Use a stick, a stick breaks, it tells you when to stop.'

'What did they do this time,' Lily asked when she saw the scratches on the girl's legs.

'Digging through rubbish bins,' Peggy replied. 'I can't be in two places at the same time, Lily. It's not easy, you know.'

67

Syringa trees in full bloom

Almost three months had gone by without any word from Kenny.

'Where's Daddy?' the children took turns to ask, and Peggy knew that they blamed her for their father's disappearance.

She packed up their belongings hastily and pretended not to hear.

'Where are you going?' Sue asked with a puzzled expression.

The sound of a key in the door made them all look up eagerly, expecting to see Kenny, but they saw their landlord instead, standing in the doorway.

'Make sure you're out by seven. The new tenants will be moving in,' she told Peggy briskly.

Her glance fell on the children and, giving in to some impulse of kindness, she helped them to carry their possessions to the roadside. The children sat beside their packed suitcases and bags and waited. Not long after the young man Peggy had been expecting arrived, dressed in tattered clothes and the wheels of his trolley rattling noisily.

'How much?' Peggy asked.

The young man's gaze sailed over their luggage and then after some inward deliberation he turned back to Peggy and named his price.

'That's too much,' Peggy returned aghast. 'Don't worry, we can manage this on our own!' Sue and Angie opened their mouths to protest, but no words came out of them.

The youth reconsidered and then threw the question back to Peggy. She told him what she was prepared to pay. It didn't make sense for the man to go back empty-handed, having already come this far, so he agreed to the price reluctantly. Then he looked at Peggy as if he didn't trust her. She pulled out some coins from her handbag and held them out to him. He had shifty eyes, and a sudden greed came into them, and Peggy, noticing, quickly withdrew her palm, her fingers folding over the coins.

'Okay,' the young man announced before springing into action and loading the luggage into the trolley with hurried movements.

Not much later, the dust stirred up as Peggy and her daughters hurried off to their new home.

'That's my new job,' Peggy told them with a smile after a long walk.

They stood hidden behind the front hedge and peered down the long driveway lined with pine trees to where two cars were parked outside a large double-storey house. A gardener dressed in khaki overalls pushed a wheelbarrow with a spade in it across the neat courtyard and in the garden three smartly dressed children rolled about on a thick green lawn, their laughter trickling lightly back to them.

The trolley driver's interest waned. 'How much further, madam?' he asked. 'I have plenty of jobs waiting for me.'

There were syringa trees, in full bloom and showing off their purple petals, planted at intervals alongside the road. Sue and Angie skipped on ahead and then raced each other to the next tree. They turned their heads back just in time to see the trolley turn off the main road and they ran back to join it. They squeezed through a lane, and when the opening became too narrow for the trolley, its owner heaved the bags off it. After he expressed concern about leaving his trolley unattended, Peggy paid him, and he left them in the lane with their pile of bags.

They dragged their belongings through a dirty courtyard with a dull and jaded pepper tree with spotted berries hanging on its branches. After passing a row of prefabricated rooms with asbestos roofs and groups of people sitting outside them, Peggy found the room she was looking for.

She fiddled with the lock of the door, and when the key turned at last, she used her knee to force it wide open. Inside the room there was a small table pushed against one wall, with a one-burner primus stove on top of it. There was also a candle with its bottom half stuck in a beer bottle.

Peggy flicked on the light switch and when nothing happened, they all looked up and saw the loose wires dangling from the overhead beams.

'We don't have a sink.' Sue stated the obvious irritably. 'And where's the toilet?'

They wandered outside in search of water and walked past an old man holding an empty one gallon bucket in his hand. He nodded to them in greeting before he placed the bucket with its opening on the ground beside his door and sat on it.

A few doors down, a woman surrounded by small children, sat spread-legged on a reed mat. They all looked up curiously at the new arrivals.

Peggy stopped to talk to a man wandering about in the courtyard and he pointed towards a building a little ahead of them.

At the entrance of the ablution block, they passed a child crouched next to a copper tap with a puddle of water below it. The child waited patiently as the water trickled out into a long-handled pot in her hands.

Inside they tiptoed over puddles of water and walked past a shower with chipped tiles that were a dirty beige colour.

Sue pulled back and wrinkled up her nose with distaste. Just then a bulky woman barrelled past her and stopped suddenly at the sight of Peggy who was holding the toilet door open and taking a peep inside. The woman cursed out aloud and stumbled back the way she'd come, her feet unsteady under her.

'At least the room is clean,' Peggy said in a cheery voice, using her arm to propel them away from the stench. They wiped their feet on some stones outside their door before going back indoors.

'We'll get a potty and a plastic tub, and we'll have our own bathroom here with a curtain,' Peggy told them brightly, going to a corner of the room and showing them.

The children looked at her despondently.

68

A day of rest

The day drew to a close, and Peggy peeped out of the window. She noticed how more and more people entered the small compound and locked the door.

Then they all stood behind the curtain and watched the men and women sprawled on the ground and drinking out of plastic tubs. As the night wore on, the lively chatter turned to brawling and cursing.

The landlady stood on her stoop and in a drunken slur told them to 'Shut up!' The patrons quieted down. She staggered back indoors, and the noise picked up from where it had left off.

Peggy shuddered and turned away from the curtain and made their bed up on the chipped cement floor.

Just after midnight, they were awoken by sharp voices calling out curt orders and the panting of people as they scrambled about. They rushed back to the window and saw figures being pursued by police officers with batons dashing across the courtyard.

One man held his arm up to deflect the baton coming down on him, while another made futile attempts to hold onto the ground as he was pulled from under a straggly shrub.

Two police dogs charged after another lot of figures amid shrieks of horror and mayhem. A whistle rang out and the two charging animals rushed back to their handlers and stood obediently as their leashes were clipped back to the collars around their necks.

An order was yelled out and the captured patrons, now quiet, formed a line. An officer pointed his baton at three strong men. They entered the landlord's house hastily and came out again carrying several cartons and the landlord, seated outside her door, burst into loud howls of frustration. The confiscated liquor was transported through a small gate that led to the main road.

'Get up!' an officer ordered, and the landlord rested her insolent glance on him.

Then she turned to her shoes beside her and put them on in her own time before she was manhandled to the road.

Now seated with her customers in the back of the police van, she croaked 'You bloody thieves, the whole lot of you, you're just after my booze!' Then she dropped her head as she wrapped a piece of paper over some dubious-looking leaves. 'Anyone with a match?' her voice raked out as the van drove off.

A few days later, a very sober landlord returned, and everything went back to how it was, with the noise and the patrons and the stench of alcohol and bodies.

'Make sure you keep the curtains drawn and the door locked,' Peggy instructed the children at the crack of dawn, before slipping out.

'You're angry all the time,' Sue told Peggy solemnly, a few months later.

It was four o'clock in the morning and dark outside and Sue was helping Peggy pack their meal for the day. Angie stirred in the bed the three of them shared.

The small candle on the table flickered and sparked before an orange flame spiralled up to show Peggy's blue cotton uniform and a similarly coloured scarf tied around her head. The dim light exaggerated her hollow cheeks and the dark circles around her eyes. She paused to look at Sue silently, but Sue could tell by the expression on her face that if she did decide to speak it would be to say something harsh to her.

'I don't want to come back from work and find the house in a mess like I did yesterday,' Peggy said instead with her glance fixed on Sue. 'I do enough cleaning at work without having to do the same here.'

Sue pulled her mouth sullenly.

'I want you both to behave,' Peggy said as she tied a white apron over her uniform. 'No noise. Do you hear me?'

'Yes, ma,' they both replied before Peggy shut the door and locked it.

There was a small pot covered with a newspaper where they went to relieve themselves and which Peggy emptied out every evening when she returned from work. There was also a five gallon bucket beside the table filled with water for drinking and washing up.

Sue crawled back to bed, complaining of boredom before they both fell asleep. The sun poured in through the window to wake them up. Then they spent the rest of the day waiting for the sun to plunge them back into darkness and after that the sound of Peggy's key in the door.

Sunday was Peggy's day off and the one day of the week Sue and Angie looked forward to. They were returning from church one Sunday when a car drove past before stopping a short distance from them.

The laughter on Peggy's face dissolved and fear took its place. The children looked at their mother curiously. The car reversed and stopped a little ahead of them and the passenger door swung open.

A smartly dressed woman with a feather in her hat stood behind the door and looked back at them.

'Well, don't just stand there,' she snapped at Peggy. 'I don't have all day!'

Peggy walked quickly towards her with her head bowed.

'And whose children are those?' the woman asked with her glance at Sue and Angie.

'They are mine, madam,' Peggy mumbled with downcast eyes.

'The gardener told me he'd seen them. I didn't believe him. And you told me you didn't have children. Am I correct in saying that?' she asked.

Peggy was silent for a moment before nodding her head.

'Well, now you can have all the free time you want. You no longer work for me as of today, do you hear me?' Peggy's employer advised her.

'I can't pay the rent or feed my children if I have no job. The children are good, madam. They can look after themselves. They don't interfere with my work,' Peggy pleaded.

'Look at your child,' she said with her eyes on Sue, 'I can't have you working for me with a child that looks like that. What would the people think if they found out? She shouldn't be here! I'm sorry, I won't have it!' the madam added haughtily.

The driver's door opened and a tall man with blond whiskers and a pale face leaned over the car to face his companion and said, 'For heaven's sake, Thelma,' speaking through his teeth. 'The children don't even live in our bloody yard. Let her stay until the end of the month!'

'You don't have to put up with the embarrassment,' Thelma retorted. 'I do!'

'She can stay until the end of the month. It's my bloody money that pays her wage,' he asserted in a firm tone. 'You can't just toss her off. She has two young children and she's still a child herself, for god's sake!'

The man popped himself back into his car and slammed the door shut. The woman turned bright red and then, exhaling audibly, relented.

'Very well,' she said to Peggy. 'Two more weeks and I want you gone.'

'Thank you, madam,' Peggy mumbled.

The car drove off and they watched it until it became a tiny dot on the long road.

'What's wrong with me?' Sue asked, looking up at Peggy. 'Why did she say, a child like that?'

Peggy looked at Sue but did not reply because how do you explain to a child who was perfect in every sense that an imperfect law said that she was not.

69

Contact with the spirit world

Peggy and the girls continued down the road, but the incident had dampened their spirits, and their mood was now sober. Peggy looked thoughtful for a moment, and then said brightly, 'Let's go and see if Aunty Lily's at home.'

The children immediately dismissed the woman and her contempt for them from their minds and chatting gaily rushed alongside their mother towards their new destination. Lily's house was in Shamrock, a suburb on the wrong side of town and only a stone's throw away from the Gwelo cemetery.

'You didn't say you were coming today,' Lily said, smiling with pleasure.

'I wasn't, but something unexpected came up,' Peggy confided to her friend.

'Something not good?' Lily guessed before taking one last drag from her cigarette and throwing the stub into a flower bed. Then she got up from her seat and said, 'Let's talk inside.'

Half an hour later, Lily said, 'It's not far from here,' as she locked her front door.

A path led them to a busy main road, and after crossing it, they found themselves at Monomotapa township. Lily pointed at the small houses all crammed together and said, 'It's over there.'

'Is that the one with a tin shack behind it?' Peggy asked after passing a few homes with curious neighbours staring at them.

'Yes, that's the one,' Lily replied before she stopped walking.

'Thank you, Lily,' Peggy said, throwing her arms around her friend.

They waited until Lily was safely back on the other side of the road before they proceeded.

'I'm looking for Mr Chifamba's house,' Peggy addressed a woman who had come out to the gate to meet them.

'You've come to the right place,' the woman informed her.

They followed the woman across the bare and sandy courtyard and were then directed to a bench outside the tin shack. A short while later, the woman advised them that their host was ready to receive them.

They entered the dark recess timidly, with their heads bowed. Peggy clapped her hands with reverence and murmured her gratitude to the spirits as she'd so often done as a child when accompanied by Esther and Clara.

The children sat cross-legged on the reed mat, and having never visited a spirit medium before, stared at their surroundings anxiously.

'What is troubling you, what has brought you here today?' A voice broke through the dark and the children trembled with fear and huddled closer to their mother.

Gradually their eyes adjusted to the dark, and they saw a man seated on a low stool with deep scars on his forehead and cheeks staring curiously down at them.

Peggy's glance travelled to the bottles filled with powdery substances soaking in liquid, and then to the roots and leaves drying out on shelves. And finally, to the animal bits: tails, feet, and even dried-out carcasses with their fur still stuck to them, hanging from nails knocked into the walls of the shed. Then, not finding the answer to his question there, she sighed quietly and dropped her eyes to the ground.

The man withdrew his gaze and tilted his head down so that his crown of feathers was now pointed toward the seated guests. He picked up a canvas pouch at his feet and methodically extracted a pinch of tobacco which he stuffed in each of his nostrils.

Then he rubbed the sides of the black shorts he was dressed in vigorously, which made his chest quiver and the beads around his neck rattle. He released a succession of loud burps that burst through the air as he adjusted the leopard hide hanging over his shoulder.

His assistant began to clap her hands, inviting Peggy to do the same, and when he spoke next, his voice came out high-pitched and quite different from the one before. He turned his gaze on Peggy, waiting for her answer.

Peggy stirred in her seat and then with her eyes turned away from him said, 'My husband and I had a disagreement, and I haven't heard from him since he left. And as you can see, I have two children to support.'

'Is this the first time he has left home?' the woman-like voice of the spirit medium asked.

Peggy shook her head and when the man's eyes remained fixed on her, she relented and elaborated about her fights with Kenny. Then she told him about her attack and the loss of her previous job.

'And I will have no job soon,' she concluded, alluding to her pending dismissal from her current employment.

The probing eyes remained on her when she stopped talking. Then, after a short pause, the voice barely audible said, 'Your problems are the work of evil people. It is my job to find that evil and turn it back to its owners.'

He picked up a bowl filled with bones and with his palm shielding it began to mumble inaudibly, before tossing out the bones onto a cowhide in front of him.

'You have no father,' the voice uttered with his eyes on Peggy, 'No,' Peggy agreed.

'I can also see that you have no mother.' Again, the murmur from Peggy.

'Your mother is just a shadow, so I think there is nothing much I can say there. But your father is right here in the room with us. He has never left your side, even though you may think so when things don't work out for you. He wants to take care of you but because your life is different from what it used to be when you were young, he cannot find the door to it. He wants to know that you accept him in your new life. Do you want him to be part of your life?'

Peggy was taken back to her childhood and her eyes filled up with tears before they trickled down her cheeks. Then she whispered, 'I want him to be part of my life.'

The message was relayed telepathically to the spirit world and its response made the man smile with amusement as he toyed with the bones on the floor. Twisting his body back, he retrieved a small hessian bag filled with crushed roots and poured some of them into the empty bowl in front of him.

His assistant crawled in with a tin mug before retreating to the doorway. He tipped the hot liquid over the contents in the bowl and allowed the roots to steep, for a moment.

Then he said, 'Your father wants to know if the pain you came with today is still in your shoulder.'

All three guests gasped with surprise as Peggy had complained often about her shoulder and Sue and Angie had taken it in turns each evening to hold a warm cloth over it to ease the pain. Peggy shifted her shoulder about, and an incredulous smile broke on her face.

'No pain?' the voice queried. Peggy shook her head. 'What about your neck?'

'Nothing,' Peggy replied with more confidence. 'It used to start from here,' she said, showing him with her hand, 'And then travel all the way down here. It was awful, but I can't feel it at all now. It's all gone.'

The spirit medium sat upright and began to stamp the ground meditatively with his walking stick. Then he said with a small smile, 'I'm pleased to hear that, and your father is happy to hear that too.'

He took a sip from the bowl before passing it to Peggy, and then he gestured to the children, who sampled it, and then squinched their faces at its bitter taste.

He passed a crumpled-up piece of paper torn off a newspaper and filled with flat wafery seeds to Peggy and said, 'You must stand at the edge of an open field, with your back to the wind, and release the seeds slowly. Tell the evil spirit that is on you that you want nothing to do with it, and the breeze will carry it away with it.'

A short pause followed. Then the man burped several times, and his assistant clapped her hands. He blinked as he emerged from his trance.

Peggy turned to her side and discreetly removed some notes from under her bodice and held them out to him. The spirit medium turned his head away arrogantly and his assistant crawled up quickly. She received the notes and after examining them, gave the spirit medium a brief nod.

Peggy sighed happily when they were back outdoors.

70

A change of circumstances

Peggy and the girls entered the sanitary lane and through the first opening on its side, they saw several dark-skinned women lounging in front of a zinc shed. One of them, with a phlegm-filled cough, ambled towards a clothesline carrying a blue plastic bucket, before stopping to yell in a throaty voice at a group of brown children playing in a dirty puddle of water.

They weaved their way through squalor and several children of various shades of brown, chasing after plastic bags tied into a ball. They turned off the lane at the next opening into a well-kept garden and found Sylvia sitting on the stoep of her house and reading a magazine.

'I was just thinking of you,' Sylvia said as she rose to her feet. She stooped down and circled her arms around Sue and Angie in turn saying, 'You must have read my mind.'

She waddled up the steps and they followed her into the house through the front door.

'Mariam!' she called out as they entered the lounge room. She dropped herself onto a sofa saying, 'Come, come,' to her visitors, 'sit, sit,' and then turning to the door yelled out, 'Mariam!'

Mariam appeared silently and stood in front of her mistress.

'Aah! Why are you just standing there?' Sylvia said to her housekeeper, giving her a severe look. 'Why don't you answer? Couldn't you hear me calling?'

The woman looked at her pleasantly, a smile playing on her face.

'We're thirsty, make some tea, and don't take all day,' Sylvia ordered, her face relaxing.

Miriam curtsied politely before slipping away quietly.

'Ashley! Alistair!' Sylvia called out, 'Come take the girls and you people can play outside!'

Two heads popped into the lounge room and the girls followed them out to play.

'Kenny sent a message. He was asking about you and the children,' she told Peggy when they were alone.

'Why?' Peggy retorted. 'He left us in the lurch, why's he interested in us now?'

'You're still his wife, and the children are his,' Sylvia reminded her. 'He came here, that night he left, looking to rent a room for you. But I was full and when I came to look for you, they told me you'd left. I didn't know where you'd gone.'

'He was looking for a room to rent, with what money?' Peggy scoffed. 'We were kicked out because we couldn't pay the rent.'

'It happens,' Sylvia told her. 'Jobs are not easy to come by. But he's working now. Shabani mine. Like I said, he was asking about you and he also sent rent money. I don't have any room right now, but Olivia is moving out at the end of next month. And if you want, you can move here until you find somewhere with more room.'

Peggy's face lit up. 'Did he say when he's coming back?' she asked.

'That's all I know. And if you want, I can speak to Olivia about her job at the dry cleaners. She can put in a good word for you if you're interested.'

Peggy nodded her head eagerly.

'Where will you live in the meantime?' Sylvia asked with a small frown.

'I'll go home for a bit, to rest,' Peggy replied.

'Home?' Sylvia asked puzzled.

'Home!' Peggy repeated with more conviction.

71

The bus terminus

A day later Peggy and her daughters cut through the market square, with its makeshift stalls, and baskets spilling with colour. There were small pyramids of tomatoes, apples, and oranges, stacked next to cucumbers on wooden tables. And resting in pails filled with water were spinach leaves and shallots. Potatoes with some earth still stuck to them and large bulbs of onions peeped out of their sacks at the people milling around them. A sweet and fruity smell permeated the air.

A stout woman scooped out a mug full of maize kernels mixed with brown beans from a round pot bubbling over an open fire and slipped them into a cone made from newspaper. A hand passed her some coins, and she counted them out before holding out the snack to it.

A man chewing sugar cane and spitting out its bits on the ground stopped suddenly to stare and Peggy drew the children closer to her. They left the market square and the stores with their Indian storekeepers overlooking it and then entered a fenced area.

Peggy found the bus stop she wanted and then after looking about her found a spot and spread a blanket on the ground. Not long after, a man dressed in a pair of navy-blue trousers, and a matching shirt and with a baton swinging against his hip approached them.

'You can't sit here,' he said authoritatively to Peggy. 'You must move on now!'

'Yes, we're going,' Peggy told him, standing up quickly. 'It's just that the children are tired, and I wanted them to rest first.'

'Go and rest outside this area,' he said, pointing around him, 'And watch out for thieves out there.'

Peggy delved into her bag and held her closed palm out to him discreetly. 'My brother,' she implored, 'it's going to get dark very soon. I just need a safe place for my children and myself to sleep. One night only.'

'Let me see your ticket,' the man said, flicking his head on either side of him to see who, if anyone, was watching before closing his hand over the closed palm.

He studied the half-hidden notes now in his possession and dropped his hand into his side pocket. Then he uttered, 'Ah,' with a satisfied grin and talking loud for the benefit of the commuters passing by, 'I see your ticket is for tonight, you can take your things over there.'

He pointed to a spot that was more appealing than the present one, so the family gathered up their possessions and took them there.

The security guard turned away, in search of someone else to harass. They caught him heading toward another family also looking for a spot to retire for the night.

72

Arriving at the village

Peggy and the girls endured a few hours of being jostled over a bumpy dirt road as they sat cramped in an old and battered bus. Then they hitched a ride in a scotch cart before trekking on foot through the bush. At last, they saw round huts and thatched roofs and then came the light and happy chatter of young voices.

As they entered a compound, the merry voices suddenly turned to shrieks of terror. The visitors watched in dismay as small bodies bolted across the courtyard and went to seek refuge indoors.

An old woman struggled up to her feet, the copper bangles around her wrists clattering as her hands went up to her mouth. Then tears began to flow unheeded from her eyes. Peggy emitted a strangled cry before rushing to the arms held open to her. For a moment the two women sobbed bitterly.

Then Esther wiped Peggy's wet face and fastened a kiss on her cheek before turning to hold Sue and Angie in a tight embrace. And although she was a vague memory in the children's minds, they felt as if they'd always known her.

The wooden beads around Esther's ankles clashed again as she led them back to the shade of her hut. She unwrapped the cloth tied around her waist and spread it over the reed mat, then invited them to sit on it.

The children who had gone indoors to hide, now feeling braver, crept out quietly and went and sat crowded around Esther.

One of them whispered something to her and Esther murmured, 'Why should you be frightened of green eyes? Who runs away from your black eyes?' before they all chuckled good-humouredly.

A week after their arrival Esther led Angie outdoors and to the edge of the courtyard where Peggy was winnowing rice in a flat round basket.

'I found her sitting with her back to the door and her eyes on the little window in the hut,' Esther told Peggy with her kind eyes on her.

'I have to lock them up in the room when I go out to work,' Peggy explained. 'It's for their safety.' Seeing the look on her grandmother's face she added, 'Sue's okay.'

'But this one is not,' Esther informed her quietly. 'Leave them here with me if you can't take care of them properly in town.'

'I would if the law permitted me,' Peggy reminded her.

The dark circles around Peggy's eyes had disappeared and her face had filled out to how it had been in her happy days with Kenny.

'You're leaving soon,' Esther commented when they were seated around the fire and enjoying roasted maize and groundnuts, and Peggy nodded.

Peggy stood beside Esther's bed and looked around the room as she packed. Next to the bed was a small table and on top of it a bottle with a wick submerged in liquid for light. A chair sat further away with Esther's wooden suitcase on top of it. And above one end of the hut, a wire was stretched across some overhead beams on which three tattered tunics hung as well as a bright floral frock Peggy had brought with her for Esther.

'You don't have much in here,' Peggy had once said of the sparsely furnished room.

'I have more than I need,' Esther had replied. Then she had told her grandchild to close her eyes and to tell her what she saw. And Peggy after closing her eyes, had shook her head to show that she did not understand.

'Empty your mind,' Esther had whispered in her ear. And after a short pause, the child had opened her eyes and smiled widely at Esther.

'What did you see?' her grandmother asked.

'I saw you, and Aunty Clara and Temba,' the child replied.

'So, how can my room be empty,' Esther quizzed, 'when every space is filled with all of you?'

The time for Peggy to leave arrived and Esther couldn't help noticing how, the older she grew, the more time she spent looking back rather than forward.

They all scrambled up to their feet as the bus arrived finally, tilting to one side as it approached. A newspaper in a passenger's hand showed military personnel standing over three men lying dead on the ground, with their rifles pointed at them.

"Three terrorists killed," it read.

Esther held Peggy tight as she drank in the smell of her granddaughter.

And Peggy felt a stab of fear at the thought that this might well be the last time they'd be together.

VII

Part 8 – A new Beginning

73

New Year's Eve

Kenny went to the couch and peered down at the girls fully dressed and lying fast asleep.

'Don't wake them up, Kenny,' Peggy urged.

'And let them miss the fireworks?' Kenny asked with his eyebrows raised in surprise. 'You know how upset they'll be.'

Kenny shook them gently and whispered, 'Fireworks, girls, come, come, time to go.'

Sue and Angie sat up rubbing their eyes and Peggy ran a wet towel over their faces. She brushed down their hair as they buckled up their shoes.

The family emerged from the sanitary lane and walked past a group of constables manning a roadblock and towards the Midlands Hotel that was decorated with tinsel and multicoloured garlands.

They took their place among other brown faces behind the brown ropes cordoning off the big white clock sitting staunchly in the middle of Main Street. Then they all turned their faces towards the light streaming out from the hotel's large windows and doors.

They caught a glimpse of women in shiny evening dresses with their hair held up with sparkling pins. And the men beside them were dressed in long-sleeved shirts, and their Brylcreemed hair sparkled under the glittering chandeliers.

'Imagine sitting there and sipping drinks out of tall beer mugs and long-fluted glasses,' Kenny murmured to Peggy with a mischievous twinkle in his eyes.

A cool breeze drifted their way carrying with it the fragmented chatter and music behind the doors. Someone leaned too close to the brown rope to get a better view and a constable wielding a baton stepped forward to caution the culprit.

Two highly inebriated men holding up another in a worse condition staggered out of the hotel singing and laughing. The man in the middle was led to a potted shrub. He belched over it and the other two turned their faces away from him. Then all three tottered back inside.

Ten minutes before twelve, the band players brought their instruments out to the veranda and the music started again. Two lines formed at the hotel entrance, men in one and women in the other. Gold and silver stilettos and black shiny shoes tucked neatly under long dinner pants tapped in time with the band. And then the two lines merged, as men with their ties discarded and their faces flushed with excitement paired off with their elegantly dressed partners.

The long and jubilant human chain spiralled towards the clock, arms, legs, and hips twisting and turning in time with the music and oblivious to the figures huddled in the dark with their eyes fixed on them.

A young boy not much older than Sue, refusing to be left out of the fun, broke out into a jig, much to the amusement of the crowd.

The vigilant constable advanced swiftly, and the crowd yelled out, 'Let him dance, why can't he dance if he chooses to?' The constable backed off silently.

The band readied itself for the big countdown, and Kenny pointed to the hotel rooftop where a head shrouded by the dark popped back and forth. A silhouette leaned back as if preparing to launch a rocket and the drummer raised his mallet and paused.

This part of the celebration was open to all, and the crowd roared, 'Ten! Nine! Eight…' And on the count of one, the drum received a merciless onslaught of pounding that was at last checked by the sudden clashing of cymbals. The children held their hands to their ears until the chime of the big clock grew silent.

Kenny pulled Peggy closer and planted a kiss on her smiling lips before bending down to cuddle the children.

On the rooftop, a rocket hissed as it soared upwards before exploding into a cluster of jewels and as they slowly died, another bolt of lightning arched up and disintegrated into a kaleidoscope of colour. Soon the sky was a battlefield, roaring and rumbling as cascading fireballs erupted, lightening up the sky and filling the air with the smell and taste of smoke. Then one by one the imposing lights vying for position under the star-studded black void began to slowly fizzle out, taking with them the remnants of the old year.

Some night revellers turned back to the hotel to be waited on by eager staff. While older guests, tired out from the celebrations, called out their farewells. Then they glided back to their luxury vehicles under the safe custody of the town's police force.

'I'm going to be just like them,' Sue announced when the family was back home.

'Just like who?' Peggy asked as she prepared the girls for bed.

'The women that were dancing around the clock,' Sue replied. 'I'm going to be just like them when I grow up.'

74

A growing family

Peggy held the new baby out and Mandy squinched her face at her two sisters as they hovered around her protectively.

'Another one!' the woman at the counter muttered with distaste and Peggy dropped her eyes. 'Same father?' the woman prodded, and Peggy nodded, her eyes still downcast.

'Have you put in a request for school uniforms?' the woman snapped, looking at Angie and Peggy murmured that she had.

The woman went to her desk and flipped through a big black book. She found what she was looking for and, handing a coupon to Peggy, said, 'You take this to the supermarket.'

Peggy, who'd been given coupons before, listened patiently even though she knew what to do with it.

They left the counter and the next person in the queue stepped up to it, and the welfare official smiled at her because she only had one toddler, and one mistake was acceptable but three went beyond a joke.

Angie was dressed in a plain green tunic with a white collar, and when the time came for her to be in the class Sue was in now, she would wear a checked uniform with fine lines of olive green and yellow. Peggy had brushed Angie's hair, and it smelled of the cooking oil she'd used to keep it in place.

When they arrived at school, Angie joined Sue in the welfare line and the school matron gave them each a blue plastic mug filled with a yellowish-brown soup. It had a horrible taste to it.

'Hold your nose and drink it with your eyes closed,' Sue told Angie.

The tears welled up in Angie's eyes and when the matron was not looking Sue quickly tipped the cup over her own mouth.

'Did she drink it all?' the matron asked when the mug was handed back to her and Sue nodded.

At break time the other day scholars unwrapped their lunch before going out to play, and Sue and Angie were back in the welfare queue. A matron in a starched pink uniform stood with a big dish in her hand, spooning roasted peanuts into their outstretched palms, while her assistant gave them each a small bottle of milk.

And when they turned the corner with their lunch, the school bullies were there to relieve them of it.

'Tell me something interesting,' Mrs Ferreira invited the class when Angie wore a uniform like Sue's. 'Something you may have seen or heard that you think will be of interest to the rest of the class.'

Angie put her hand up eagerly and the teacher, drawn in by her enthusiasm, gave her the nod to go ahead. Angie sprang out of her seat and went to stand in front of the class so that they were now all looking at her.

She began to tell them about their visit to the spirit medium and how he had given Peggy medicine to wash away her bad luck.

'Stop! Stop! Stop!' Mrs Ferreira yelled, holding her ruler over Angie's head. 'This is a civilised school, and we don't believe in that rubbish,' she stated sternly. 'I don't want you to ever speak about such things on these grounds.'

Angie looked back at her confused, because their luck had changed after that. And Peggy still carried the small pouch of herbs the witch doctor had given her for good luck, in her handbag.

'Don't listen to what she tells you,' Peggy retorted when Angie told her mother. 'We both know the truth.'

And every day the girls brought home something new about how this great country of theirs was saved by strangers from across the sea and when Peggy shook her head at them sadly to refute their newly found knowledge, they were angered at what they saw as their mother's ignorance.

In the classroom, the teachers worked tirelessly to mold the children into what they said they should be, and on the playground, there were other lessons to be learned, too.

'Can we play?' Angie and her friend Olga asked two girls twisting a rope and watching three others skipping back and forth over it.

'Nah, you can't,' all of them answered, without looking their way.

'Why not?' Olga asked, looking at them curiously.

'Because you have kroes hair,' the girls told them.

Angie did not know what kroes meant, and neither did Olga.

They turned to look at each other and saw the frizzy bits of hair that instead of flowing down their shoulders, defied gravity and shot upwards around their face. Then turning away without arguing, they went in search of those girls whose hair resembled theirs.

They were distracted for a moment by a group of boys standing in a circle. And through the gaps in the bodies, they spotted Amos, a long-standing resident of the special class, prancing about and challenging two frightened-looking Indian boys in front of him to throw the first punch.

One boy began to cry, and the circle broke up, so they carried on walking until they found three girls with frizzy hair, playing a game of hopscotch drawn in the sand.

'You want to play?' they asked without waiting for Angie or Olga to ask, and the two friends' faces lit up with pleasure.

Sports Day came before the year ended and Peggy, although reluctant as usual, this time accepted the invitation to attend.

And when she arrived in her brown shoes, which were chipped in the front, Sue said, 'Why can't you dress like the other mothers?' who were wearing stockings and high heels.

When the races had ended and the parents were being treated to tea, Peggy stood on her own, feeling out of place. While the other mothers flicked back their curls with their ring-clad fingers and spoke in shrill voices, and looked past her as if she wasn't there.

75

Whatever it takes

In Gwelo, the town council found itself suddenly inundated with complaints about the increasing number of brown children plaguing the urban areas.

'I'll take my business somewhere else if you don't take care of this problem,' Mr Richards warned, his eyes darting towards a group of brown children lingering outside his store.

The councillor's glance swept over the odd bunch of ruffians, all aged under twelve. His gaze rested on one dirt smudged face which appeared to have an uncanny resemblance to the esteemed butcher.

The men exchanged a knowing look. Then the elected member said, 'Don't worry John, we'll do whatever it takes.'

'It's not a township,' leaders of the coloured community assured their people when the housing project was completed, 'It's a suburb.'

And although the houses did not look any different to those in the townships where black people lived, that assurance was enough to appease those keen to hold on fast to their second-class status.

'Time to ship out the rats and sanitise the sanitary lanes,' the mayor chuckled in a private joke, as he signed off the eviction notices.

'Nashville!' a brown leader declared, making the suburb sound better than it looked, as he snipped a pink ribbon with a pair of scissors.

And the Gwelo river gushed as it went about its business of keeping the town and the suburb apart.

'I saw it in my dreams,' Peggy told her family excitedly, and not for the first time, as they packed up and got ready to leave.

'Why can't we just go and live in Nashville like Aunty Sylvia?' Sue muttered crossly.

'And live squashed up like sardines?' Peggy lashed back with irritation as an engine started up and they sped off in the opposite direction.

The car bumped and heaved as it left the two strips of tarmac and civilisation behind, and the wheels rattled as they landed on the corrugated dust road. Then it began to descend a slope, and their stomachs dipped with it. Peggy held her swollen belly tightly in both hands as they grated over a ridged bridge before they began to ascend again. The engine groaned with despair as Kenny kept it in one gear, and the children, tired out by the long ride, flopped back in their seats with boredom, while the younger ones fell asleep.

The short reverie was broken by the sudden screech of tires. The children fell against each other as the car left the road and went to rock back and forth in front of a rusted old gate.

'Go and open it,' Peggy said, turning back to look at Sue and Angie.

The girls scrambled out of the car and tugged at the gate.

'Lift it!' Peggy yelled out to them, through Kenny's half-open window, and the gate edged back slowly.

'You're going to have to do something about that gate,' Kenny muttered as he shoved the gear stick around before stamping hard on the accelerator.

The car leapt forward, but only for an instant, before Kenny's foot shifted and came down heavily on the brake pedal. A cloud of dust burst out and enveloped the two girls who were still struggling to drag the gate back into its place. Then the car skidded before coming to a decisive halt beside the yellow chipped walls of the house. Four doors flew open and released a bundle of bodies.

The family crowded behind Kenny as he struggled with the lock of the back door and once the battle was won, they all trooped in behind Peggy who led the way with an animated look on her face. She showed off the scullery with its dirty old sink and stood proudly in the kitchen, oblivious to the gaping cracks in the walls. They paused in the dining room and turned their curious eyes up to the sagging ceilings above where a string of white ants zigzagged over the half-eaten boards.

Then they tramped their way down a long passageway that had three bedrooms leading off it, their feet crunching over the loose wooden tiles. The front door swung out onto a veranda and beside it was another door. This one opened into a lounge room with a fireplace built with brick and painted a dull maroon colour. This room was in a better condition than the rest of the house except for a large crack in the wall that started from the ceiling and ran parallel to the chimney and down to the floor.

'Where's the toilet? There's no toilet in the house,' Sue yelled as she stepped back outside.

'What are you shouting for?' Peggy who was now pulling weeds from a flower bed edged with pointed stones and bits of bricks countered as she straightened up. 'Everything is a fight with you!'

'Where's the toilet, Ma,' Sue repeated.

Peggy pointed to a small building standing on its own.

'Does it flush?' Sue asked, and Peggy shook her head, before turning to Kenny and asking, 'Did you remember to bring the box of old newspapers?'

'It's in there,' Kenny replied, pointing to the offending structure with his chin.

76

A long bicycle ride

At five thirty, the next morning, Peggy walked with the girls to the top of the hill.

'Remember to ride single file,' she reminded them as they hopped onto their bicycles.

She stood in her nightgown and watched as Sue's headlight lit up the gravel and showed them the way, and Angie's reflectors waited to light up for any vehicle that came from behind. And when they had reached the top of the next hill, Peggy turned back home, confident of help reaching the girls if they needed it, from the houses that were lined alongside the road.

They reached the school and finding the main gate shut pushed their bicycles reluctantly to the small gate at the side entrance where Fatima, the head girl, and two of her prefects were waiting to take down the names of all the latecomers.

"We had to stay for detention," Sue told Peggy crossly when they reached home at last.

'Then we'll wake up earlier tomorrow,' Peggy replied determinedly.

Many weeks later the girls were on the way to school when Sue suddenly turned off the road and forced Angie to stop with her.

'I can't take any more of this! I can't believe—' Sue sobbed with her head on the handlebars, when her voice was drowned out by the blaring sound of a horn and they found themselves caught in a pool of light.

The truck charged towards them, and then hurtled recklessly past them, taking with it its cargo of cattle before showering them with dust and pebbles.

'Come on, Sue,' Angie urged when her sister had stopped her coughing and spluttering. 'We have to go, or we'll be late again.'

'I don't care!' Sue replied, rubbing her eyes. 'Why did we have to leave our house in town for this?'

'Well, it's only until the end of the year and then you're off to high school,' Angie reminded her.

Sue pushed her bicycle back on the road and they waited for Lovemore to charge past them with Mandy in the back carrier of his bicycle and Julien in the front, before riding on.

77

Making history

The house quivered with excitement as Sue prepared to return to boarding school. And when Sue went on about going to watch movies and having brown cows at Wimpy with her friends, Angie swallowed her disappointment because a new school had been built and she wouldn't be joining her.

Sue, looking smart in her school blazer and hat, weaved past her similarly dressed peers before going to find the compartment allocated to her. She dropped her bags off and then after chatting gaily with her classmates went to stand with her family on the platform where the excitement and chaos continued.

There were hugs and tears as trunks were loaded onto the train and those scholars still on the ground boarded the train hurriedly as it slowly edged forward. Here and there a woman dabbed her eyes with a handkerchief. Sue's family waited until the guard's van became a blurry image before they made their way back home in a sombre mood.

School for Angie started the day after. Their first assembly was held on a patch of dusty ground in front of a classroom block. The school had no name and no uniform, and the students had been told to come dressed in casual clothes. After assembly, the headmaster took them on a tour. There were markings on the ground showing where the future classrooms would be erected and patches of cleared ground for a tennis court. A hole had been dug where the swimming pool would go.

They were separated into two age groups. The older group were in their second year of high school. And Angie stood with the group that the headmaster told them was 'fortunate to be making history as the first form ones of the new school.'

'Your parents have got their wish. They have finally got what they've always wanted,' the headmaster told them proudly, just as a dust devil raced over some patchy grass and nipped at their heels before disappearing around the classroom block.

And looking at the faces around her, Angie knew that they were all there through no choice of their own.

78

The farmer's visit

Peggy straightened up in the shoulder-high maize crop with a hoe in her hand and watched as a white utility vehicle went to park alongside her vegetable garden. The driver disembarked, and Peggy, now crouched in the field, asked the gardener still standing upright and staring ahead, 'Who is it?'

'Magirazi,' the gardener offered with his eyes on the visitor.

'Magirazi?' Peggy repeated. 'Why would he stop here? Boss Kenny had a puncture, and he drove past him without even stopping to offer him help. He could see he was pushing his bicycle. Why couldn't he have just stopped and asked what the problem was or given him a ride?'

Mr Van Niekerk was the farmer's name, but most of the locals, unable to pronounce it, called him Magirazi instead, because of the thick spectacles he wore.

The farmer, dressed in a beige shirt and matching shorts, crunched over the dry earth in his beige veldt-schooners and an army of blackjacks lying there sprung up to bite the thick socks wrapped around his ankles in retaliation. A second later, his companion ambled towards him in a sleeveless tunic and they both stood viewing the vegetable garden with their sun-toasted hands on their hips. Then Mr Van, as others called him, sensing the eyes on him, turned to the maize field and caught Lovemore staring back at him.

The farmer drew himself up to his full height, and with his face twisted in a scowl yelled out, 'Come here, boy!' in a commanding voice.

'Go and see what he wants,' Peggy ordered, her hoe picking at the weeds around a mealie stalk.

Lovemore scrambled through the field and slipped through the fence, before going to stand a short distance from the farmer with his head bowed and his hands pressed together.

'Is this your garden?' the farmer snapped, and the gardener shook his head before darting a glance at the mealie field.

'Then who's the bloody owner?' the visitor demanded.

'I'm the owner,' Peggy volunteered quietly, from the other side of the fence.

Mrs Van Niekerk, who had turned to look at Peggy, snorted before shaking her head with disgust.

'Is this all your land?' the farmer asked, pointing to the maize field and the cattle kraal next to it, and Peggy looked at him silently.

'Do you have title deeds?' he persisted, becoming more irritated.

'Yes,' Peggy replied faintly.

'I want to see them,' the man barked, his cheeks now a bright red colour.

'Why do you need to see them?' Angie, who was now almost as tall as Peggy, asked gazing at the speaker defiantly.

'Because I don't believe that that piece of land belongs to you,' he replied, ignoring Angie now standing at her mother's side and addressing Peggy.

In the distance, a car changed gears from the top of the hill and came down it in a loud howl before skidding off the main road in a cloud of dust. The gardener turned and was ready to scoot to open the gate where Kenny was now parked, when Angie's voice rang out to stop him.

'That farmer is being aggressive to Mummy!' Angie shouted out to Kenny even before she reached his car.

Kenny, exhausted and hungry after his night shift and now finding an outlet for his irritation, swung his door open with more force than was necessary. He marched ahead of Angie and swung his arm out to the intruders while bellowing out, 'Bugger off! Who are you to come asking to see my title deed?'

Angie who had never witnessed her father raising his voice to anyone in anger before, looked at him with alarm.

'This is private property, and I don't take orders from you!' he continued with his nostrils flared, jabbing the air with his finger.

Mr Van, who'd been standing with his hands on his hips, now dropped his arms to his sides.

A black Alsatian with bits of tan, which only moments earlier had been flopped down against one of the milk cans in the back of the ute, now scrambled up and bared its teeth at Kenny. Then it began to bark at him aggressively as it tugged at its leash.

Rasta and Busta, who had been strolling in the yard, pricked their ears at the commotion, before charging through the fields and making futile attempts to climb into the back of the pickup.

'Julien! Dexter!' Peggy yelled out. 'Come get the dogs!'

A loud whistle rang through the air, and the dogs turned around, and after a second whistle scuttled towards it. The boys pounced on the dogs and dragged them away by their collars.

Mr Van held his hand out to Kenny and said something to him in a strange language, and Kenny responded in the same guttural tones of the Afrikaner. After a short hesitation, they shook hands.

'I know this land,' the farmer said after a short conversation in the same dialect and reverting to English, with his arm stretched towards the cattle kraal. 'All this here is O'Donnell's land.'

Kenny brushed his face with his hand and gave Peggy a look that said, 'I told you so,' before turning back to the farmer.

Mr Van walked briskly to his Mazda pickup and returned with a map. 'Come,' he said, 'I'll show you.'

His wife pulled the hat hanging behind her neck onto her head and the four of them marched alongside the fence, and when they reached the cattle kraal, they stepped through the strands of wire. The others stood back and watched as the farmer began pacing through the tall, coarse grass and stopping to consult his map. He stooped down and scratched the hard earth with his brown fingernails before shifting his position and scraping the ground with the heel of his boot.

'Here,' he said after a short pause, 'here's one of them.'

He kicked aside a small pile of rocks and revealed a small iron peg, before moving on again and after scratching around, uttered, 'Here's another,' until it was obvious that Peggy had indeed helped herself to a little more than an acre of O'Donnell's land.

Back on the main road, the farmer removed a handkerchief from his pocket and wiped his forehead saying, 'This is where your land ends,' and pointing to the end of Peggy's vegetable garden.

'All this,' his wife reiterated in a querulous tone and gesturing at the mealie field and cattle kraal, 'doesn't belong to you. You can't just take over land as you choose!'

Kenny eyed her, and she relaxed the scowl on her face.

'You need to remove these fences,' the farmer declared firmly as a parting shot at Kenny, before starting up his vehicle and leaving them standing there in a gloomy silence.

And then Kenny, remembering the small khaki envelope in his breast pocket, pulled it out and gave it to his wife saying, 'I'm on RDO.'

Peggy opened the envelope and took out one note from it, and Kenny received it with a grin, before calling out to Lovemore to go on an errand for him.

Later that afternoon, Kenny dragged a garden chair across the yard to the orchard and unwrapped the brown paper around the bottle Lovemore had brought back with him. Then, looking around him, he spotted Myles playing with his toy cars in the dirt.

'Bring me a jug of water and an empty glass,' he called out to Myles. And Myles, eager to get back to his toys, came running back to him with a glass in his hand with water sloshing out of it.

Kenny eyed the half-full glass and said to him with a smile, 'That's not what I said, you little monkey, I said bring a glass and a jug with water.' Myles stared back at him. Then, chucking the water out and putting the glass down next to the bottle, Kenny said, 'Tell Spiwe to bring a jug with water in it,' before settling back in his seat.

A short while later, the maid strolled up to him with an empty water jug and he turned an exasperated look at her.

'Don't forget the spirits,' Peggy reminded him as she set a side table down next to him before making her way to the fields.

Kenny poured a drop of brandy into the lid of the bottle and poured it out on the ground.

'Kenny!' Peggy called out when she returned from the field. 'Go inside, it's dark out here.' Then she yelled, 'Spiwe! Come and pack all these things away,' as she stepped over the empty bottle on the ground and helped her husband up to his feet.

They stumbled indoors and when she had lowered Kenny onto the bed, he shook his head and speaking in a slurred voice said, 'The Van Niekerk's have over five thousand hectares of land. Remember, Peggy, we drove down there to see it for ourselves. So why should half an acre be such an issue with them?'

'And it's not like O'Donnell is even in the country,' Peggy agreed. 'I mean, that land is vacant up to the river. Surely, they can't force us off, after all these years, not when the owners are not interested in it anymore?'

A week later the McAlister's received a visit from the rural council, who supervised the pulling down of their fence.

79

Arrival of the phone

Two technicians arrived just before midday, when Peggy was in the milk shed serving a customer and Kenny was at work. The men looked around at the neatly kept garden and then up at the old house with its faded and chipped paint. Then the driver went to the back of his utility van and pulled out a ladder.

'Where's your dining room?' his companion holding a toolbox in his hand, asked.

Dexter pointed towards the back door, and the man gestured back at him with his head. The child ran on ahead and the two men followed behind him. The other children, now feeling braver, came out of hiding and followed the pair.

The men tramped over the polished veranda floor and looked about them as they walked past spotless furniture that was old and dented. They gazed at the walls scarred with grey cement filling old cracks and then up to where the ceilings should have been and saw exposed timber beams that smelled of used engine oil. Then, with their curiosity quenched, they took their tools to one corner of the room and began to fiddle with some wires.

When the big black phone had been installed, the children followed the men out to their work van and watched it silently as it drove off.

Just then an unfamiliar sound belted through the house and the children looked at each other with frightened eyes. Sue pushed Angie forward and although not much frightened her, even this was too scary for her. She sidestepped her sister's efforts and went to stand a short distance away.

'Pick it up!' Peggy cried out, dropping the milk jug on the kitchen table and rushing into the dining room.

Julien, the man of the house when Kenny was away, stepped up bravely to the bleating monster and yanking the receiver up, held it up in front of him.

'Talk! Talk!' Peggy yelled from a safe distance.

'Hello! Hello!' Julien said to the air.

A barrage of abuse hurtled out from the receiver. 'This is not your call! Put the bloody phone down!'

Julien flung the receiver down like it was a piece of burning coal and rubbed his hands together. The telephone remained silent for a moment, and just as they were about to drift off, three loud rings blasted out, and everyone rushed towards the door.

Peggy put on a brave face and held the receiver like Julien had and said, 'Hello! Hello!' in a dull tone.

A woman's voice yelled out, 'This is a party line!' and Peggy was about to throw the phone down when the voice carried on talking. 'Only pick up the phone when you hear three long rings. Not short ones, long ones like the ones you heard when I called you,' the voice shouted.

Peggy nodded.

'I said, do you understand me?' the voice yelled.

'Yes, madam,' Peggy shouted back at the unknown voice with her eyes on the children, before shaking her head at the complexity of what she was being asked to do.

Then, turning to Sue, she asked, 'What did she say?' as she carefully replaced the black handpiece back on its cradle with a worried look on her face.

'She said we must count the rings, and only answer the phone when there are three rings,' Sue replied, and Dexter imitated the rings, and they all burst out laughing.

VIII

Part 9 – Upheaval in family life

80

Hard-earned coins

Peggy, dressed in her striped going-out dress and her brown shoes which were chipped in the front, sat beside Kenny in his old car, as they drove into town. When they arrived, she picked up the parcel she had brought with her and he remained behind, parked on the side of the road.

She walked past a new building that had gone up on the spot where their old, rented house once stood. When she reached the launderette where she once worked, she followed a lane that took her to the back of the shop.

'I'm leaving,' Mrs Wilson said to Peggy through the fence, as she unlocked the back gate. 'We're going back home.'

'To Australia?' Peggy asked, astonished.

'Where else?' Mrs Wilson replied with a resigned tone. 'It's not safe here anymore.'

Peggy followed the elderly woman up a flight of stairs and a voice on the radio said, "Terrorists have attacked a school in Lupane killing three children..."

'As you can see, this is all gone,' Mrs Wilson said, stopping to turn the radio off and waving her hand around the kitchen and dining area.

Peggy looked around the familiar flat that she'd often cleaned when business in the laundry downstairs was slow.

Eileen went to fill a kettle with water and Peggy asked, 'And the surgery?' as she unwrapped a home-baked cake she had brought with her.

'That's all sorted. Brian found a good doctor to replace him,' the woman replied. Then, seeing the frown forming on Peggy's face, added quickly, 'Don't worry, he's from overseas, and with different ideas from this lot.'

After tea, the women strolled into the lounge room and Eileen said in her familiar crisp bursts, 'I spend good money on all this, but it must all go. It's just too expensive to ship back home. I'll give you the first choice if you want it, but it won't be cheap!'

Peggy did not need any convincing.

A few days later, Mr Kashish arrived with his son in his white pickup and declined Peggy's invitation to come indoors, preferring to lean against his car as he conducted business.

There was a quiet hum between them before Peggy asserted, 'No!' firmly and shook her head. She called out to Angie to bring a pencil and a piece of paper.

'Write down three goats, for this price,' Peggy yelled out, holding up her fingers to show the amount.

Angie pressed the paper down on the bonnet of Kenny's car and after performing a quick calculation, shouted out the figure to Peggy.

'Add on one sheep,' Peggy said, and this one had a different price, so Angie, after jotting it at the bottom of her list, used her fingers to work out the new total.

'How much now?' Peggy asked, glancing at Angie.

Mr Kashish's son walked over to where Angie was standing and peered over her shoulder. And seeing the total she had to be the same as the one he had already calculated in his head, nodded.

'Put another sheep,' Mr Kashish ordered, his English more broken than Peggy's, and Angie assumed that's what he'd asked her to do.

'No!' Peggy, who understood him better, retorted with a shake of her head. 'That's the price. If I add another sheep, then you must pay for it!'

They reached an impasse, and Peggy offered him a cup of tea. There was a flick of anticipation in his son's eyes and Mr Kashish licked his dry lips, but after a slight pause where he fought the invisible boundaries imposed on him by his religion, he shook his head with regret.

'Water?' Peggy offered, and finding even that to be unacceptable, he shook his head resolutely. Peggy's jaw tightened at the snub, but only briefly.

Then they resumed the task at hand, goats and sheep numbers increasing or decreasing until Angie was quite lost as to where they all stood.

After some hard bargaining, sweetened by a promise of fresh green stalks of garlic, they reached an agreement and made their way to the kraal where the unfortunate animals were unknowingly awaiting their fate.

'I've got the money, madam,' Peggy yelled into the mouthpiece, even before Mr Kashish had turned his truck around and driven out. 'Don't sell anything in the lounge room, I'm taking it all!'

'What about the bed in the guest room?'

'I'll take that too!' Peggy replied, breathless with excitement.

Eileen Wilson replaced the receiver and uttered a sigh of relief.

That same day, farm labourers handed over their hard-earned coins and trickled out through the back gate carrying bits of old furniture, to make space in the lounge room for Peggy's 'new' furnishings.

81

Special visitors

Angie was on her way home from school when Lovemore came pedalling fast from the opposite direction, with an empty plastic container sitting in the front carrier of his bicycle. He raised his hand in greeting as he rode past her swiftly with a wide grin on his face.

Further up the road, Peggy passed Kenny's car parked on the side of the road with its nose pointed homewards and its windows wound up. And Angie was sure that it had run out of petrol, as it often did.

When she turned into the driveway, Kenny, who was still dressed in his work clothes, rushed out from behind a bush to open the gate for her.

'Did you see Lovemore,' he yelled out impatiently, and Angie told him she had.

'Where?' he asked and Angie, pushing her bicycle beside him replied, 'Just before MacDonalds' gate.'

Angie raised her eyebrows at the open lounge room door and Kenny shook his head. When they reached the back veranda, he gave her a look to warn her of the whirlwind inside before wandering off and leaving Angie to step indoors on her own.

'Why are you using dirty water to wash those cups?' Peggy demanded, not expecting an answer from the maid, whose sullen face was turned purposely away from her.

She thrust her hand into the greasy water and yanked out the plug, saying through a clenched jaw, 'Get hot water outside and wash all these dishes again!'

The water gurgled down the drain and Angie slipped into the bedroom she shared with her sisters, unnoticed.

Much later the front gate rattled, and Kenny sped towards it, grabbed the bicycle off Lovemore, and rode off in a hurry.

'Did you put petrol in the car?' Peggy asked the gardener as he came down the driveway swinging the empty plastic container in his hand.

'Yes, madam,' he replied, without breaking his stride.

'Hurry up and come and sweep the front yard!' Peggy yelled at the quickly retreating figure. 'Did you hear what I said?' and the disgruntled gardener murmured inaudibly.

Half an hour later, Kenny returned with the bicycle in the boot of his car.

That evening an unfamiliar car turned off the main road and swung in through the open gate. The dogs locked up in a shed at the rear of the property began to yelp with agitation.

Kenny, who was now looking smart in a freshly ironed shirt, stood on the newly polished front stoep and, gestured to the driver as he guided him around the front rockery. The car came to a stop behind the tall trees in the front yard. Doors were opened and banged shut and Sue, giggling lightly, leaned towards her father and gave him a peck on his cheek.

Then she turned to the young man with reddish hair and the old couple with worried looks on their faces behind them and introduced them to Kenny in her put-on posh voice. The men shook hands, but the woman turned her face away from Kenny.

Peggy pulled back from behind the curtain as the group trooped into the lounge room and returned to the kitchen where she had prepared a tray of refreshments. Sue breezed in later wearing a soft scarf around her neck to keep the brown mole she shared with her father hidden from view and stood watching as Peggy and Angie got the tea ready.

'So that's him?' Peggy asked.

'You saw him,' Sue returned in her normal voice and smiled back at them. Then she asked, 'What do you think?' although the smile on her face said that she already knew.

'He's handsome,' Peggy replied with a happy gleam in her eyes.

Angie was about to say that she thought he was handsome too, but Sue already had her back turned to them.

'I hope the tea's coming soon,' Sue said, speaking loud enough to be heard in the lounge room and flicking back her hair with a manicured finger. 'I'm famished!'

The word meant nothing to Peggy, so she turned to Angie to explain.

There were conditions to the visit. Peggy had been allowed to carry the tea tray in but was not allowed to stay. And as she was eager to see Sue's future-in-law's close-up, she felt grateful for the small concession. When she came through the door, Sue's young man sprang out of his seat to assist her, when a small dry cough cackled through the still air. He turned to his mother quickly, his eyes pleading with hers. She stitched up her lips and the young man cowered back on his seat.

The visit was over a lot sooner than expected, and the rest of the family listened to their quiet chatter on the front veranda, from behind closed doors. When Peggy ventured to peep out, she saw that the woman had distanced herself from the others and was standing stiffly beside the car door.

The men shook hands, and Sue gave Kenny another peck on his

cheek. The young man circled his arm around Sue's waist and the three of them walked off to the car. Kenny took back his post on the stoep and they all watched the car as it glided out through the gateway.

Dexter came darting out from the back of the house and went to shut the gate. Kenny waited until he had joined him before the two of them walked towards the front door.

'They're gone,' Peggy said as she went to meet them.

'Yes,' Kenny replied with a small smile.

Then they all slipped into the lounge room as if in a trance.

'Where will she live?' Angie asked abruptly, her voice betraying her angry feelings, causing both her parents to turn towards her with startled looks. 'I mean, if we are not allowed to talk to her or to see her, where will she live so that we can make a point of not going there?' Angie went on in a determined tone.

Peggy's face clouded over.

'Your sister is doing what she feels is best for her, and whether we agree with her or not, we must respect her wishes,' Kenny told his family firmly.

Angie was trembling with fury. She wanted to say more, she wanted them to fight for her.

'I want a sister I can talk to, and spend time with, not someone who is ashamed to be part of our family and who pretends that we don't exist. No man is worth that sacrifice,' she cried with smouldering eyes turned on Peggy accusingly.

The tears trickled down Peggy's cheeks, and Angie felt terrible for being the cause of them.

82

Conscription papers

It was 1976 and a special assembly had been called at Angie's school.

'Some of you young men will have received your conscription papers. We don't discuss politics at school, and I only mention this to wish the boys well,' the headmaster told the students in a sombre tone.

A teacher approached, and Amos, now finally in high school, but stuck in the same class for the last four years, began to fidget uncomfortably.

'Got your call-up papers, son, I hear,' Mr Rogers said.

Amos paused for a second before bending down to the satchel on the floor beside him. He opened the flap and whipping out a large envelope with 'Rhodesian Army Headquarters' stamped on it, held it out to the teacher.

'You have to learn to read now that you're going to be in the military,' Mr Rogers told him opening the khaki envelope and reading through the call-up papers. Then, turning back to the young man, he asked, 'When?' and Amos replied, 'April 15,' with his hands at his side.

'Are you afraid?' Mr Rogers enquired, no longer smiling.

Amos was silent for a moment and then, speaking as one did in a rehearsed speech, he said, 'I'll catch the train to Bulawayo and then we'll be taken to Llewellin Barracks.'

Mr Rogers nodded pensively.

An uncertain look overshadowed the boy's face and Mr Rogers, noticing it, threw his arm around Amos with the papers still in his hand.

'Don't worry, son,' he told him in a firm tone, 'you'll be fine.'

A ripple of panic ran through the students looking on.

'Things are heating up,' Kenny commented grimly when Angie took the news home with her that day.

83

The lollipop

Back in the village, a little girl, not more than four years old, ran out of the compound and stood at the edge of some bushes. In the compound, a woman's voice rang out and the child turned her head back and shouted, 'Mama!'

'Where are you?' the woman asked. 'I want you to come now!'

The child was about to do what she'd been told when a hand came out and stopped her. It was not a threatening gesture, just a slight movement of the hand to discourage her from going.

A boy sent on an errand instinctively melted back into the trees. Then, leaving the empty milk jug hidden under a shrub, he crawled around some bushes to take a closer look. He saw a bearded man dressed in denim shorts and a camouflaged shirt crouched in front of the child. And above him, another man, similarly dressed and sitting on a rock and looking out while at the same time listening in on the conversation between his companion and the little girl below.

The man, with his arms and face blackened, offered the child a lollipop, a bright red one. She accepted it and looked at it, not knowing what to do with it, and he held out his tongue and used hand gestures to show her what to do. She gave the lollipop a tentative lick, before

306

slipping it through her lips and savouring its flavour.

'Do you like it?' the man asked in a slightly accented tone, and the girl nodded her head at him shyly.

The girl turned to leave, and again the man's hand came out to detain her.

'Look,' he said, speaking to her kindly and holding out a small box towards her.

The girl stopped licking her lollipop and took a curious step forward.

'See this here,' he said, showing her a button on the tape recorder he was holding.

His finger pressed down on the button and music trickled out of the machine, township music, the kind the child had often heard playing on her father's radio. He danced with his upper body and the man sitting on the rocks above them clapped his hands softly.

'You dance too,' the man coaxed her.

She was wearing a string of beads around her neck and nothing else except for a ragged skirt, which was tucked under a rounded stomach with a protruding navel stuck below it. The child started to sway her body in time to the music, the rags around her waist twisting and turning around her body, her small round face bright with excitement.

'You like it?' the man asked before pressing the button again, silencing the music. The little girl nodded. 'You want to try it?' he asked, holding out the tape recorder to her and showing her where to press.

The little finger zoned to where she'd been shown, and the music flowed out again. The child swayed her body again and smiled happily at their encouraging faces. The man turned off the tape recorder.

'Because you've been so clever,' the man said, fiddling with the equipment in his hand, and pausing now and then to look at her with a smile on his face, 'this is what I will do.'

She looked at him expectantly.

'I will give it to you,' he stated as he slapped the back of the recorder shut. Then he said, teasing her and pretending to keep it, 'Are you sure you want it?'

The child put the lollipop in her mouth and held out both hands eagerly.

'Okay, if you insist,' he said.

The woman in the compound called out again.

'Mama!' the girl replied absentmindedly.

'I want you to surprise your mama,' the man said to the child. 'Don't show it to her now. Hide it, and then when she comes to the kitchen, press the button so the music can play, okay?'

'Okay! the girl replied obediently.

When she turned to leave, he said to her, 'Do you know what to do?'

Her finger moved towards the button and both men sprang to their feet, and the one next to her said, 'No! No! Not now!' The girl grinned at their nervousness and took her finger away.

The men watched the child as she skipped down the patchy path toward the compound.

'Where've you been,' her mother asked angrily when she saw her coming up the path with her hands behind her back. 'Go and bring me water from the kitchen,' she demanded before turning back to her chores.

The little girl took the recorder into the kitchen and came out carrying a mug with water and the men at the top of the hill leaned back in their makeshift seats and waited and something made the boy wait too. The mother gave the mug back to the child who returned to the kitchen with it.

And then without warning the world below the boy's eyes exploded, tearing the hut the girl had just entered apart. Her mother, who had been scrubbing pots earlier, now lay on the ground with the baby still strapped to her back.

The two men, now joined by others the boy had not seen before, came charging down the hill, discharging their rifles as they screamed and tossed grenades into the compound. Smoke billowed out of blazing thatched roofs and the air was filled with the sound of screaming and the smell of burning flesh interspersed with the crackle of firearms. The boy turned away from the carnage and lost his footing. He rolled down the hill, tipping over rocks and stumps, his arms grabbing wildly at whatever was in reach. Then he crashed into a tree and lay there stunned for a moment.

In the compound, armed men talked excitedly, peeping into structures still standing and prodding bodies on the ground with their rifles. An old man with his limbs blown off groaned on the ground where he lay.

'Make sure you finish him off,' the man in charge ordered and the boy recognized the voice as the person who'd been talking to the little girl earlier.

More shots rang out in the compound. The survivors, bleeding and dazed, most of whom were old women and old men, were rounded up and ordered to sit on the ground with their hands in the air. A baby bawled out for its mother, and no one went to attend to it. A radio crackled to life and the man in charge shouted into it and not long after a helicopter hovered above open ground and the men with rifles scrambled into it. Then it whisked up into the blood-red sky, leaving behind it the burnt-out huts.

And below it, a blackened village slowly began to stir.

'Temba!' Clara cried out in surprise. 'What are you doing here at this time of the night?'

'Sipho,' Temba said with a glance at his son, as they sat in front of the fire in the kitchen, 'tell Grandma what you saw.'

A few weeks later, Clara and her family were herded out of their homes and resettled in a village with barbed wire running around it.

'A protected village for your own safety,' the army corporal told them, his nervous eyes alert.

And the people understood that to mean that it was themselves that they were really protecting.

84

Returning the favour

Sue arrived in a taxi for her last visit, before travelling to her new home in England.

'I'm the happiest I've ever been,' she announced with her emerald-green eyes twinkling under the overhead light. 'Can you believe that I actually had lunch in the Midlands Hotel and the staff didn't even blink an eye.'

Sue's face in the mirror was the same as the face in the locket Peggy kept locked away in her wardrobe. Sonia, the woman of French and English heritage, who Africa had enticed and held on to so greedily. But today Europe was claiming back what had once been taken from her. And Sue was returning there in her grandmother's place.

Without warning the warmth behind Sue's smile froze, leaving a red gash behind, and dampening the earlier glow in her eyes before her face crumbled. A second later, she tore at the clips holding up her hair, kicked her heels off irritably and began to tug at her pantihose before peeling them off with frantic movements. She unclipped her necklace and placed the thick pleated chain gently on the dresser. She turned to the pearls hanging from her ears and then to the threads of gold around her wrists before slipping off the diamonds and sapphires around her fingers. And when she'd removed all her jewellery, the mirrored table glittered back at her with its newly found wealth.

Tears that had been slowly welling up broke through their banks and trailed slowly down her cheeks. Peggy and Angie, pinned to the bed with shock, watched her with panicked looks, as she began to undress. She ripped the front of her dress apart and tugged at the lacy bra under it.

'Look at me,' she implored, fixing a stony glance first on Peggy and then on Angie. 'Look at my eyes,' she said, anger simmering inside them and drawing closer to the bed. 'See what colour they are!'

Taking a step back she said, 'Look at my skin,' as she twisted her arm towards them and forced them to drop their eyes from her face and to look at her arm. 'Now tell me, which part of me is supposed to be black? The part that says you are not all white! You tell me that!'

They looked at her without understanding her anguish.

Then she rummaged through the pile of old clothes that she'd contemptuously flung on the floor earlier. Finding something suitable she slipped a grey shapeless tunic over her head.

Her body was trembling, and she was no longer the sophisticated woman who had walked in through the front door in her silver stilettos, but the child they both remembered from so long ago.

And then like the child she still was behind all the pretence, she threw herself on her mother, her body quivering with all the bottled-up emotions that she'd hidden so well, until now. She sobbed, clinging to Peggy as she'd done when as a child Kenny had left them and they'd all thought he was never coming back, and Peggy broke down too. And the room shuddered as all three bodies folded into each other, their faces washed in tears.

A few hours later Peggy came through the door saying, 'He's here,' at the sound of a car coming down the driveway.

'I'm ready,' Sue, standing in her heels in front of the mirror, murmured.

The old tunic had been thrown back on the floor and she was looking as she had when she'd first arrived.

'Are you sure this is what you want?' Angie asked, going to sit on the bed.

'Yes, I am sure,' she replied in a sing-song voice as she dabbed her face with powder.

After applying a fresh layer of lipstick and adjusting the scarf around her neck, she gave Angie a quick hug before striding towards the front door where her young man was waiting for her.

85

An untimely loss

Angie's face flushed with embarrassment when she saw her father's car parked outside the school gates. She pretended not to see Kenny and he blew his horn. A group of boys hanging around the school entrance yelled out to her, and she had no choice but to wheel her bicycle towards him.

'Mummy is by Aunty Lydia's house,' Kenny said as he opened the boot of his car and put Angie's bike inside.

Kenny jumped back in his car, and Angie, aware of what was to follow, stood outside as he began to crank the ignition. He turned the key back and forth and pumped the accelerator pad with his foot. And soon, the noise of the engine and the smell of petrol began to attract more than its fair share of attention.

After a short pause, he scrambled back out and said, 'Shoosh, I think the battery's flat,' before holding his hand up to the students gathered at the school entrance and calling out, 'Give us a push, boys!'

Angie cringed inwardly as the boys, some of them prefects, approached the car reluctantly to offer their assistance.

'Jump in, jump in,' Kenny insisted and to avoid any further embarrassment Angie slipped into the front seat sheepishly and tried to hide her head under the dashboard.

Angie listened to the quick patter of the boy's feet on the tarmac as they pushed and panted outside. The car made a few false attempts to start, bucking on the road as she'd seen an angry horse behave. Then a cloud of black smoke blasted out of the exhaust and some of the boys began to cough. Eventually, the engine came alive, and they tore off down the road. The boys stopped running, and Kenny thanked them by thrusting his arm out through his window.

'Did you hear about Ashley?' Peggy asked Angie as she came through the door.

'Come sit,' Lydia broke in, as she shifted on the couch to give Angie room.

'A training accident,' Peggy said.

'They threatened him, told him that the only way he was going to go home would be in a body bag,' Alistair told them bitterly.

'And I warned you about what could happen to you if you go on about this equal rights business,' his mother countered.

'Someone had to,' Alistair retorted. 'That's what Ashley always used to say.'

'And look where that got him,' Lydia reminded him. Then she turned to Peggy and said, 'Alistair called his father one day and told him that Ashley had been threatened about his anti-racism views. Alan told him to tell Ashley to take the threats seriously. Alistair told Ashley and Ashley wouldn't listen. He was like that, stubborn.'

'You don't understand,' Alistair said as he stood up. 'We are all soldiers, and yet the army doesn't see it that way. They see three separate races: white, brown and black. We don't eat the same food, or sleep under the same roof, and our wages are not the same. So how can we be expected to fight for a system that is designed to keep us down?'

Peggy and Lydia turned away from him and looked at each other and the door clicked as it closed behind Alistair.

'He's heartbroken,' Lydia said to Peggy. 'They'd been friends since childhood and were like brothers. I'm afraid for him sometimes, worried about what this will do to him.'

'Lydia said Felix is angry, and it is right that he is,' Kenny told Peggy on their drive back home. 'That was no accident. You can't line up men and then use live ammunition to fire above their heads.'

'A convoy travelling from Salisbury to Kariba got hit, but not a word about poor Ashley,' Kenny said the next day, his voice raspy with emotion, as he folded the *Bulawayo Chronicle* in his hand.

86

Last farewells

It was the day of Ashley's funeral and every seat in the church had been taken up, leaving others to linger outside the doors.

Felix was sitting on the front bench with his arm around Sylvia, and with close family members on either side of them. The organ started up and twelve soldiers dressed in bush camouflage came down the aisle carrying Ashley's casket and placed it on a table in front of the altar. The music stopped, and Felix went to stand behind the microphone. The church grew silent.

Felix cleared his throat and thanked the congregation for their support. Then, leaning towards the microphone, he said, 'My son never ceased to amaze me. Being accepted into the University of Rhodesia is an impossible feat for our people, as you all know, but he did it. And who would've thought that someone like him, with parents like us, with no real paid work and running a shebeen to make ends meet, could achieve that? But that's what Ashley set out to achieve and achieve it he did.' Felix paused with a fond smile on his face. 'He refused to take no for an answer, and he's like... he was like that. He got that from his mother, never giving up, so I blame her for that.'

A chuckle rippled through the church and put a smile on Sylvia's face.

Then Felix drew himself upright and bodies stirred in their seats. Those who knew Felix well knew that he was not one to mince his words.

'My son joined the army not because he was forced to,' Felix began with a hard stare at the people in front of him, 'but because he was proud to serve his country. But he was also conflicted about fighting to uphold the laws that divided its people. So, he tried to make changes from within the military force. But in the end, he was not only fighting the enemy that was threatening from outside our borders but also the one entrenched within the fabric of our society. And for that, he will always be a hero in my eyes. Some of you have sons who served with Ashley. They were there training with Ashley when it happened, and they blamed themselves for what happened to him on that fatal day.'

He looked around the church and then at his wife, and then said, 'I want to say to you that you have nothing to feel guilty about. Yes, someone shot my son, but it wasn't any of the lads ordered to fire those shots above their mate's heads that day. I have reason enough to believe that the shot that killed my son was not fired by any of those young men. That shot was deliberately fired by someone who had been ordered to put an end to my son's life.'

The men dressed in their camouflage uniforms fidgeted uncomfortably.

'Yes, we've all been sworn into secrecy by the military,' Felix continued. 'We've been told not to discuss what happened that day. But we are all family here, and it is only right that you all go home knowing that no one here is to blame for what happened to my son that day.'

There were murmurs of solidarity and others of anger at the military among the mourners.

After the service, the hearse crawled out of the cathedral grounds, followed by an old and battered bus hired to ferry some of the mourners. Other old cars joined the shabby-looking procession.

Half an hour later, the hearse drove halfway around the traffic circle and then turned off down a road leading to the cemetery. And just then a police officer stepped away from three parked squadron cars and planted himself in front of the oncoming traffic.

He directed the hearse off the road, and then, motioning irritably, ordered the rest of the procession to do the same. The drivers left their engines idling for a short while and then, concerned about conserving their fuel, switched their engines off.

'How long are they going to make us wait?' Peggy asked, dabbing her face with her handkerchief.

'For as long as they want to,' Kenny replied as he loosened his tie.

Twenty minutes later a convoy of gleaming black cars with flags flying on either side of them crawled up the road, followed by a mounted cavalry with their full military uniform decorated with medals. Then came a long line of luxury civilian vehicles.

The procession proceeded up the road before turning to the cemetery on the left with its white brick wall and the two imposing white pillars at the entrance. The hearse and horses slipped through the black spiked gates and disappeared, and the luxury vehicles went to park alongside a lush green curb.

The police officer waited until all the important people were neatly tucked away behind the tall walls before stepping back on the road and giving the signal to the parked vehicles to proceed.

Kenny cranked his engine and around him ignitions were turned on and vehicles bumped their way back onto the road. His foot pumped the accelerator furiously and the car spurted and shuddered.

'I told you to leave the car at the cathedral. We could've easily caught a lift with Lydia and Alan,' Peggy complained.

'It just needs a little push,' Kenny replied, his face red with exertion.

A door was thrown open and then banged shut. Kenny looked up quickly, then he pulled the key out of the ignition and rushed after Peggy.

They turned to the cemetery with its sagging wire and rusted gates, and Peggy gave Kenny a pointed look as they walked past Alan's car, which was old and dusty like the rest. Kenny accepted the blame for declining Alan's offer of a ride by dropping his eyes.

They picked their way past the scraggly trees and untidy-looking graves with their faded plastic flowers and broken vases and went to join the people already gathered beside a fresh mound of earth.

The priest shuffled in after, circling a crudely built brick headstone and stepping over a beer bottle with dead flowers sticking out of it. He breathed heavily as he took his place at the head of the newly dug grave before dropping his glance to the bible in his hands.

'Let us pray,' the priest began, and the mourners bowed their heads and a loud crackle of gunfire from the other cemetery with its ornamental headstones and shady red gum trees rang out.

Here and there, a woman clutched her chest with fright before chuckling with embarrassment. The priest showed his irritation by biting his lip.

'Let us pray,' he attempted again after a short pause and a loud horn belted out from the other side. A flutter of voices rose.

The priest stood back, and a gentle hymn started up. And it was only when the ceremonies were over on the other side, that the burial rites could begin.

Sylvia began to weep audibly with her face buried against Felix's shirt as the coffin, accompanied by a sorrowful song, was lowered into the grave. And just then a passing cloud shed some of its moisture and left wet splashes in the dirt before sailing across the blue sky.

'Tears from heaven,' someone whispered.

Then the priest and his helpers left, scuttling past a line of rusted metal plaques sticking out of the hard ground, as they quickly made their escape.

Gradually the mourners pulled themselves away from the small mound of earth with its plastic wreath, carrying with them memories of a young life that had started with so much promise, only to end so abruptly.

Heavy rain came down a day after the funeral and persisted for a few days. Inside the house, where the McAlister's were forced to wait it out, streams of water poured in through the chinks in the roof and were caught by several enamel bowls placed strategically on the floor.

Towards the afternoon the rain had only just turned into a drizzle when a car hooted at the gate. Kenny peeped out through the kitchen window and saw Lovemore dash from his kia to open the gate. A car edged forward, its wheels sinking further and further into the muddy driveway, before stopping. The driver shouted through his window before reversing back to safety. After a quiet chat with Lovemore, Kenny left the house and tiptoed around the mud to the waiting car.

'The Rhodesian front has been playing us, Kenny,' Felix said as he opened his door. 'You can't still be supporting them surely? That business about us being classed as Europeans is just on paper but look how we live man!'

But the iron curtain had done its job, and most only knew what the authorities fed them and it came as no surprise to Felix when Kenny replied, 'I understand Felix, but sometimes it's better to go with the devil you know.'

A low murmur of voices ensued, and then Felix shook Kenny's hand before driving off.

'Alistair has deserted the army and joined the Freedom fighters,' Kenny whispered to Peggy on his return and Peggy cupped her mouth with her hand.

A few weeks after, Amos strode into the schoolyard dressed in bush camouflage, and staff and students went to crowd around him.

'What's your rank now, son,' Mr Rodgers asked with a smile on his face.

'Corporal, sir!' Amos shouted as he saluted him.

IX

Part 10 – Changing times

87

An end to school life

Mr Parker, the physics and chemistry teacher, walked to the blackboard and scribbled on it, 'The principles of energy.' He turned to face the students and said, 'Today we will demonstrate how energy moves from one source to another.'

Then he strolled up to a table and stooped to examine a tripod with an unlit candle under it. Stepping away from it, he said, 'Kinetic energy is the result of colliding molecules,' and then throwing the question to the faces turned towards him said, 'Right or wrong?'

Angie stirred uncomfortably in her seat, as she dug through the information that she had learned parrot fashion and stored in her brain and came up with a blank.

'Anyone?' Mr Parker pleaded desperately with the wall of impassive faces staring back at him. 'Can someone say something, please?'

Thirty-five bodies sweated under the question, and then to everyone's relief, a hand went up and a voice quivering under the weight of all that was riding on it said, 'That's right, sir!'

Mr Parker glared at the speaker for a moment, and then turning back on the others, said in a tired voice, 'What about the rest of you, do you agree with Ben?'

And feeling the pressure, a few, 'yes sirs,' and 'no sirs,' were whispered around the classroom. Mr Parker dropped his head with despair.

To be fair to the students, Mr Parker had talked about moving water and windmills but the only windmills the students had ever seen were in the pictures of the book he had held up to them as he walked around the classroom. The same book which now sat closed on his desk.

'And you expect to pass your exams?' the teacher asked, as a slow red flush began to grow under his collar. 'Let me save you the trouble of answering that. Not one of you, not even you, Ben, has any chance in hell of passing your finals, mark my words!'

With a careless sweep of his hand, the experiment he had so painfully set up clattered off the table and landed in an untidy heap on the floor. A loud gasp rose in the room, and Mr Parker, without a backward glance, simply walked out through the door.

'Kept walking until he reached Chaplin High,' Ben told his peers a week later, and someone said, 'It figures, he never stopped talking about that school.'

'It's the heat,' Kenny stated when the Ordinary levels results were released, and only four students out of thirty-five got the required five subjects to pass. 'Chaplin High had sprinklers running on its rooftops during the exams and where were the sprinklers for our kids?'

The teachers were disappointed, as could be expected, but remained hopeful. And the four, excluding Angie, who had managed to secure sufficient grades to move to Matric level were paraded at a special assembly where their parents, all of them influential in the community, looked on proudly.

'Isn't this your Mr Parker?' Kenny asked holding the *Gwelo Times* up to Angie.

Angie peered at the physics and chemistry teacher smiling proudly at the camera and standing beside a small group of equally proud students and nodded her head. Underneath the photograph, a caption declared, 'Chaplin High does it again! All twenty students pass their Ordinary level with flying colours!'

And proving what everyone in the town already knew, that a cool rooftop was all that was needed for academic excellence.

Meanwhile, at Nashville High two classroom blocks had been added to the school to accommodate the increasing number of students. And in the year that Angie repeated her studies the tennis court went up. And the hole that had been dug for the swimming pool was covered up and turned into a soccer field.

And when some, including Angie, managed to scrape through their Ordinary level at the end of that year and escaped their humiliation into the working world, the majority writing exams for the first time failed and were forced to sit the same exam again the following year.

And so, the pattern and excuses continued, and those with the final word patted each other on the shoulder, for managing to keep things moving, according to their plans.

88

Silence from afar

Peggy unlocked her wardrobe and pulled out a small suitcase. She dug through all the important paperwork; marriage certificate, birth certificates, and title deeds until she reached the bottom and pulled out a plastic bag with a wad of papers in it. She picked out the one she wanted and handed it to Angie. Angie saw Sue's name at the top and her phone number. She turned the letter over and saw that it had been sent to Sue's father-in-law's address.

Angie dialled a number, and a posh voice answered a short while later

'Is that Sue?' Angie spoke into the mouthpiece. There was silence on the other end of the line. 'Daddy's not well,' Angie said into the emptiness. 'He's been diagnosed with sclerosis of the liver. They say it's something that will get worse with time.'

Then she gave more details about Kenny's diagnosis, and the sound of quiet chatter mingled with laughter drifted in through the earpiece.

After a short pause, a voice on the other side of the line said, 'I'm sorry, I think you may have the wrong number. Please don't call back.'

Angie waited until she heard a click before she replaced the handpiece on its cradle. She felt the tears threatening to come so she kept her face turned towards the wall until it was safe for her to turn around again.

'Did you speak to her?' Peggy asked, touching her shoulder lightly. 'What did she say?'

'She sends her love,' Angie replied quietly.

'Is she coming home?' Peggy asked, her face brightening.

'She'll try to,' Angie murmured without looking at her mother. 'Plane tickets are expensive.'

Peggy's face dropped and then lifted again as she said, 'But if she says she'll try and come then I am sure she'll come,' her voice full of hope.

Angie walked away quickly as her anger towards Sue began to stir up again, conscious of her mother's eyes on her back.

89

The dark days

The coloured community was a mishmash of Bantu, Asian, and European, with tones of pale café au lait so that you could hardly tell, to coffee with just a dash of milk. It was a tapestry of tight and springy strands uncoiling leisurely into those that were soft and silky.

It was a race with a mixed heritage, a unique blend of cultures and histories, that gave it a broader perspective and understanding of the world. And had it been allowed to embrace its ancestry; its blended heritage would have proved to be its greatest privilege and the core of its strength. But instead, it was denigrated for the interracial relationships that had created it. And manipulated to despise one side of itself, while the other was taught to detest it. And in the end, it was left to rattle in emptiness, eternally shackled to those it had been groomed to emulate from infancy.

It was a race that floundered as it tried to find its own identity, adopting those traditions that had been forced on it and making them its own. Its people clinging onto each other for support, as it limped towards preserving itself, through self-isolation.

For Angie, being part of the coloured community meant that the negative stereotyping of being brown was now a burden she did not have to carry on her own. But it was a community that strived for whiteness. And mornings became an art of patience for her, as she carefully reshaped her generous lips into a thinner version of themselves and used concealers to draw in her protruding cheekbones and bulbous nose.

But hair was the community's potent symbol of identity and its weapon. It dictated a person's position in the social hierarchy and was used to form cliques. Straight hair was the pinnacle. It excused dark skin and unattractive features and catapulted its owners to the top of the pile. Frizzy hair like Angie's was a source of shame, revealing that part of themselves they were desperately trying to ignore.

'You just have to apply the straightener to your hair every two months,' Lucy said as she lathered the relaxer cream over Angie's bushy curls.

The battle to tame Angie's hair had begun and bits of cream splattered around. Some found her forehead and the back of her neck and scorched the flesh under it. Angie squinched her face with pain. Her eyes burned and turned red and puffy as the chemical's pungent fumes filled the small bathroom and irritated her throat.

'Remember to wash your hair every week and to always sleep with curlers,' Lucy said brushing Angie's hair with her fingers and leaving the relaxer caught in a stream of cold water to ooze through them.

Then, on went the horrible pricky orange rollers and the hairpins that took great pleasure in puncturing Angie's already bruised and tender scalp.

'Better, don't you think?' Lucy asked as they stared at Angie's hair hanging limply over her shoulders.

'But why straight!' Angie moaned as she squeezed her head through an old nylon stocking Lucy had given her to keep her curls in check at night.

Six weeks passed, and Angie watched in horror as the beast began to flutter back into consciousness. Here and there, bits of hair sprang out haphazardly and were quickly doused back into place with blobs of grease. And as the weeks passed and the relaxer wore off, Angie's hair grew stronger, retaliating aggressively, and becoming as unruly as it chose. Angie soon found herself at the losing end of a full-fledged battle and left with little choice, resorted to her trusted tube of chemicals, to beat her hair back into submission.

'It's not fair,' was Angie's eternal cry. 'Why can't I just let my hair be the way it was meant to be!'

It wasn't just the loss of free time and money that Angie resented, but the extreme levels of anxiety that came with trying to keep her hair straight. It controlled her existence, kept her on edge, and then without warning it would frizz at the slightest change in the air, undoing hours of curling, swirling, and styling and leaving her exposed.

'You can't ever tell anyone you use a relaxer,' Trudy warned, 'That's a secret you never reveal!' And Angie understood that to be yet another rule.

'Straight hair comes with compliments and fun times with friends, and not a bad trade-off,' Angie conceded inwardly.

It was the weekend, and she was seated, cramped on torn covers in the back seat of an old Zephyr, surrounded by the sound of happy chatter.

'White people lived there once,' Lucy said bringing Angie back to the present as they drove past Cranborne Park and then pointing towards Arcadia, and Braeside.

'We moved in, and they moved out, so now we get to use their sports clubs and swimming pools,' Trudy shouted from the front seat.

'And here we thought that they'd be only too happy to live next door to their kin,' their afro'd driver laughed.

They rattled over a railway line and Lucy pointed out Hillside saying, 'That's where most of them ended up.'

'Salisbury!' the train conductor shouted as his hand banged against the second-class compartment door. And when Angie, still breathless with excitement from her day out with friends returned to Belvedere, she found Peggy waiting for her outside the girl's hostel.

'Back so soon,' Angie thought miserably, conscious of how her mother had a way of blurring the lines between brown and black, that her new life was trying so hard to define.

Peggy's striped dress and the brown shoes that were chipped in the front, which she only wore when the need to leave home came, looked shabby and out of place. Her nails were chipped and her face burnt from spending too much of her time outdoors. She looked nothing like the other mothers who came to visit their daughters and Angie in her embarrassment led her mother hastily to a table in the furthest corner of the lounge room.

Peggy who was excited to see her daughter, began chatting happily as she unwrapped the plastic bag in her hands. The smell of boiled mealies filled the lounge room and Angie flinched uncomfortably.

'Please speak in English, mummy,' she implored in a low tone a short while later, as two young women seated at a table next to theirs, looked their way and sniggered.

Peggy switched languages, and Angie cringed at her mother's broken English. Peggy noticed for the first time her daughter's discomfort and stopped talking with her eyes on her.

Then she said, 'Is it so bad that I am here because I missed you? Are you ashamed to be seen with me? That I work in the fields and that your father takes care of chickens to give you what you have now?'

Angie started and was aggrieved at how much like Sue she had become. Behaving the same way Sue had and which she had criticised Sue for. Then she stared back at her mother, torn between her love for her family and the life she craved for. Her gaze dropped and her eyes welled with tears, unable to put into words the struggles she had with her conflicting identities and her sense of belonging.

Peggy had her troubles too. And when she returned home after her short trip, the dark days always close at hand, crept up slowly before they came to claim her completely. The fire in the wood stove stopped burning and no pots bubbled on the electric stove indoors. And for days, the children were forced to tiptoe in the dark and dreary silence, as their joy was gradually sucked out of them.

'Lights out!' the matrons yelled, and Peggy whimpered with heartache.

'Peggy!' Kenny whispered, 'can you sit up? Here, let me help you up.'

The haze fogging Peggy's brow lifted briefly, and she saw Kenny seated beside her with a bowl of porridge in his hands.

'Look at us, Kenny, no parents, and no family. Children shouldn't be dragged away from their homes. It's cruel!' Peggy mumbled miserably.

'We're your family now Peggy, me and the children,' Kenny told her soothingly.

'But they don't have grandparents, and how are we supposed to bring them up properly, without our parents to show us?' Peggy persisted before the black cloud draped itself back around her.

Then she curled up into a ball and resumed her sobbing.

And Kenny knew that at times like these, there was nothing he could do to ease her pain because the love Peggy yearned for was different from the one that he could give her.

Kenny had his memories too, of long nights and cold dormitory beds. Flashbacks of his mother sitting outside the hostel gate with a parcel on her lap, and his heart leaping with joy at the sight of her.

'She's not the right colour,' they said. 'Move forward, not backward,' they told him. And when he was finally allowed to go and see her, he pretended not to know her.

'Gwelo!' the train conductor yelled, his keys rattling against Angie's door, just as Kenny arrived at the station to drive her home.

Peggy is herself again, her reed broom swishing back and forth over the courtyard in the early morning as it swept away the evil left behind by the spirit world. Then the children rose and dressed in their tattered clothes, played barefooted in the dirt. And here, away from that other world, Angie could be herself and feel no shame.

That afternoon on the back veranda Kenny leaned forward in his chair as if to say something, then thinking better of it leaned back again without saying anything.

'What did the doctor say?' Angie asked when he remained silent.

'Nothing, I'm fine, nothing wrong with me,' he replied irritably, refusing to look at her.

'When's your next appointment?' Angie persisted.

He grunted and pretended not to hear her. 'How about a cup of tea?' he asked instead, getting out of his seat and sitting back down again.

Angie entered the outside kitchen and shoved a log in the wood stove before dragging the big black kettle to the plate that received the most heat.

'Why isn't the electric kettle working?' she asked when she was back in her seat.

'It's the water,' Kenny replied, pointing to the well. 'The limestone builds up until the kettle can't take it anymore.'

'Mummy said you have an appointment with the specialist,' Angie stated and when he remained silent, she returned to the kitchen to get the tea tray ready.

'Have you got the wardrobe keys?' Angie yelled out to him after, from the kitchen door holding out an empty sugar canister.

'Shoosh,' he exclaimed. 'Finished already. It was full this morning when I had a cuppa.'

'Empty now,' Angie confirmed. 'Does Mummy still keep the bag of sugar in her wardrobe?'

'She's coming now,' Kenny said, rising to his feet and suddenly coming alive.

'Mummy!' Angie yelled out to Peggy and the world at large, 'we need sugar to make tea!' and Kenny's voice echoed hers.

90

Against the tide

Jonas the new gardener had his back to Angie as he banged the kitchen drawers with easy familiarity and when he found the containers he'd been looking for, he dropped them carelessly on the kitchen dresser. Then he helped himself to powdered milk and sugar, and the tin mug rang out ruthlessly as he stirred it with a tablespoon. Then he drove a sharp-tipped and serrated knife through a loaf of bread and began to lather the chunks he had chopped off generously with butter and jam.

He slurped loudly from his mug and Angie darted a look of disgust his way before going to join Peggy outside.

'Lovemore used to do that,' she commented as Peggy shovelled ash out of the wood stove. Her mother pretended not to hear her.

She did not see the new gardener for the rest of the morning and when Angie next set eyes on him, she found him lounging in a wheelbarrow in the courtyard with his feet up against the trunk of the jacaranda tree.

'Jonas was in the kitchen this morning,' Angie said, turning to Peggy.

'Oh, he was just making his tea, 'Peggy replied without concern.

'Are our gardeners allowed in the house now?' Angie asked.

'Times are changing, things are not like they used to be,' Peggy replied.

And she was right of course, it was 1979. The whispers of a shift in political power were growing, and attitudes were changing, except of course in the town of Gwelo.

'Out, out!' the store owner yelled, shoving Peggy and Angie out of his store.

Peggy mumbled something about a belt before she dropped her gaze and Angie stared at the shopkeeper aghast.

'What belt is this?' he snapped with twisted eyebrows when he joined them on the pavement.

Angie pointed it out to him.

'You won't have trouble finding one down there,' he growled with his arm stretched towards downtown. 'It may not be as good as the one in the window, but it's good enough for the likes of you!'

In Lower Gwelo, Mr. Van, as he was called by some, sat stone-faced as he learned about the abduction of five of his employees and the threats that had led to the desertion of the rest of his workforce.

'Two farms gone just like that,' he muttered.

'It's time to walk away now,' his son the auctioneer advised him bleakly.

'Bloody terrs,' his father cursed. 'If I lose this farm, then I lose everything!'

'You better come, because I'm not coming back,' his wife warned him over the phone from the right wing of the auctioneer's large double-storey house.

'This is Pete,' his son huffed from the short walk to the front door of the farmhouse and gesturing to a bearded young man beside him. 'He'll manage the farm and take care of everything for you.'

Mr Van conceded. This wasn't farming anymore, sleeping with one eye open and a rifle at your side. And even though he refused to admit it, he knew that he'd lost his nerve. He'd grown old.

Pete sat patiently in a vehicle mounted with a machine gun and a cannon, as his new boss took his last walk around the small fortress that had once been the family home. Fond memories of happier times flooded back to Mr Van and caught at his throat and almost made him refuse to go. Then the reality of steel bars around buildings, the walls built of sandbags and the barbed mesh wire rolled around everything made him stride to the waiting vehicle with a new resolve.

The two white men sat in the front with their rifles resting beside them and their pistols strapped around their waists. And behind them, a squad of black militia were seated with their rifles propped up between their knees.

They drove alongside the security fencing with armed personnel patrolling it for several kilometres. Then the meshed wire turned abruptly marking off Mr Van's farm, before it raced off again in the opposite direction, and as far as the eye could see, making its owner drop his face as they left it behind.

They drove in silence, then the farmer leaned forward to scrutinise a fast-approaching structure made of crumbling bricks, twisted metal, and blackened windows.

'Bad business,' he muttered as they drew closer. Then, recognising the black face behind the steering wheel of a battered Land Rover, he acknowledged his neighbour with a smile saying, 'Good man.'

A black hand was raised, and Mr Van received a hearty wave in return.

The farmer was unarmed and unable to defend himself or his store as the law did not permit him to own a weapon. He was an exceptional farmer with an excellent crop, but a man with limited resources because only those local markets dictated by the law were open to him. Nor could he earn foreign currency, even before sanctions were imposed, because the law prohibited him from exporting his produce.

And for a man who lived under the same conditions as his peers, and to be treated as poorly as he had, and to still bear no malice, was a good man indeed.

The armoured vehicle rushed past trees and bushes and as the old house with its faded yellow paint and cracked walls came into view Mr. Van told Pete about the time he had to intervene to save O'Donnell's land from squatters. Peggy, who had lost the field and the cattle kraal, and who was now tending her vegetables stood upright in her garden as the vehicle drove past. The children in their ragged clothing and playing barefooted in the yard stopped and gazed in awe at the armoured vehicle. And the black militia sitting in the back waved and the children cheered with glee until the vehicle was out of sight.

At the Midlands hotel, a long queue of vehicles formed, and the police escort milled around as they readied the convoy for the journey to Salisbury. And the auctioneer seated in a gleaming grey hummer, waited patiently for his father to arrive.

And all around the country, a sea of black heaved and panted, impatient to take back what once belonged to it

91

A call from overseas

The intercom in the girls' hostel beeped a few times before the matron's sharp tones cut through the silence.

Angie looked up subconsciously and the voice slashed the airwaves once more announcing, 'Telephone, Angie, telephone!'

Angie picked up her key and, locking her room, rushed down a flight of steps. The matron, still not accustomed to having brown faces instead of white, glared at her from her glass office. She waited until Angie entered the telephone cubicle, then banged the phone down even before Angie had the receiver against her ear.

'Angie! Angie! Is that you?' a voice from the past, her sister's voice, called out urgently.

'Angie speaking,' Angie replied, trying to stop the dull thumping of her chest.

'It's Sue,' the voice uttered unnecessarily because it was a voice Angie would recognise anywhere. 'It's your sister, Sue!'

'How are you?' Angie asked with a palpitating heart.

'I'm happy,' Sue replied in her posh voice. 'We have so many friends!'

The line went quiet, and then, speaking in her normal voice, Sue said, 'Oh, Angie, what have I done?'

There was a flood of tears, and Angie asked, 'What's it like, living in England?' as she tried to stem the sobbing in her ear.

'Tough,' Sue admitted. 'Just the pretence of it all.'

There was another bout of tears, and then, hearing a faint drumbeat in the background, Angie asked, 'Where are you calling from?' Sue named a place in London that meant nothing to her.

'Is that where you live?' Angie asked and Sue replied, 'Good heavens, no!' condescendingly.

'Why are you there then?' Angie asked curiously. 'Are you visiting friends?'

'I'm downtown. How could I possibly have friends here?' Sue snapped back. Then her tone softened, and she said, 'But you should see it, Angie. It's like being back home. Real people, just like when we were growing up. This is where I come when I am tired of the whiteness. Of not being who I am,' she confided.

Sue was sobbing quietly now, and Angie began to comfort her as she'd often done when they were children.

'Remember the underground toilets near the Midlands Hotel,' Angie said, her tone light. 'Remember them? Whites only!'

'I remember!' Sue replied, chortling as she recalled the memory of the security guard standing at the gate and blocking Angie from entering with her.

'You told him you were the mayor's daughter, and you threatened to get him fired if he didn't let me in and he believed you!' Angie reminded her.

'I made the right decision, Angie,' Sue said, sobering up, and Angie knew that Sue was no longer talking about the security guard. 'I never quite fitted in. You know that don't you?'

Angie murmured and then Sue said, 'We decided not to have children, even before I left home. We figured it would be too risky. Did I tell you that?'

'No,' Angie replied, 'You know that you stopped confiding in me when you met Tim.'

Sue let that slide, and said instead, 'How are you, how is everyone at home?'

'Do you want children?' Angie asked stubbornly. 'If deep down you want children, then you must have them. Do what makes you happy, give yourself that at least.'

'A weight has just lifted off my shoulders,' Sue told her sister after a long pause. 'I can sense your smile, are you smiling?'

'Yes, I am,' Angie replied.

'I think mummy hates me!' Sue blurted out, before sobbing again.

'No, no,' Angie told her firmly. 'Why should she?'

Sue continued to sob quietly.

'Do you remember the driveway around the rockery in the front yard? We used to ride our bicycles around it, do you remember that? Angie asked.

'I do,' Sue whispered back.

'I was carrying Maisy on the back carrier, and we'd only gone round the rockery a few times when there was this awful howl, and my bike suddenly stopped. Somehow, Maisy's foot had ended up in the spokes of my back wheel. Mummy came dashing out of the mealie stalks and, coward that I was, instead of staying to help, I sprang off my bike and ran off to save my skin. I waited for that dreaded peachy stick, but it didn't come. Mummy knew that it was an accident, and I would never hurt Maisy on purpose. I think she knows us better than we think. She told me often that leaving home was the right decision for you.'

'You're saying she doesn't hate me?' Sue asked.

'I know she doesn't,' Angie replied with confidence.

About the Author

Mavis Stewart was born in Rhodesia, now Zimbabwe. She is a first-time author. She has a degree in accounting and although her entire career has been in finance, her passion has always been in writing. She is an Australian citizen and resides there with her family.

www.ingramcontent.com/pod-product-compliance
Lightning Source LLC
Chambersburg PA
CBHW010256100726
47904CB00011B/2626